THE MURDERS AT
SUGAR MILL FARM

What Reviewers Say About Ronica Black's Work

A Love that Leads to Home

"If you love a slow-burn romance where the characters are carefully dancing around each other while being incredibly adorable, this story is for you. It was an emotional read for me, and if you want a good heart-wrenching story, read it."—*Hsinju's Lit Log*

Freedom to Love

"This is a great book. The police drama keeps you enthralled throughout but what I found captivating was the growing affection between the two main characters. Although they are both very different women, you find yourself holding your breath, hoping that they will find a way to be together."—*Lesbian Reading Room*

The Practitioner

"*The Practitioner* by Ronica Black is the angsty sort of romance that I can easily get lost in. I wanted to fill a tub and bathe in all the feelings. Hell, if I had one of those fancy, waterproof Kindles, I just might have."
—*Lesbian Review*

"The beginning of this novel captured my attention from the rather luscious description of a pint of Guinness. I cannot tell a lie, I almost immediately wanted to be drinking it. ...The first scene with the practitioner also pulled me in, making me sit up and pay attention to what was happening on the digital page. The relationship was like a low simmering fire, frequently doused by either Johnnie's personal angst, or Elaine's. This book was an overall enjoyable read and one which I would recommend to people wanting characters who practically breathe off the page."—*Library Thing*

Snow Angel

"A beautifully written, passionate and romantic novella."—*SunsetX Cocktail*

"*Snow Angel* is a novella, and it flies by. It draws characters and scenes in large strokes, and it's good fun if you'd like a quick read that's particularly escapist."—*The Lesbrary*

Under Her Wing

"From the start Ronica Black had me. I loved everything about this story, from the emotional intensity to the amazingly hot sex scenes. The emotion between them is so real and tear jerking at times. And the love scenes are phenomenal. I feel I'm raving—but I enjoyed it that much. Highly recommended."—*Kitty Kat's Book Review Blog*

"*Emily*" in Women of the Dark Streets

"A darkly disturbing brush with questionable magic that leads to an astounding one-eighty-degree turnaround after an apparent attempt at suicide. Mindboggling!"—*Rainbow Book Reviews*

The Seeker

"Stalkers, child kidnappers and murderers all collide in this fast-paced, dual-plotted novel. This is not Black's first novel, and readers can only hope it will not be her last."—*Lambda Literary Review*

"Ronica Black's books just keep getting stronger and stronger. ...This is such a tightly written plot-driven novel that readers will find themselves glued to the pages and ignoring phone calls. *The Seeker* is a great read, with an exciting plot, great characters, and great sex."—*Just About Write*

Flesh and Bone—*Lambda Literary Award Finalist*

"Ronica Black handles a traditional range of lesbian fantasies with gusto and sincerity. The reader wants to know these women as well as they come to know each other. When Black's characters ignore their realistic fears to follow their passion, this reader admires their chutzpah and cheers them on. ...These stories make good bedtime reading, and could lead to sweet dreams. Read them and see."—*Erotica Revealed*

Chasing Love

"Ronica Black's writing is fluid, and lots of dialogue makes this a fast read. If you like steamy erotica with intense sexual situations, you'll like *Chasing Love*."—*Queer Magazine Online*

Hearts Aflame

"Sleek storytelling and terrific characters are the backbone of Ronica Black's third and best novel, *Hearts Aflame*. Prepare to hop on for an emotional ride with this thrilling story of love in the outback. ...Along with the romance of Krista and Rae, the secondary storylines such as Krista's fear of horses and an uncle suffering from Alzheimer's are told with depth and warmth. Black also draws in the reader by utilizing the weather as a metaphor for the sexual and emotional tension in all the storylines. Wonderful storytelling and rich characterization make this a high recommendation."—*Lambda Literary Review*

"*Hearts Aflame* takes the reader on the rough and tumble ride of the cattle drive. Heat, flood, and a sexual pervert are all part of the adventure. Heat also appears between Krista and Rae. The twists and turns of the plot engage the reader all the way to the satisfying conclusion." —*Just About Write*

"I like the author's writing style and she tells a good story. I was drawn in quickly and didn't lose interest at all. Black paints a great picture with her words and I was able to feel like I was sitting around the camp fire with the characters."—*C-Spot Reviews*

Wild Abandon—*Lambda Literary Award Finalist*

"Black is a master at teasing the reader with her use of domination and desire. Black's first novel, *In Too Deep*, was a finalist for a 2005 Lammy. ...With *Wild Abandon*, the author continues her winning ways, writing like a seasoned pro. This is one romance I will not soon forget."—*Books to Watch Out For*

"This sequel to Ronica Black's debut novel, *In Too Deep*, is an electrifying thriller. The author's development as a fine storyteller shines with this tightly written story. ...[The mystery] keeps the story charged—never unraveling or leading us to a predictable conclusion. More than once I gasped in surprise at the dark and twisted paths this book took."—*Curve*

"Ronica Black, author of *In Too Deep*, has given her fans another fast paced novel of romance and danger. As previously, Black develops her characters fully, complete with their quirks and flaws. She is also skilled at allowing her characters to grow, and to find their way out of psychic holes. If you enjoy complex characters and passionate sex scenes, you'll love *Wild Abandon*."—*MegaScene*

"Black has managed to create two very sensual and compelling women. The backstory is intriguing, original, and quite well-developed. Yet, it doesn't detract from the primary premise of the novel—it is a sexually-charged romance about two very different and guarded women. Black carries the reader along at such a rapid pace that the rise and fall of each climactic moment successfully creates that suspension of disbelief which the reader seeks."—*Midwest Book Review*

"Ronica Black has proven once again that she is an awesome storyteller with her new romance, *Wild Abandon*. With her second published novel, she has crafted an erotic, sensual and well-paced tale. ...Black is a master at teasing the reader with her use of domination and desire. Emotions pour endlessly from the pages, moving the plot forward at a pace that never slows or gets dull. But Black doesn't stop there. She is intent on giving the reader more. *Wild Abandon* hints at a plot twist early on, and while we know who it involves, we do not know what will happen, and how, until the last minute, effectively keeping us spellbound."
—*Just About Write*

In Too Deep—*Lambda Literary Award Finalist*

"Ronica Black's debut novel *In Too Deep* has everything from nonstop action and intriguing well developed characters to steamy erotic love scenes. From the opening scenes where Black plunges the reader headfirst into the story to the explosive unexpected ending, *In Too Deep* has what it takes to rise to the top. Black has a winner with *In Too Deep*, one that will keep the reader turning the pages until the very last one."
—*Independent Gay Writer*

"...an exciting, page turning read, full of mystery, sex, and suspense."
—*MegaScene*

"...a challenging murder mystery—sections of this mixed-genre novel are hot, hot, hot. Black juggles the assorted elements of her first book with assured pacing and estimable panache."—*Q Syndicate*

"Black's characterization is skillful, and the sexual chemistry surrounding the three major characters is palpable and definitely hot-hot-hot...if you're looking for a solid read with ample amounts of eroticism and a red herring or two you're sure to find *In Too Deep* a satisfying read."
—*L Word Literature*

"Ronica Black's debut novel, *In Too Deep*, is the outstanding first effort of a gifted writer who has a promising career ahead of her. Black shows extraordinary command in weaving a thoroughly engrossing tale around multi-faceted characters, intricate action and character-driven plots and subplots, sizzling sex that jumps off the page and stimulates libidos effortlessly, amidst brilliant storytelling. A clever mystery writer, Black has the reader guessing until the end."—*Midwest Book Review*

"Every time the reader has a handle on what's happening, Black throws in a curve, successfully devising a good mystery. The romance and sex add a special gift to the package rounding out the story for a totally satisfying read."—*Just About Write*

By the Author

In Too Deep
Deeper
Wild Abandon
Hearts Aflame
Flesh and Bone
The Seeker
Chasing Love
Conquest
Wholehearted
The Midnight Room
Snow Angel
The Practitioner
Freedom to Love
Under Her Wing
Private Passion
Dark Euphoria
The Last Seduction
Olivia's Awakening
A Love That Leads to Home
Passion's Sweet Surrender
A Turn of Fate
Watching Over Her
The Business of Pleasure
Something to Talk About
Passionate Pursuance—Novella in Decadence
The Murders at Sugar Mill Farm

THE MURDERS AT SUGAR MILL FARM

by

Ronica Black

2023

THE MURDERS AT SUGAR MILL FARM
© 2023 By Ronica Black. All Rights Reserved.

ISBN 13: 978-1-63679-455-6

This Trade Paperback Original Is Published By
Bold Strokes Books, Inc.
P.O. Box 249
Valley Falls, NY 12185

First Edition: December 2023

Credits
Editor: Cindy Cresap
Production Design: Susan Ramundo
Cover Design By Tammy Seidick

Acknowledgments

I would like to thank my friends and family for their continued love and support throughout the writing process. Also, thank you so much for your feedback on this book, it helped me more than you know.

Thank you to everyone at BSB. I'm very lucky to have such a supportive publisher.

PROLOGUE

The man lowered the window on his early model Chevy sedan as it crept along in virtual silence down the dirt road. He extinguished his headlights, allowing the brightness of the moon to illuminate his path between the two sugarcane fields. He inhaled deeply as the wet heat infiltrated the inside of his vehicle. He felt closer to his lovelies in the heat. Could almost imagine the sweet stink of their rotting bodies. But the sweet stink didn't come tonight. It had been too long since his last kill. Now they were bones and bones didn't smell. He'd have to get out and handle them if he wanted to feel close to his lovelies now.

He slowed as he neared the familiar clearing and turned off the engine. Then he crawled from the cab and carefully closed the door. His footsteps made crunching noises as he walked a few feet into the rows of standing cane. It didn't take him long to find her.

The last girl.

She was easy to spot with his low beam flashlight.

He knelt, nearly breathless with excitement. The thigh bone felt light in his hands as he maneuvered it from the ground. Soon the bone would change. Soon the entire field would change. It would burn and the bone would be charred. Just like the others. He brought the femur up to his mouth and stuck out his tongue. He swore he could still taste her. Beyond the dirt, beyond the bits of leaves, he could still taste her.

Perfect, flawless. Smelling like the innocent angel she'd been. God, he could still feel her porcelain skin. She'd been the softest one to date. So soft. So, so soft. Even when she'd been trying to scream, the taut muscles in her beautiful neck had still felt soft beneath her glorious skin. Soft as they strained. Soft as they fought for life.

In the end he had won of course. And he'd had to rid himself of her. Which was why he was here. This was where he'd left them all. In the sugarcane field so they could be surrounded by something as sweet as they had been.

He couldn't believe they hadn't been found, but then again cane harvesters don't discern bones and the fires took care of the flesh.

It was the perfect place to leave his lovelies.

He gave the bone one last, long lick and rubbed at the stiffening between his legs. She made him hard. Even in death. Especially in death.

He rubbed the heel of his hand against himself as he returned the bone to the ground. He closed his eyes and unzipped his pants, ready to bring himself to climax, but a barking dog in the distance startled him and he froze.

"It's just a dog," he whispered. "An annoying ankle biter."

He closed his fly and walked without the use of his flashlight back to his sedan, blowing a kiss back to his girls as he crawled inside. Then he started the engine and sat for a moment, thinking. When he eventually turned around and switched on his headlights, one thing came to mind.

It was time for another lovely.

CHAPTER ONE

One Month Later

Come on.
Come on, you can do it.
You're strong.
Fucking superhero strong.

Lyra Aarden clenched her eyes and pushed herself onward, the muddy ground sucking at her sneakers as she ran. She opened her eyes and glanced at her Fitbit. She'd only run two miles.

Fuck.

She wasn't going to make it. Her knee was hurting, and running down the road through the burnt sugarcane fields hadn't been such a good idea after all. The black was everywhere, and ash blew in the wind. It blew for miles, even settling up against the base of her brother's house, a sight that still amazed her. Didn't anyone care about the ozone? Or breathing for that matter?

I do, so why am I running right through it?

The answer came quickly.

Because I was curious.

She'd noticed the ash lining the house, resting on the bushes and on the windshields of the cars. Louie had told her it was from the burnt sugarcane, and she'd wanted to check it out. Now she was beginning to regret it. It was affecting her breathing and her damn knee...she wasn't going to make it all the way around her planned trek. She was going to have to turn around.

Fuck.

She closed her eyes again and thought back to her conversation with her brother earlier that morning.

"You're taking two water bottles?" Louie had asked as he poured himself a cup of coffee.

Lyra considered ignoring him, but when she saw him lean on the kitchen counter to sip from his mug, she decided against it. Seemed he was going to hang around for a while rather than retreat to his office to work.

"It's hot out," she said.

"I thought you were used to it."

"I'm used to Arizona heat. Not this crazy shit."

Louie laughed. "A little too humid for you?"

"Just a little." She pulled the brace on over her knee and strapped it into place, then stood to test it out. She grimaced as she bounced, the stab of pain from her bursitis already making itself known.

"What the hell are you doing anyway?" Louie asked.

"What's it look like?" She did some toe raises as she allowed Louie to take in her attire. A sports bra and running shorts.

"It looks like you're going to try to run."

"Ding, ding, ding! We have a winner."

He smirked and took another sip of his coffee.

Lyra grinned at him and he narrowed his eyes. "You're nuts, you know. Going out running with that bum knee. It's too soon."

She lifted her leg behind her for a hamstring stretch. "My other injuries have healed. All that remains is a little knee irritation."

"It's too soon to run."

He was referring to the accident. The one that had nearly taken her life. He refused to believe she was fine now.

"Let me be the judge of that, okay?" She stretched the other leg and examined him in silence. He was a good-looking guy, close to her height, and blond like she was. But everything else about him was vastly different. From his eye color to his personality, to his views on life in general. In fact, the only thing left that they had in common was their sense of humor. That had bonded them wholeheartedly. She wasn't sure what she'd do if she couldn't hear Louie's laugh ever again.

He sipped more of his coffee. "If that won't stop you, then this should."

"What's that?" She pulled her arm across her chest for an additional stretch.

"It's not safe. Young women go missing here in this parish."

She scoffed. "You're going to have to try harder than that, Lou. I'm not buying it."

"I'm not lying. Look it up, it's true."

She strapped her phone into an armband and popped in her earbuds. "Later. Right now, I've got to get going." She turned to walk out of the kitchen. Louie called out after her.

"What's the hurry? You're on vacation!"

She opened the front door and that time didn't rise to the bait.

She shook the morning and the conversation with Louie from her mind as she refocused on the path. He'd been right about the vacation. Technically, she was supposed to be resting and recovering some more from the accident. But she was finding that her visit to the small town of Sugar Mill Farm was becoming boring and mundane. While she loved the scenery and the culture of Southern Louisiana, she was finding her days to be more of the same. But then again, what did she expect from a town the size of Sugar Mill Farm?

Truthfully, she wished she was on another field study. Somewhere exotic. Like the last trip she'd been on before the accident. She'd gone to Thailand to help out a colleague from another university. They'd excavated an Iron Age cemetery at an ancient monastery in Promtin Tai and had also visited other temples in and around Bangkok. She recalled how the villagers visited, and even held ceremonies at the site when they were there. She'd met so many wonderful people and learned so much from the skeletal remains they'd unearthed. It had been the trip of a lifetime and she wished it had never ended. If it hadn't, she never would've been in the accident. She never would've had life-threatening injuries, or injuries that still caused her trouble, like her knee.

She was deep in thought about her painful knee when she tripped and fell headfirst into the edge of burnt cane. She landed hard and she lay stunned for a moment before the pain set in.

The first thing she noticed was her jaw. It hurt like hell. And as she slowly pushed herself up, she had trouble getting her bearings. Her arms were skinned, and she rubbed her jaw and tasted blood. "Shit." She felt her teeth to make sure they were still there. So far so good. But the blood.

"Ow." She'd not only hurt her jaw, she'd scraped the skin and bitten her lip. Damn, it hurt.

She spat and held her head. The world came into focus around her once again. Something off-white stood out against the blackened cane on the ground. She blinked against some blowing ash and looked harder. She brushed herself off and checked for more wounds. When she didn't find anything other than her sore knee and some more scrapes, she limped over to the object slightly protruding from the ground.

Her highly trained eyes honed in. She stepped closer, disbelieving what she was seeing. She crouched, afraid to get too close, and grabbed a rare rock. She used it as a tool and rooted the object from the mud and covered her mouth in shock.

"No way."

Quickly, she looked around, as if she'd see someone nearby. Someone she could share her shock with. But she was alone. Just her, the bone, and the burnt sugarcane.

She stood and walked the few steps back to the clearing. She glanced around again, suddenly very unnerved. She unstrapped her phone and paced as she dialed nine-one-one. Her heart raced and her mind flew as the line rang.

How could this be?

Was she seeing correctly?

Was this real?

A woman answered on the other line.

Lyra sucked in a big breath and said something she'd never thought she'd say outside of work.

"I just found human remains."

CHAPTER TWO

In the name of the Father, Son, and Holy Spirit," Danica said as she knelt in the church, made the sign of the cross, and kissed her rosary.

She took a deep breath and reminded herself that she'd promised her mother she'd come. She had to do this in order to pacify her, just like she did by attending Sunday mass. It didn't seem to matter to her mother that her heart wasn't always in it. All that mattered was the saving of her soul.

She pondered her sins, preferring to pray about them rather than go to the confessional. Besides, her long-time priest, Father O'Toole, could probably recite her sins by heart by now. It wasn't like there were any new ones on the list.

She drank. Every day to wind down. To help clear her head. Her ex, Shawna, thought it was becoming a problem, but she wasn't keen to agree with her. At least not yet. She enjoyed having sips of whiskey when needed. It soothed her and, in her opinion, helped her work. Plus, it helped her feel connected to her late father, who'd also favored whiskey. She even had one of his old bottles left at home that she liked to drink from.

She imagined what Father O'Toole would tell her. He'd ask if she could control the drinking. Or if it controlled her. She wasn't sure how to answer. But she didn't feel the need for AA or anything like that. After all, she wasn't that far gone.

She continued going down the mental list of her sins.

She cursed a lot.

Took the Lord's name in vain. Another habit she wasn't ready to concede.

And of course there was the big one. Her homosexuality. There was no way she was going to try to control that. That was who she was. How she was made. So how did one control who they were in their core? As far as she was concerned, God didn't make mistakes.

She closed her eyes and prayed. Prayed for the sake of her mother. Her mother who prayed desperately for her soul. She prayed her mother would ease up and accept her for who she was. She prayed for peace, and most of all, she prayed for help with her current case.

There were five girls missing now in Sugar Mill Farm. Five girls in three years. Not a trace of them had been found. She had nothing. And it was eating her alive.

"Please help me find the girls," she whispered.

She crossed herself again as she finished.

"My God, I am sorry for all my sins, confessed and forgotten. Amen."

There. She felt better. Even though she came mostly at the behest of her mother, she really did find solace in church. She just wanted to come on her own terms. Not her mother's. Maybe in due time.

She stood as her phone alerted. Frazzled, she pulled it from her waist band and read the text.

She blinked in disbelief and hurried from the church.

Half an hour later, she turned down the dirt road to the cane fields that were the namesake of the town, Sugar Mill Farm. She passed through the police barricade and headed through the fields toward the half dozen police vehicles. Surrounding her were the burnt remnants of sugarcane, and in the distance she could see a cane harvester, and someone she assumed to be the operator, standing next to it arguing with a deputy. It was harvest time, which meant the fields had just been burned to make harvesting the cane easier.

She squinted through her dirty windshield and turned on the wipers to help clear off the ash and some remaining dead love bugs. She blasted her A/C knowing in just a minute or so she'd have to step out into another unseasonably hot Southern Louisiana day. But that wasn't weighing on her mind much at the moment.

She slowed her vehicle and put it in park behind the others. Then she gently ran her fingertips over the wallet-sized photo she had of the latest missing girl, Tina Givens. She kept it on her instrument panel in her car so each time she checked her speed she'd be reminded of Tina.

She closed her eyes and said a short prayer.

Voices carried to her as she crawled from the unmarked police cruiser and walked toward the white tent-like structure being erected. CSI personnel covered from head to toe in the white "bunny" suits were already on scene, and her pulse thudded as she considered what they might have already found.

"Is it her?" she asked as she wove her way through more personnel.

She stared down her partner, Grady Devereaux, as she waited for an answer.

"It's bones and they're burned, so it's not Tina Givens. Last fire here was too long ago. But…"

"But what?" Tina had only been missing for three days, so Devereaux was right. The remains couldn't be Tina.

"Preliminary says the remains belong to a young woman."

Danica straightened a little, the disappointment leaving her in an instant.

"As in, this could be one of the other missing women?"

"Could be."

She pushed her way past him and tried to get a look at the scene, but CSI techs were blocking her view.

"Who called it in?" Danica asked.

Devereaux removed his eyeglasses and tried to wipe the steam off with his tie.

"The farmer?" She glanced back toward the harvester, but he was nowhere near the remains.

"Nah, he claims he hasn't seen anything. Been harvesting these fields for years and has never come across anything suspicious."

"Well, if the fields are already burnt, then that makes sense." She thought for a moment. "I don't understand. We searched these fields, Devereaux. Numerous times."

He shrugged. "Maybe the perp was wise to us and put these bodies here after we searched and just before the burns."

She chewed her lower lip. "I suppose."

Devereaux gestured toward a woman across the clearing, beyond the perimeter tape. She was talking at a deputy, much like the farmer had been doing back at the cane harvester.

"That's who called it in."

"Who is she?"

"Some hotshot bioarchaeologist from Arizona State."

"Bioarchaeologist? What's she doing here?"

"She was jogging."

"Through the burnt cane?"

"Guess so. Said she was curious."

Danica laughed. But then the woman turned and she got a good look at her, and suddenly she felt like she needed to go right back to church for an actual confession. The woman was covered in dried mud and smeared ash. The side of her face had a considerable scrape, along with her arms. She was incredibly beautiful nonetheless, with her chin-length blond hair, her tight-fitting sports bra, and her unbelievably high running shorts showing off her lean legs. She was a knockout and Danica had to swallow hard as she left Devereaux to talk to her.

"I've got this, Michaels," she said, dismissing the young deputy who was with her. He tipped his hat, seemingly more than happy to be dismissed, and walked away.

"Hi," Danica started. "I'm Detective Danica Wallace with the Louisiana State Police Bureau of Investigations. I understand you're the one who discovered the remains?"

"You could say that," the woman said. She narrowed her light brown eyes at Danica and placed her hands on her hips. "You're a detective, you say?"

"Yes, ma'am."

"Sorry, it's just…you don't look like a cop."

"I don't?" She actually got that a lot. But she was still surprised to hear this woman say the same thing. She seemed to be really taking her in and Danica wondered what all she was thinking.

"No, you're too beau—"

She stopped and appeared to be somewhat embarrassed. She covered that up though, by narrowing her eyes again.

"You're upset," Danica said, not quite sure if she was reading her right. But nevertheless she wanted to comfort her. "It's understandable. Finding remains can be traumatizing."

The woman rubbed at the dried mud and ash on her arm. Danica noticed that she was bleeding from her deep scrapes.

"Do you need EMS? You look hurt."

"No."

"You sure?"

"I just took a little fall as I was running. I'm fine."

"If you change your mind, just say so."

Her face softened. "Thank you." But then she shook her head, as if to break herself from a trance.

"I'm more concerned about the femur I saw when I fell. It was near where I landed and I recognized it as human right away, so I called it in."

"Yes, Detective Devereaux tells me you're a bioarchaeologist. From Arizona is it?"

"Yes."

"So you were able to discern that the bone was human."

"Correct."

Danica pulled her small notebook from her back pocket. She began making notes. "Can I get your name, Ms...?"

"Aarden. Lyra Aarden. Double a's. But my name isn't what's important."

"Sorry?"

Lyra pointed toward the white tent. "I tried to tell them. But they pushed me back."

Danica glanced back at the tent. "Tell them what?"

"That there are more than one set of remains."

Danica blinked at her. "Come again?"

"There are more bones just a little farther into the cane. And from what I could make out without touching them, you've got more than one body there."

The cane field seemed to spin, and Danica struggled to remain present. She couldn't believe what she was hearing. Could it be true? If so, what did it mean? Could it possibly be her missing girls?

She steeled herself, not wanting to get too carried away. After all, she'd been let down in the missing women case more times than she'd like to admit. It was safer to remain detached and cynical.

"You could see the bones from where you fell?"

"Not all of them. Not initially. They're partially buried."

Danica waited for her to continue.

"After I found the femur and called it in, I walked farther into the cane and spotted more bones. From what I could see, I'm fairly certain there's more than one set of remains."

"From what you could see?"

Lyra stared at her. "Yeah."

"Do you realize you may have compromised a crime scene?" Christ, this was all she needed. An armchair detective disturbing a crime scene. One that could be vital to her missing persons case. The attraction she felt for her threatened to diminish.

"This ain't my first rodeo, Detective. I've been on more excavations than you have crime scenes."

Feisty, huh? Okay. I can handle that.

"I seriously doubt that. And even if it were true, you should know that the first rule at a crime scene is to touch nothing."

"I know my way around unearthing remains. I was careful not to disturb anything other than the initial bone, which I uprooted from the mud with a rock."

Danica lowered her notebook and Lyra sighed. "Can you please go ask them if they've come to the same conclusion I have?" She paused, and when Danica didn't say anything, she continued. "Look, I know my stuff, okay? I'm a bioarchaeologist. That means I study human remains and learn all about them, from their diet to their lifestyle, to their death. Understand? I work at Arizona State. You can call them if you'd like."

"I might do." It would be interesting to find out if she was really as well versed in human remains as she said she was. But she knew she wouldn't call. She just didn't have the time, especially since she wasn't ever planning on seeing her again.

"Well, could you hurry? Because I really want to know what all they've found."

Danica considered her qualifications for a moment and then glanced behind her and called out. "Yo, Devereaux? Any further word on the remains?"

"Like what?" he called back.

"Just ask them."

Devereaux leaned into the tent for a few seconds and then withdrew. "The bones are scattered. It's going to take a while to gather them all."

"Anything else?"

"Like?"

"Another body."

"What?"

Danica marched to the tent and stood at the threshold. "Have you stumbled upon any other bones?" she asked. "As in another set of remains?"

The numerous technicians looked up at her.

"You're kidding, right? We're doing all we can to unearth this one at the moment."

"Well, is it possible? That there's another set somewhere close?"

"Sure, it's possible. But we haven't found anything so far. We literally just got here, Detective."

Danica left the tent and returned to Lyra. "Nothing so far."

"They're there, I saw them. Tell them—"

Danica motioned for her to calm down. "I understand. But they haven't found anything further so far." Danica tilted her head in empathy. Lyra, despite her good looks, appeared to be tired and roughed up. She looked like she could use a nice, hot shower and something cool to drink, despite her having two water bottles at her hips. She was either on a very long run or she wasn't used to the Louisiana heat. "What brings you to Louisiana?"

Lyra seemed surprised at the question, and she looked as though she had to think for a moment.

"I have family here."

"First time visiting?"

"For an extended stay, yes. Why do you ask?"

"Just curious. So, a bioarchaeologist, eh?"

"That's right."

"So you know bones?"

"You could say that." She looked beyond Danica to the tent. "Where's your forensic anthropologist? Does he ever come on scene?"

Danica glanced back at the tent with her. "Doesn't look like she's here. But rest assured, she'll come when called."

"Oh, it's a woman."

"Mm-hm."

Danica wasn't sure why she was asking. Maybe she really was well versed on crime scenes. "Listen, why don't you let me hold down the fort here and you go on home and get cleaned up? We'll contact you if we need anything further."

"They're there, I'm telling you. You've got quite a surface scatter to check."

Danica nodded. "And I'll be sure they check thoroughly, trust me. We'll let you know if you can be of further assistance. Did you give Deputy Michaels your contact information?"

"I—yes."

"We'll also need a DNA sample from you as well as photos of your shoes."

"That's fine."

Danica turned and called for a technician, instructing them on what was needed.

"Mary here will take care of you," Danica said, introducing her to the tech. "When she's finished you can go ahead on home. Deputy Michaels can give you a lift."

"Can you call me no matter what? I really want to know if I'm correct."

"Technically, I'm not supposed to share information on a case. But in this instance, and considering that the press will find out eventually, sure, I can give you a call." Danica closed her notebook. It wouldn't be right away and she wouldn't be able to share much, if anything at all. But at the moment it seemed to calm her down. "Sound good?"

Her defenses seemed to drop along with the relaxation of her stance. "Sure," she breathed.

"I'll be in touch." Danica left her and returned to the scene. She was sliding on shoe covers when Devereaux approached.

"She seems like a real piece of work," he said as he stood next to her. "Real intense."

"She's alright. Just a little curious. And given her field of specialty, I can't say I blame her."

"Yeah, well, you got the toned-down version. When I first got here she was up in arms."

Danica looked back at her and saw Mary swabbing her inner cheek for DNA.

"She seems cooperative," Danica said. "So, that's good."

"She's a know-it-all. That's the last thing we need."

"She'll cool off. Probably forget the whole thing before long."

"I hope you're right."

"Me, too." She didn't need a know-it-all up in her case at the moment. She had enough to worry about.

A technician popped his head out from the tent. "Detectives, we've got something."

"What is it? A piece of jewelry? Clothing?" Danica asked, knowing that would go far in proving whether or not the remains belonged to one of the missing girls, but also fearing that the cane fires had destroyed any such evidence.

"A second body," the technician said. "Just like you said."

Danica almost swayed in disbelief. "You're kidding."

"No, ma'am. We've got more than one body here."

Danica watched as Lyra walked with Deputy Michaels to his cruiser. She had a considerable limp and Danica wondered just how badly she'd hurt herself on that fall and just what all she really knew about crime scenes.

"Who the hell are you, Lyra Aarden?"

CHAPTER THREE

Dr. Eleanor Stafford sipped her La Crema Russian River Valley pinot noir as she adjusted her sound system. She settled on Mo-Town classics and began to hum to the Temptations as she returned to her sofa to study the paperwork on her coffee table. The work was tiring but interesting, so she was never upset at having to work late into the night. In fact, some nights she looked forward to it. It helped occupy her time and chase away the loneliness she sometimes felt.

She grabbed some popcorn from the bowl next to the wine and held up a dental X-ray against the overhead light. She examined the identifiable defects as she ate. There were five filled cavities and a bridge for the front teeth which was found intact with the body. She lowered the X-ray and slid on her reading glasses. Then she read the ante-mortem dental records and the report from the forensic odontologist. She scanned through them quickly and smiled as she confirmed his conclusion. They were a match.

They'd identified yet another body, this one without DNA testing. She was still smiling when the doorbell rang. A quick glance at the clock left her feeling surprised. It was after ten.

She headed for the front door. To her continued surprise, she saw her ex-lover, Detective Danica Wallace, through the peephole.

She unlocked the door and opened it.

"Danny," she breathed. "It's been a while since I've had a late-night visit from you."

"You mean you're getting them from someone else?" Danny said with a smirk.

"Uh, no."

Danny leaned against the doorjamb in a relaxed manner. "That's too bad."

"Is it?"

"Sure. You deserve love just like everyone else."

"Right, like you're getting with Shawna?"

A look of sadness overcame her as she reached out to remove Eleanor's reading glasses. "Still forget to take these off, I see."

Eleanor slowly drew away. "I didn't forget." She walked back into her living room, allowing Danny to follow. She had no idea why she'd come over, but the past led her to believe that when she showed up late, sex was most likely on her mind. Though it had been over two years since Danny had come on to her, she wasn't up for a one-night stand, regardless of how attractive she was.

"Shouldn't you be at home with Shawna?" Eleanor asked, returning to the couch. She reached for her pinot noir and tried not to gulp. Danny's presence always got her flustered, much to her dismay. Why did she still have to be so damned beautiful, with her shoulder-length dark hair and captivating hazel-blue eyes?

Danny crossed the room slowly, allowing Eleanor plenty of time to take in her beauty. She stopped by the sound system and leaned on the entertainment center much like she had the doorjamb. Only this time there was no smirk. Just an overwhelming sense of sadness.

"Shawna's gone," she said softly.

Eleanor sat in silence for a moment, unsure what to say. "Was it a mutual thing?"

"No. She ended things. Just like you did."

Eleanor sipped more wine. "I'm sorry to hear that, Danny."

"Yeah, me too."

"Do you want to talk about it?"

She sighed. "Not much to say. She said she was sick of me and she left. End of story."

"I'm sorry," Eleanor said.

"Guess I'm still a screwup. Can't keep a woman."

"You are not a screwup, Danny."

"Ha. That's not what you used to allude to."

"I never thought you were a screwup. You were just younger than you are now, more frivolous. And you couldn't leave your job at the office. Not to mention the drinking."

"Are you kidding me?" Danny asked as she whipped her head around. "Who's the pot calling the kettle black?" She gestured toward her papers and files on the coffee table.

Eleanor gathered them up and slid them aside. "I work late, yes. But I don't let it get to me like you do."

"And the drinking?"

"I have a glass of wine. Two some nights. But never more than that and some nights not at all."

"Right, so you've got it all together."

"That's not what I'm saying."

"Yeah, well you sound just like Shawna."

"So, you're still bringing your work home and drinking?"

Danny drew away from the sound system with a pinched look on her face.

"Like I said, I'm still a screwup." She held her hand up to keep Eleanor from responding. "But that's not why I'm here. I didn't come here to discuss me or us."

"Oh?"

Danny sank down on the chair next to the couch. "I need information. On the cane field remains at Sugar Mill Farm."

Eleanor chuckled. "Oh, good God, Danny."

"I need it as soon as possible, El."

"And you'll get it as soon as we write up our profile."

"Well, what do you have so far? Surely you can tell me that."

"We've had the bones for a day, Danny. And I haven't been to the scene yet."

"Are there more than one set of remains? Can you verify that?"

Eleanor sighed. "Danny, what's this about? Why the full-court pressure?"

"My missing persons case. I need to know if these remains belong to any of my girls."

"*Your* girls?"

Danny waved her off. "So to speak."

"Danny, you're taking these cases to heart, aren't you? Probably aren't sleeping well on top of the stress."

"I'm sleeping fine."

"I can tell by the dark circles under your eyes that that isn't the truth. And I know how much time you've spent on those big searches, looking for those girls at all hours of the day and night."

"Yeah, well." She shrugged.

"I understand your need to know about the remains, but I don't want to give you inaccurate information or guesswork on my part. Give me a chance to do my job."

"When? When should I come back?"

"To answer your questions? I don't know. Midweek? You can *call* midweek."

"You mean you're leaving it for the weekend?"

"I have other work to catch up on first." She held up the files. "I can't just drop everything for you and your caseload."

"You have no idea how important this is, do you? I've got five girls missing, El. Five. I've got mothers crying and cursing at me. Families devastated. Young children missing their mother."

"I'm sorry, Danny. But you're going to have to wait until next week. Midweek is probably the best I can do and even then the information will be incomplete."

"You mean midweek is the best you *will* do."

Eleanor stood. "I think it's time for you to go."

"Look, I'm sorry," Danny said, hanging her head in her hands. "I'm just—I'm being a total ass and I'm sorry."

She glanced up at her with an expectant look.

"A little bit, yeah."

"You're right. These missing women are eating me alive. I'm just so stressed."

Eleanor felt for her. She could see the misery in her tired eyes. "Maybe you should take a break. Take the weekend and do something you enjoy. Like take your mountain bike out for a ride."

Danny sighed. "I don't know. I'll think about it."

"I hope so. You really look like you could use the rest."

"I just need to know if she's right," Danny said, standing as well.

"Who?"

Danny shook her head as if frustrated. "The woman. From Arizona State."

"What woman?"

"The one who found the bones. She claimed there were more than one set of remains."

"How would she know?"

"She's a bioarchaeologist."

Really? That's interesting.

"Why do you care if she's right?"

"It's not about her, per se. I just really need to know if there's more than one body. And if so, who do they belong to."

"What did the techs say?"

"They also said there was more than one set."

"Then she's probably right."

"But you can't say yet?"

"I haven't even done a preliminary examination."

Danny sighed again.

Eleanor studied her. "I'm assuming in being a bioarchaeologist that she didn't disturb the remains?"

"She said she didn't."

Eleanor headed for the door, hoping Danny would follow. She was drained from a hectic work week and she knew she couldn't help Danny any further without wanting to take her in her arms to help ease her pain. And they both knew, due to their past, that it was best if that didn't happen.

"I'm sorry I don't have any information for you, Danny."

Danny followed and then stopped in front of her. "I really need your help on this one, El. If not for me, then for the missing young women."

Eleanor met her soulful eyes and nodded. "Call me, next week."

Danny nodded. "Okay." She reached up and lightly grazed Eleanor's cheek. "Again, I'm sorry. I really didn't mean to come here and act like an ass."

Eleanor clutched her hand in hers. "I know."

"We'll talk soon," Danny said. She then walked out the door and waved good-bye.

CHAPTER FOUR

Lyra was once again lost in her thoughts as she approached her parents' house for Sunday brunch. She was thinking about her recent fall, and how her hip and knee still hurt, not to mention her jaw and her arms from the numerous scrapes and abrasions. Louie had had a fit over her injuries and insisted she go to the emergency room, but she'd declined, and instead tended to herself. She was sore, but she wasn't nearly as sore as she had been after her car accident. A flashback of her pulling out from the four-way stop entered her mind and then she flinched as she recalled the full-sized SUV running the adjacent stop sign to broadside her. The impact had rolled her car and she'd been stuck upside down, hanging by her seat belt. She could still hear the Jaws of Life as the firemen worked to free her.

She shook the memories from her mind and inhaled. She had her folks to contend with now and that in itself might be a chore.

I can do this.

I can.

Just like running.

I just hope I don't fall on my face here as well.

She steeled herself and knocked on the door.

The morning was damp but a little cooler than it had been the previous days. She eyed the potted plants on her mother's front porch and knelt to rearrange two carved pumpkins that were sitting on the edge. By the look of the rough carvings, she could tell it had been her nieces who'd done the work. Or maybe her mother had. She wasn't exactly known for her pumpkin carving skills. Either way, the pumpkins had seen way better days.

She'd have to buy her nieces more so they could carve some for Louie's front porch. They still had plenty of time before Halloween.

"Lyra," her mother said as she opened the door. "What in the world are you doing knocking on the door? You know you're welcome to just come right in."

Lyra kissed her mother on the cheek. "I know, Mom. I was just being polite."

"Well, stop," her mother teased her. "We'll have none of that."

Some things never changed. Like the smell of her mother's biscuits for example. Nothing in the world could beat it.

"Smells great," she said, heading for the kitchen. She did her best to try to hide her limp, but she knew her mother would notice.

Her mother touched her arms, and when Lyra turned toward her, she held her face. "What happened?"

"Oh, it's nothing," she said. "I just took a little spill."

"A little spill?" She gently touched her jaw. "Looks like you got in a fight the way you're all bruised and scraped up."

"I'm okay."

"And your knee?"

"It's just irritated."

"Do you need your cane?"

"I'm fine."

"I hope so. You were doing so well."

"I still am. Just a minor setback." She smiled and rested her hand over her mother's.

"Okay, I'll leave you be about it."

"Thanks. What all do we have going on here? Looks like a huge breakfast."

"Just a little Sunday brunch."

But Lyra knew that was hardly the case. She noticed the steaming bowl of scrambled eggs, the plate of bacon, the tray of biscuits, and the jars of homemade jam. Her mother had gone all out, just like she always did when she was expecting company.

"Oh, Mom, you've got blackberry," Lyra said, picking up the dark jar of preserves.

"Of course. It's your favorite. I was going to send some home with you."

"Thank you," she said, kissing her on the cheek again. She looked very similar to the way she'd looked when Lyra last saw her, with shoulder-length gray hair, light brown eyes, and an elfish grin. She stood just a bit taller than Lyra and had a thin build. Some might even say she was slight. But her mother always argued that one, refusing to believe it.

Lyra stroked her hair. "You finally stopped dying it," she said. "It looks great." Lyra liked her gray hair and had told her for some time just to let it take over.

"You think so? I don't look too old?"

"Mom, you always look beautiful. Honest."

She did. Her mother could still turn heads.

"Well, you look pretty good, too." Her mother stroked her face. "Despite looking beat up."

"Yeah?"

"Oh, yes. Although you're still a little skinny." She poked her ribs playfully.

"Hey, I'm eating."

"You better be."

Lyra laughed, still grateful to be out of the rehab facility where she'd spent weeks in recovery from the accident. She'd lost thirty pounds while there, the food having been terrible and well, she hadn't felt much like eating at first. The pain had been nearly unbearable.

"Dad here?" Lyra asked. But she knew the answer. She could hear the television and feel the sucking of the good energy. He was there. He was always there.

"He's in the living room."

"There must be a game on," Lyra said. "Or a pregame show." Her father rarely left his chair when she came. Especially if there was a game on. It had been this way for about ten years now. Ever since she'd disappointed him in telling him she was gay.

"You know him," her mother said.

Yeah, she knew.

"Go say hello."

"I don't want to bother him." She didn't want to say hello at all. She feared rejection, feared his cold reaction to her. She was thirty-two years old and still couldn't get over it.

"Oh, go say hello. You won't bother him. He'll be happy to see you."

Yeah, right. Fat chance of that.

Lyra headed for the living room, leaving her mother to set the table.

She found her father in his favorite armchair with his sock-covered feet up on the ottoman, cup of hot coffee in his hand. He was in his khaki shorts and white undershirt. But he appeared to be fresh from the shower with wet, slicked back hair and the scent of his Nautica cologne lingering in the air.

"Hi, Dad." She didn't bother sitting. The ice in the room was already hanging off the furniture in sickles.

He made a noise. Almost like a grunt. He didn't bother to look over at her.

"So you're in town, eh?" he said.

"For a while, yeah."

"You don't have to work, or what?"

She stood in silence for a moment. "I've been off due to the car accident. Remember? I've been recuperating." She didn't mention having to learn how to walk again which he damn well knew.

"Hmph," he said, as if it wasn't a good enough excuse. He slurped his coffee and scratched his temple. She stared at the sun reflecting in his golden hair and it made her hate her own blond locks. Why did she have to look so much like him?

At least I don't act like him.

Lyra stood there awkwardly, feeling like she was six years old again and wondering what the hell she'd done wrong.

"Well, I just wanted to say hi."

He finally glanced over at her. His look was not one of approval.

"You look perfectly healthy to me."

She shifted some on her feet, feeling defensive. "I'm getting there."

He looked back to the television, not mentioning her bruised and scraped face.

"Saints are gonna kick Arizona's ass today. What do you think about that?"

She wasn't sure what to say. He was obviously trying to get her goat, but she wasn't going to give him the satisfaction.

"That's nice, Dad. Well, it was good seeing you." She swallowed the ball in her throat and returned to the kitchen.

Her mother had the table set and was busy making her father a plate.

"You go ahead and have a seat, I'll be right back." She winked at her and disappeared into the living room. Lyra made herself comfortable at the table and sipped her juice. Her hands shook from the brief conversation with her father. Why did she still let him get to her? Why?

Her mother breezed back into the room like nothing in the world was wrong.

"There, now. You ready to eat?"

"Dad won't be joining us?"

"He likes to watch the football. You know that."

"Yeah, I know. I just thought that maybe since I lived so far away and wasn't here very often that he might like to join us." She was trying to get her mother to see how ridiculous her father was. How rude and selfish. But if she noticed, she never said. She just always smoothed everything over when it came to him.

Her mother took a bite of eggs and changed the subject. "So, you like staying at Louie's? Because you're always welcome here, you know?"

"Louie's is great." She loved seeing her nieces and she got along with her brother just fine. Besides, there was no way she was going to stay at her folks' house and be iced out by her father for weeks at a time. She wouldn't wish that on her worst enemy.

"The girls love having you," her mother said. "They miss their auntie Lyra."

"I miss them, too." She opened the blackberry jam and spread some on her biscuit. "They've really grown since I've seen them last."

"They sure have."

They both ate in silence for a moment.

"How are things, Mom?" Lyra asked softly.

"Oh, they're good, honey. They're good." She smiled.

"I mean with Dad."

Her mother looked down at her plate. "They're fine." She took another bite. "Why do you ask?"

Are you kidding?

"Because of the way he is with Louie and me. He's so, I don't know, pissy. And I know he can be that way with you, too."

"Oh, he's just tired."

"Tired? From what? He's pretty much retired." He worked as an engineer four days a week now. Pretty much ran his own schedule.

"All those things he builds while he's tinkering around out in that garage. He built the girls that tree house, you know? Did you see that?"

"I did," she said. "It's neat."

"He worked hard on that."

Lyra picked at her food. "So, he's good with the kids?"

Her mother looked offended. "Of course he is. They just adore him."

Lyra nodded. "That's good." At least there was that. If he'd treated them anything less than that she and Louie would not take that lightly.

Her mother handed her another biscuit and changed the subject again. "Do you know how long you're going to stay?"

"I'm not sure." She chewed quietly. Her folks had followed Louie to Louisiana five years before and they acted like they'd never lived anywhere else. Arizona seemed to be a distant memory to them now. "I'm getting really antsy about getting back to work."

"Oh, I hope you don't go too soon. Seems like you just got here."

"I'm not planning on leaving anytime soon. I'm just getting antsy. I kind of stumbled upon something the other day that really got my head going again."

"What was that?"

"Louie didn't tell you?"

She shook her head.

"I found some human remains."

Her mother stopped chewing.

"Sorry, maybe we shouldn't discuss it." She'd forgotten how bothered her mother was by talk of bodies and bones. It was the reason why she hadn't told her in the first place. While she supported Lyra and her choices in life, including her job, she wasn't very keen on discussing it.

"Where was this?" she asked, incredulous.

"The cane fields at Sugar Mill Farm. You know, that dirt road that runs through there?"

"That's right. I just read about that in the paper this morning."

"You did?" Lyra hadn't heard anything and she'd been anxiously awaiting some sort of news. But the detective had yet to call, and nothing had been reported to the public as far as she knew.

Her mother rose and returned with a newspaper. She unfolded it and pointed to the headline as she handed it over.

HUMAN REMAINS FOUND AT SUGAR MILL FARM

Lyra snatched the paper and read furiously. She felt her skin heat as she skimmed the article. "Unbelievable!" She refolded the paper and smacked it down on the table. "Just unbelievable."

"It is rather disturbing."

"That's not what I mean," Lyra said. "Damn it." She pushed her plate away.

"What?"

"She was supposed to call me," Lyra said. "That damn detective." Why hadn't she called? Had she forgotten? It wasn't likely considering how they'd interacted. Not to mention how they'd both fought an obvious attraction. She'd never seen a cop so striking before and she'd suspected, by the way the detective had looked at her, that she'd felt similarly. She might not have had a relationship in a while, but she could still tell when a woman was interested.

"What for?" her mother asked.

Lyra shook the thoughts of the attractive detective away, reminding herself that she was frustrated with her.

"To tell me if my observations had been correct. I'm the one who found the bones and identified them as being two sets of remains."

"Well, what does this mean?" her mother asked. "They said something about a serial killer in that article."

"I don't know, Mom, but I'm dying to find out." She finished her juice in one shot and ate her eggs and played with her bacon. She tried to enjoy her meal and her mother's company, but she couldn't get her mind off the bones in the sugarcane field. After a short while that felt like an eternity, she pushed away from the table. "In fact, that's exactly what I'm going to go do," she said as she thought out loud.

"What?"

"Find out."

"Find out what?"

Lyra stood and pointed at the paper. "What's going on with those remains."

"How?"

"By going straight to the head honcho."

"Who is that?"

"According to that article her name is Dr. Eleanor Stafford. She's head of forensic anthropology over at Southern Lafayette University. She's the one examining the bones for the investigation."

"Do you think she'll talk to you?"

Lyra shrugged. "I don't know. But it's not going to hurt to try."

"I wish you wouldn't get involved."

"Why? This is what I do, Mom. What I live for."

"I know, but you're on a break. Take some time for yourself, honey. Relax. Heal."

"I've done enough of that," Lyra said, kissing her good-bye. "I can't sit still any longer." She headed for the door. "Thank you very much for brunch. It was delicious."

"Don't you want to take this jam?" She hurried over to Lyra while screwing on the lid to the Mason jar.

Lyra took it and kissed her again. "Thanks."

And with that, she left her mother standing in the middle of the kitchen, waving after her just like she'd done for the past ten years.

She nodded.

"Okay," he said. He dropped his hands and stood beside her, excited to see her reaction. She staggered a little as she stared at the made-up table. The candles flickered and the scent of the steaks filled the air.

"I did this just for you," he said, waiting for her to at least smile. But she did no such thing. Instead, a tear fell down her face and she staggered again. He steadied her and led her to her chair. "Here, perhaps you need to sit to fully enjoy the experience." She sat and continued to stare. More tears fell from her eyes.

"You're so moved you're crying," he said as he settled in directly next to her. "I understand. It's a very moving occasion. It's our first dinner date."

He spread the paper napkin across her lap for her and then did the same to himself. Then he cut her steak and forked her a bite. He brought it to her mouth and waited. She didn't budge.

"Come on," he said softly. "You've got to at least try it. I worked so hard on it, just for you. Even got out grandmother's special china."

He touched the bite to her lips. Slowly, she opened her mouth and he fed her the steak. She took it in and chewed. Another tear fell down her face and she shuddered as if cold.

"There," he said, lowering the fork. "How is it? Good?"

She swallowed and nodded. He smiled, pleased.

"I marinated it overnight. I used balsamic vinegar, olive oil, Worcestershire sauce, beef broth, dried rosemary, garlic, and salt and pepper to taste." He brushed some hair back away from her eyes. "What do you think?"

Her eyes shifted over to his but then moved away quickly. She nodded again.

"You can speak," he said. "I'll allow it for now."

She blinked and spoke with a meek voice. "It's good."

He beamed. "That makes me so happy." He brushed back more hair. "You ready to try the rest?" He buttered her potato and handed her her fork. "Go ahead," he said. "Eat."

She took the fork with a shaky hand and forked herself some green beans. She brought the bite slowly to her mouth and took it in. She chewed long and slow and swallowed.

"Good?"

She nodded.

"That's my own secret recipe, but I'll tell you. I cook it with tasso and some Slap Ya Mama seasoning. But you can't tell anyone about the seasoning. I've got a reputation to keep and it would upset grandmother."

He cut himself a bite of steak and tried it. "Mm," he said, eyes rolling. "You're right. That is so good." He took another bite and watched her closely.

"Here, have some wine." He handed her the glass. But her hand shook so badly that she spilled. "That's okay," he said. "Take a sip."

She turned her head away, refusing.

"Now, now," he said. "You must drink."

But she kept her head turned in defiance.

His impatience grew. "Drink," he said yet again, firmer this time. She refused.

He slammed his hand down on the table and she jerked. "Damn it, I said drink!" He grabbed the glass and wrapped his arm around her face, holding her firmly in his grip. He pushed the glass to her lips and tilted her head back, forcing her to drink. She choked and tried to spit it up. But he kept on, insisting she get the majority of it down. When he finished, he set down the glass and breathed deeply.

"See? That wasn't so bad, was it?" He wiped her face with her napkin. "There was no need to fight me. I'm always going to win, you see."

"Here," he picked up her fork and placed it in her hand. "Eat, it's getting cold."

She sat very still, trembling. He sighed and pulled out his knife. He set it on the table. She lifted her fork and got herself another bite.

"That's it," he said. "Let's enjoy our dinner." He took another bite himself and chewed quietly.

His lovely was eating, Margo Smith was on the radio, and his heart was swelling with pride.

It was turning out to be a wonderful evening.

CHAPTER SIX

Dark, full clouds hung heavy overhead as Danica wove her way between people at Southern Lafayette University. It was early morning and she was headed toward the science building, the place Eleanor called home, with a caramel latte in hand. She moved along at a hurried pace, grateful for her coffee, but more grateful to be speaking with Eleanor about the skeletal remains at Sugar Mill Farm. She'd decided earlier, and given that they now knew for certain that they had at least two bodies, that merely calling Eleanor for info was no longer going to cut it.

No, now she needed more than just a quick rundown. She needed everything, and she needed it fast. As for Eleanor approving of her just showing up instead of calling, well, that remained to be seen.

"She'll have to get over it. I've got a case to work."

Eleanor had never really appreciated her showing up on campus unannounced. She'd said she was a distraction, to both her and her students. And then there was the lab. It irritated her when Danica showed up there. Eleanor was a studious worker, a hard-nosed scientist, and she did not like being disturbed when she was working with remains.

But desperate times…

Danica pulled open the door to the red brick science building just as a light drizzle began to fall. She hurried down the hallway to the lab and stepped out of the way as the door opened and one of Eleanor's students walked out.

"Hi," the young woman said. She glanced at Danica's latte and leather satchel. "Detective Wallace, right?"

"Right."

"Haven't seen you in a long while."

"It's been a minute, hasn't it?" Danica couldn't remember her name, but she really didn't have the time to converse with her anyway.

"She in?" Danica asked.

"The 'bone whisperer'?"

Danica chuckled. She'd forgotten that the kids called her that.

"The one and only."

"Is she expecting you?"

"It'll be a nice surprise."

The young woman pointed at the DO NOT DISTURB sign. "Enter at your own risk."

"I'm sure I'll survive." Danica entered the lab. An angry voice called out to her.

"That better not be anyone but Allison with my latte!"

Danica made her way to the last table in the room, bypassing the numerous human anatomy charts and drawers full of skeletal remains. She nodded hello to more students huddled over a computer as she continued on. Dark gray bones displayed on a white sheet welcomed her with their silence. They appeared to be charred, leading her to believe that they had to be from the cane fields at Sugar Mill Farm.

Movement from Eleanor's office got her attention and she smiled when she saw her. She wanted to douse the flames before they even got started.

"Sorry to disappoint," Danica said. "But I did bring you a latte." She held up the coffee cup.

"Bullshit," Eleanor said, shoving her hands into her lab coat. "You got that for you."

Danica set the drink on the counter between them, upset at being pegged so accurately for her self-centeredness. Why hadn't she thought to get Eleanor one?

Because your head is in the clouds on this case, that's why.

"Sorry, El. My head—"

"I know. It's fine. What are you doing here? I thought we had agreed you would call."

"I need more than a phone call, El. You know that. Besides, I was in the neighborhood."

More movement came from behind Eleanor and a familiar looking woman stepped out of her office. She froze when she saw Danica.

"Detective. I didn't expect to see you here," she said.

Danica swallowed the ball in her throat, totally confused and somewhat annoyed.

"The feeling is mutual." What in the world was Lyra Aarden doing there? Had she missed something? She looked to Eleanor for an explanation.

"Right. You two have met," Eleanor said.

"Yes, Ms. Aarden and I met at the crime scene at Sugar Mill Farm." And damn it if she wasn't still extremely easy on the eyes. Extremely easy.

"Then no introductions are necessary," Eleanor said.

But Lyra, who was also sporting a lab coat, spoke up. "Uh, actually, I don't really remember your name," she said, eyeing Danica. "It was all so confusing and chaotic at the crime scene."

Danica stared her down. Was she fucking with her?

"Dr. Aarden, this is Detective Danica Wallace."

Lyra gave a nod. "Right. You were supposed to call me."

Ah. So she *was* fucking with her. She was pissed about the phone call.

"Call you?" Eleanor asked. She turned the pearl necklace around her throat in her customary nervous gesture. "What for?"

Danica noted the red rising to her cheeks.

Could that be...jealousy?

Lyra spoke. "I asked her to call me to update me about the remains. I was curious to know if my observations had been correct about there being more than one set of bones. But I never got that phone call."

Eleanor adjusted her glasses and retrieved a pair of nitrile gloves from a box hanging on the wall. But instead of slipping them on, she handed them to Lyra, then retrieved a pair for herself.

"The detective is very busy," Eleanor said, snapping on the gloves. "So, I'm sure she had good reason for not returning your call."

Danica cleared her throat. "I *have* been busy." *But I purposely avoided making that phone call because this is a sensitive case, one that needs to be kept confidential. So, again, why are you here, Lyra Aarden?*

"See? Just as I'm sure she's busy now. Too busy to stay." She gave her a stern look over the frame of her readers. She edged down to the end of the counter and adjusted the arm of the lamp as well as the camera. The bright bulb illuminated the set of bones, laid out perfectly, awaiting more scrutiny.

"Actually," Danica said, following her and Lyra to stand across from the bones. "I came for information."

"Like I said before, a phone call would've sufficed," Eleanor said.

"I tried to call you Monday. You didn't answer. I even left a message."

"You left four messages."

"I wanted to be sure you knew I called."

"I knew, Detective," she said, still being formal. "I just was rather busy myself and Monday isn't midweek, as you know."

"I'm aware, but I needed, and still need, all the information you've gathered *now*. Not later. And I wanted to see what you've found for myself." She stared down at the discolored bones. "Is this one of the bodies from Sugar Mill Farm?"

"Yes," Lyra surprised her in saying.

Danica met her gaze. As captivated as she was by her beauty, she could no longer hold back her curiosity. "I'm sorry, but why exactly are you here?" She didn't mean to come off as rude, but she was beyond curious, and she had to admit, a little jealous. Lyra was working closely with Eleanor and that, for reasons she didn't care to think about, didn't sit quite right with her.

"Dr. Aarden is here to help," Eleanor said.

"Come again?"

"She called me, gave me the rundown on her qualifications, and offered her help. I said absolutely," Eleanor said.

"You mean you're going to help with *this* case?" Danica asked in disbelief.

"For as long as Dr. Stafford needs me."

"And I will need her, Detective. Especially now that we know there are numerous bodies, and we suspect there may be more."

Danica rubbed her forehead, frustrated at having Lyra Aarden in her life in the near future, and also in learning about Eleanor's suspicions. Lyra would most definitely be a distraction, and Eleanor's suspicions about numerous bodies? That meant they had a lot of work to do together. The three of them. And she was already feeling a little uneasy about Lyra working so closely with Eleanor. Especially since she herself felt such a strong attraction to Lyra.

"Is there a problem?" Eleanor asked.

Danica blew out a breath. "Nope. Nothing." Lie. Big, huge lie. But she wasn't about to share her thoughts.

She forced a smile and dug in her satchel for her notebook and clicked on a pen. "What have you got for me?"

"Well, so far we know that this particular set of remains belongs to a female," Eleanor said, adjusting the camera again. She then motioned toward the large monitor directly next to them.

Lyra spoke. "See, you can tell by the pelvic bone. There are six different areas where you can identify a female. Here"—she gently lifted the bone—"here, and here. And also…" But Danica was no longer paying attention to the pelvic bone on the screen or to what Lyra was saying. She was too busy staring into her eyes. Her incredible light brown eyes. She'd noticed them before. But why be spellbound now? When she had a case to work and a million things to do? And was she mistaken, or was Lyra seemingly lost in her gaze as well?

This was not going to be easy.

"Don't you want to write this down? Detective?" Eleanor was speaking to her.

"Sorry?"

"Your notes. Don't you want to take some?"

Danica focused on her blank sheet of paper. "Did you get an age?"

"Early twenties," Eleanor said.

Danica held her hand up at Lyra, stopping her from interjecting and explaining further. "I don't need an anatomy lesson, thanks."

Lyra looked to Eleanor. "I was just trying to be helpful."

"Yeah, well, you can help Eleanor. I'm good." She smiled, trying to show she meant well. But Lyra didn't return it.

"Anything else?" She pointed the question to Eleanor.

"We can't determine race without a skull." She paused for a moment and then continued. "The bones have been burned, clearing them of all flesh and tendons. Not to mention any clothing. We will grind the femur for trace element analysis of course. But there is something else." She held up a finger and looked to Lyra who grabbed a small manila envelope.

"This was found along with the bones in the surface scatter." She opened the end of the envelope and turned it upside down. A thin chain, that looked at one time to be sterling silver, slid out into her gloved hand. She held it up for Danica to examine.

"A necklace," Danica said. She reached out, wanting to get a better look at the dangling charm, but Lyra drew away.

"Sorry, you need gloves."

"Just show me the charm."

Lyra displayed the necklace along the palm of her hand.

"What is that? A bird?" Danica asked as she studied the small charm.

"A hummingbird," Eleanor said.

"Interesting." Danica made notes and snapped a photo with her phone. None of her missing victims had worn any such necklace. If they had, their family and friends hadn't mentioned it. Her stomach knotted as she considered that this may be another dead end too. "What else?" she asked.

"The other set of bones," Eleanor said. She crossed to an elongated box sitting on another table. Lyra and Danica followed. "Female. Early to mid twenties. Only we found some of the skull with this one."

"Race?" Danica asked.

"Caucasian. We also have a bit of the jaw." She carefully held up the skull and then the portion of the jaw from inside the box.

"Which means teeth," Danica said. "We need to get those to the odontologist." Dental records could prove that the bones belong to one of her missing women.

"Patience, Detective," she said softly. "We'll get there."

"As you can see, there is considerably less material to work with with this set of remains," Lyra said. "So, it's good we have the skull and teeth."

Danica peered inside the box. "Can we get any DNA on either set of remains if needed?"

Eleanor spoke. "It could be difficult because the bones are burned. Therefore, our best bet is the teeth or finding some identifying marks."

"This is the bone I saw that led me to believe there was more than one set of remains," Lyra said. She reached in and held up the bone.

"Another pelvic bone," Danica said.

"Right. Bringing the total in the surface scatter to three. So…"

"More than one body," Danica finished for her.

"Correct."

"We have yet to test for the isotopic signature on the remains, but we'll let you know as soon as we know something."

"Remind me, that'll tell me what, exactly?" Danica asked.

"We use it to see how old the bones are, as well as the victim's diet and lifestyle," Lyra said. "It's really quite fascinating."

"Mm," Danica said. "Sounds like loads of fun."

"It is," Eleanor added.

Great, you two will have a ball.

Danica's phone alerted and she slid it off her belt loop to read. "Holy shit."

"What is it?" Eleanor asked.

"The techs found another necklace." She held her phone out for Eleanor and Lyra to see.

"Oh, my God," Lyra said.

"It's gotta be the same killer then," Eleanor said.

Danica saved the photo of the blackened necklace and hummingbird charm and put away her phone. She'd call Devereaux just as soon as she left the lab.

"You got anything else for me as far as these remains?"

"We'll be in touch," Eleanor said.

Danica grabbed her satchel. "Please do." She winked at Eleanor, trying to play it cool, despite her trepidations about her working with Lyra Aarden. "See ya, El."

"Good-bye, Detective."

"Dr. Aarden."

"Detective."

Danica headed out, exiting through the door to the lab. But to her surprise, she heard someone call out after her.

"Detective?"

Danica turned in the hallway and saw Lyra gently closing the door behind her.

"Dr. Aarden." She had no idea what she could possibly want, and she tried hard not to openly stare at her. "What can I do for you?"

"I just wanted to make sure there was no issue between you and me."

Danica blinked, unsure she'd heard her correctly. "Why would there be?"

"Because you didn't call and because, well, because I'm working this case. Your case."

Danica appreciated the communication and she decided to be frank with her. "I didn't call because—"

"You forgot."

Hardly.

"No, I just need to keep the facts of this case confidential. We're talking about people's lives here. I'm sure you understand."

Lyra nodded and Danica continued. "It was nothing personal."

"And you're okay with my working the case now?"

Danica smiled. "I'll admit it took me a little by surprise. But if you're as qualified as you say you are, and Eleanor approves, then I guess it's okay."

"You guess?"

"Yeah, I guess."

"I'll grow on you," Lyra said, returning the smile. "You wait and see."

Danica chuckled softly as she left. *That's what I'm afraid of.*

CHAPTER SEVEN

Eleanor pulled into the parking lot and killed the engine. She hadn't looked forward to going to lunch like this in years. Not since she and Danny had first started dating and she wondered briefly what it meant, if anything.

It can't mean anything. We're working together.

She glanced over at Lyra and smiled. "Here we are."

Lyra squinted through the windshield. "And where are we, exactly?"

"Thibodeaux's. Authentic Cajun cuisine. Thought I'd give you a little taste of what you've been missing." And she was so excited to do so. Thibodeaux's was her favorite restaurant, and she couldn't wait to share it with Lyra and hopefully get to know her better. So far, the younger woman was proving herself to be more than adequate in the lab and the two of them were getting along splendidly. It was so nice to have an equal, someone who shared and understood her passion for bones.

"I've had some Cajun food before," Lyra said.

"Not like this you haven't. Not from what you've told me. And this is the best."

They climbed from the car and walked underneath an overcast sky to the door. Eleanor held it open and allowed Lyra to enter first. It felt nice to open a door for a woman again. Especially one so beautiful and intelligent. She thought back to the days of working lunches with Danny and the way she and Danny would rush to open the door for the other. It had made her feel so special and so cared for. She wondered what Lyra felt, if anything. By the appreciative look on her face, she mused that she felt something similar. She'd have to be careful not to take things too far. Eleanor followed her to sit at one of the numerous tall tables.

"I like the atmosphere," Lyra said, taking in their surroundings.

"It is interesting, isn't it?" The restaurant had an old-fashioned feel to it, much like a Cracker Barrel, only with Cajun decor.

"Very rustic."

"Very Cajun."

A waitress took their drink orders and they both sipped from their complimentary waters.

"What a day," Lyra said as she looked over the menu. She sounded a bit tired, but she didn't look it. In fact, she looked really good, with some color from the sun tinting her cheeks and a lively sparkle to her eyes. "It felt good to be back in the field though, even if it was a bit different than what I'm used to."

"I'll drink to that," Eleanor said, raising her glass.

They toasted and sipped more water as the waitress brought their iced teas.

"Mm, it's sweet," Lyra said as she took a sip.

"Did you want it unsweetened?"

"No, this is fine. I just keep forgetting that they sweeten their tea down here."

"It is the south, you know." She smiled at her again. Lyra returned it.

"Somehow I don't think you're going to let me forget it."

"Not a chance." Eleanor winked.

"So, have you lived here your whole life, then?"

"French Cajun born and bred. From my mama's side."

"Ah."

"What about you? Were you born in Arizona?"

Lyra grinned. "Desert rat born and bred. From both sides."

"Interesting. So how do we compare to Arizona?"

"Not even close."

"No?"

"The differences are too great to compare. Both have their good qualities."

"And bad?"

"Uh-huh." Her mouth dropped open at the menu. "Gator bites? Are you serious?"

"Don't knock 'em till you try 'em."

"No, thanks."

"Come on, you've got to at least try them."

But Lyra shook her head. "No way."

"I'll order some in case you gain some courage."

"Yeah, fat chance."

"You really that picky?"

"Yes."

"That's too bad. I was going to cook for you one night here soon."

"You were?"

"I can't now, can I? You're afraid to try new things and I make a killer Cajun cuisine."

"I can make an exception."

Eleanor wondered what prompted her to change her mind so quickly. Was she just being polite?

"Oh, okay." They both smiled and continued to study their menus.

"I don't do that often, you know."

"What? Cook for strangers?"

"I'm normally a very private person." She led a very quiet life. One filled with work and tending to her little garden at home. She was used to the solitude and if she were honest, often times really enjoyed it.

"Well, then I consider myself honored to be invited."

"You should be."

Lyra chuckled. "Is your cooking that good?"

"Sure is. Ask anyone."

"I don't know anyone."

"You know Danny."

"Danny?"

Shit. "Sorry, Detective Wallace."

"She's had your cooking?"

Eleanor hesitated, unsure how much she should share. But she knew she'd already given herself away and Lyra was looking at her so hopeful. "She has and she loves it."

Eleanor set her menu aside as Lyra studied her. Had she said too much?

"You two know each other well."

We do.

"We go back a ways." She avoided her eyes, now fearing she had indeed said too much. "How about some oysters to start with along with the gator bites?"

"I don't think I'd like oysters, but you go ahead."

They sat in silence for a moment before Lyra spoke again. "Do you not want to talk about it?"

"Hm?" Eleanor finally glanced up and found Lyra looking at her with empathy.

"Detective Wallace. Do you not want to talk about her?"

"We can talk about her." But she still wasn't so sure. Sharing that Danny liked her food was one thing, but sharing their past relationship was another.

"It's a touchy subject. I can tell."

Eleanor sipped her tea and fought flushing. *Ah, hell. She'll probably hear it from one of the students at the university anyway.* She swallowed hard and confessed. "We used to date."

"Oh?"

"You seem surprised," Eleanor said softly. "Is that because I'm obviously older than her or because of our sexuality?"

"Neither."

"Then what?"

"It's just that—you two seem like you don't get along all that well. You seem completely opposite actually."

"We are."

"But I suppose that could be what drew you to each other."

Now Eleanor did blush.

"I'm sorry, I'm getting too personal."

"No, you're fine."

But they sat in silence for another long moment.

"It must be difficult to work with her," Lyra said, obviously feeling her ground on how much she should say.

"It can be."

"Your sexuality doesn't bother me, by the way."

"No?"

Lyra shook her head. "I'm gay."

Eleanor felt the heat in her cheeks turn into an inferno. "Oh."

"You didn't know?"

"How would I?" She'd suspected, with the way she and Danny had interacted, but she hadn't been sure.

"I don't know. Sometimes you can tell."

"I would never assume. Not in this day and age."

"Probably wise. So, it doesn't bother you, then? My being gay."

"Why would it?" Lyra had just learned she was gay. So why wouldn't there be a problem?

"I don't know. Three lesbians working a case together." Lyra laughed softly. "Could get complicated."

"Why is that?"

This time Lyra blushed. "Nothing. Never mind."

"No, say it."

"I—it's nothing. It's just that—you're both very beautiful and then there's the fact that you've been together before…"

"Oh, I see. You're speaking of romantic complications." Eleanor nervously sipped her tea. The mere thought of the three of them involved in some sort of love triangle set her tummy all a tumble. "We'll just have to control ourselves, won't we?"

"I didn't mean to offend."

"You didn't." She set her glass down and cleared her throat. The waitress returned and Eleanor ordered the oysters on the half shell and the deep-fried gator bites. Lyra ordered a salad, obviously wanting to play it safe from any questionable cuisine.

Eleanor handed over their menus and then tried not to stare at Lyra. But it was difficult now that there wasn't the distraction of the menu.

"What?" Lyra asked, catching her eye.

"Nothing. I was just thinking."

"Yes?"

That you're incredibly beautiful as well. Especially in that summer copper tunic offsetting your eyes. But I can't think like this. I have to stop. It's unprofessional.

"That it's nice having your help on this case."

Lyra smiled. "I hope I'm being helpful."

"You are."

Another brief silence ensued, and Eleanor noticed that Lyra was still sporting her blush. She hurried to change topics to hopefully put both their minds at ease.

"So, what do you think about the Sugar Mill Farm remains? Specifically, the perimortem trauma?"

"Oh. Well, the broken hyoid bones suggest strangulation."

"Mm-hm. What else? What about antemortem trauma?"

"The healed tibia of body number two suggests an earlier break. Perhaps a childhood accident."

Eleanor nodded. "Remind me to call Danny—er, Detective Wallace, about that. She needs to be filled in on what all we've discovered since we last saw her."

"It could go a long way in helping to identify the victim."

Eleanor sipped her drink. "Definitely."

The waitress brought the oysters and Eleanor carefully lifted one to her mouth and swallowed it down. It was delicious. "You sure you don't want to try one?"

Lyra raised her eyebrows as she studied the appetizer. "I suppose I could, I guess."

Eleanor grinned. "That a girl. Live a little." She nudged the plate closer to her and watched as Lyra selected an oyster and brought it to her mouth. She wrinkled her nose a bit and seemed to hesitate.

"I promise you won't regret it," Eleanor said with a chuckle.

Lyra shrugged. "Here goes nothing." She downed the oyster and shook her head a bit and then blinked as if surprised.

"Well?" Eleanor asked.

Lyra visibly swallowed again. "It was—not too bad."

Eleanor laughed. "Bravo!"

Lyra joined her but then took a drink of water as if maybe she feared the oyster would suddenly become distasteful even after she'd swallowed it.

"Don't tell me you've changed your mind," Eleanor said, still laughing.

"No, it's just—" Her blush returned. "Shut up," she said with a smile.

"I'm sorry," Eleanor said, "it's just that you're adorable." She really was. And Eleanor was thoroughly enjoying watching her, which could become a problem if she let it. She let her laughter die down.

"I'm just a little unnerved with unusual cuisine," Lyra said.

"I can see that." The waitress delivered the gator bites. "You brave enough for one more taste test?"

"Oh, gosh. I don't know. Alligator?"

"Aw, come on, you've come this far." Eleanor lifted an eyebrow at her.

Lyra studied the fried bits of gator. Hesitantly, she reached out with her fork and stabbed a bite.

"Dip it in the spicy rémoulade sauce."

Lyra looked at her as if truly afraid.

"It's just mayonnaise, mustard, horseradish, pickle relish and seasoning."

"Horseradish?"

Eleanor laughed again. "Just try it."

Eleanor intertwined her fingers under her chin, completely amused. She hadn't had a meal this entertaining in a very long time.

With one last look at Eleanor, Lyra dipped the gator in the sauce and then put it in her mouth and chewed. A cautious scowl came across her face and then something happened. She relaxed and swallowed.

"See," Eleanor said. "Not too bad, eh?"

"Yeah. It wasn't too bad. Tastes a little like chicken."

"And the sauce?"

"Spicy but nice."

Eleanor beamed. "Please, have some more."

"I think I will. Thanks."

"My pleasure." Eleanor happily watched her eat and then continued with their conversation, trying not to get too caught up in the pleasure of watching her. "What about postmortem? Anything catch your interest?"

"Well, the killer obviously placed the bodies in the cane fields so the fires would destroy any evidence."

"And what does that tell you about him?"

"That he's at least somewhat intelligent. Cunning. Careful."

"Mm-hm."

"Anything else?"

"He's probably from the Sugar Mill Farm area. He knows that field. Probably knows when and where the fires will be set."

"Very good."

"Thanks."

"You rival Detective Wallace with your observations."

Lyra let out a long breath. "Really?"

"She's very good at discerning crime scenes. You and she should have a conversation."

"I'd love to. But I don't think that'll ever happen. She doesn't seem very fond of me."

Eleanor sipped her tea and chuckled softly.

"What?" Lyra asked.

"I think you're misreading her demeanor toward you."

"What makes you think that?"

Because I know her very well.

"She has no reason whatsoever to dislike you, so reason stands that maybe she likes you just fine. She's just focused on her case."

"I don't know. I'm sensing some unfavorable vibes."

Eleanor swirled her drink straw. Truth be told, she'd noticed the same. But should she share that with her? If she did, she'd have to come up with a reason as to why. Which wouldn't be good for any of them if they all continued to work together. Because the only reason she could think of as to why Danny was acting so off-putting toward Lyra was simple. She found her attractive. Danny had behaved the same way when they'd first met.

"She's under a tremendous amount of stress," Eleanor said.

Lyra studied her closely, as if trying to suss out the truth. "I hope you're right. I really would like to have a conversation with her."

Eleanor cocked her head. "Oh?"

"Sure. She seems very knowledgeable and she's, I don't know, nice."

Nice?

Eleanor couldn't help but wonder what all had transpired between them when Lyra had gone out after her at the lab. By the wistful look on Lyra's face, something had definitely changed. She wanted desperately to ask, but she didn't want to come off as too concerned about it. So instead she handed the waitress her glass for a refill and moved on. "Let's continue our conversation about the remains."

"Okay."

Eleanor watched as Lyra's salad was delivered. It looked delicious even though it didn't have all the typical Cajun ingredients that her meal had. "We have to expand the search and as you know it's going to take some time."

Lyra swallowed a bite of lettuce. "And you're sure you're okay with my helping out with that?"

"Absolutely."

Eleanor considered her luck in having Lyra's help. Unearthing and examining the charred remains would go a lot faster with her know-how. And, if she were being honest, she liked having her around for another reason too.

She briefly closed her eyes and tried to shake the thought from her mind. She had to remain professional and focus solely on the case. But she had to admit, she was enjoying her time spent with Lyra and the fluttering of butterflies in her stomach suggested that there was a deeper reason why. A reason, she knew, that she might not be able to ignore, no matter how hard she tried.

She opened her eyes and found Lyra watching her closely. Eleanor spoke, hoping to cover her obvious ruminations.

"I'm so glad you're willing to help. Because if indeed these deaths are all related, then we have a serial killer loose in Lafayette Parish."

Lyra set down her iced tea with a concerned look.

Eleanor continued, deadly serious.

"And that, my new friend, is terrifying."

CHAPTER EIGHT

Danica sat very still on a light blue sofa inside Mrs. Naomi Given's modest clapboard-sided home. Mrs. Givens was crying quietly in an armchair, dabbing her eyes with a wadded up tissue. Next to her, perched on the armrest, was her oldest child, her son, Oliver. He spoke to Danica as he rubbed his mother's back in a soothing manner.

"You're sure?" he asked, wiping away one of his own tears.

"She fits the pattern," Danica said.

"What pattern is that?" he asked.

"Late teens, early twenties, Caucasian female with dark hair and eyes."

"And?" he said with sarcasm. "Didn't you forget poor? Or lower class, as you people like to call it?"

Danica looked at him with empathy. He was right. No sense in hiding it.

"She fits the demographic of our other victims."

"I don't understand," Mrs. Givens said. "You're saying she's absolutely not one of the bodies you've found, but you think she was taken by the same man that killed those other girls?"

"That's correct."

"But you can't be sure," Oliver said. "I mean, what if you're wrong?"

"I hope I'm wrong," Danica said. "But she was last seen walking alone at night, just like the other women. She's been missing for days now, with no word."

"So? She could've just run away," Oliver said, defiant.

"Do you think she had reason to?"

"My baby didn't run away," Mrs. Givens said. "I know that for a fact."

Danica nodded. "I have something to show you," she said. "Could be an important clue." She stood and approached the two of them, holding out her phone. "Have you ever seen a necklace like this?" She showed them a picture she'd found online of a stainless steel hummingbird necklace. It was identical to the charred one they'd found in the cane field.

They both looked at it for a long moment and shook their heads. "Nah."

"Why?" Mrs. Givens asked.

"A necklace similar to this may be linked to the case." She didn't want to reveal more.

"That's it? You came just to show us that?" Oliver asked.

"I'm sorry," Danica said. "I wish I had more news."

He shook his head as his mother broke out into louder sobs. "I know this isn't your fault, Detective, but your sorries don't mean shit."

"It is your fault," Mrs. Givens said, looking up at her with watery eyes. "You said you'd find her, bring her home. You said so!"

Danica sat and felt heat rise to the center of her chest. Her heart thudded as guilt rushed through her. Mrs. Givens was right. She had said that. She'd promised her in fact. A big mistake. Why had she done it? Why? She knew better.

Danica cleared her throat. "You're right. I did say those things. I'm sorry." She rubbed her palms on her thighs, hoping to wipe off the sweat.

"Well, do you at least have any leads?" Oliver asked. "I mean, who this guy is?" He choked up and covered his mouth with his fist. "Do you know how he takes them? Why he does it?"

Danica swallowed hard.

"I mean, how did he kill those girls?" he asked.

Danica looked to Mrs. Givens. She couldn't tell them. It would jeopardize the case. Even if she thought they could handle hearing it, which she didn't.

"I'm afraid I can't share any further information on the case."

Mrs. Givens, a woman in her fifties, sitting in the worn out armchair in her worn out house dress, burst into body shaking sobs.

Danica clenched her hands together in her lap and stared at the floor. She studied the pattern of the old rug and then watched as the Givens' family dog, a little mixed breed they called Tigger, tried his best to jump into Mrs. Givens's lap. He was just as disturbed by her crying as Danica was, and neither of them, it seemed, could bring her any comfort.

"What kind of monster does this kind of thing to another human being?" Oliver seethed. "To someone like—" He choked up again. "Tina. She never hurt anybody."

Danica nodded, understanding his point. Tina had been a first-year college student at the University of Louisiana. A young Rajin' Cajun, she'd been vibrant and beautiful, a kind soul in every way possible. She not only had gone to school full time, but she'd volunteered at the local animal shelters and at a nursing home, where she read to residents on a weekly basis. From what Danica could gather, she had been loved and beloved by many. This would be a hard loss. A real motherfucker of a loss. And she felt solely responsible.

"I know this is difficult," she said carefully. Oliver clenched his jaw as if he were steadying himself.

Danica stood, knowing it was time to take her leave. She straightened her blazer in a nervous manner and gripped her car keys in her pocket.

"Again, I'm sorry," she said softly.

"You will find her, won't you?" Mrs. Givens said, her voice trembling.

Danica resisted the urge to comfort her with another promise. "I will do my damndest, Mrs. Givens."

Oliver rubbed his mother's back again and pulled her close.

"We're counting on you," he said. "To find her."

Danica nodded.

She gave them one last look and then turned to leave. And as she walked through the door and closed it softly behind her, she prayed to God above, the one she didn't always believe in, that he would help her this time around.

Tina Givens and the young women in this parish depended on it.

Danica walked zombie-like into headquarters and answered her ringing phone from her back pocket.

"Please have some good news for me, El. I've had a hell of a day." She plopped down in her desk chair and opened her bottom drawer. After giving a careful glance around the room, she pulled out a half full bottle of Knobb's Creek whiskey and poured some into her Styrofoam coffee cup.

She took a sip, wished it was her late father's more expensive whiskey, like the one she had at home, and readied herself for Eleanor's news.

"You went to see one of the families, didn't you?" Eleanor asked with obvious sympathy in her voice. "That's always hard on you."

"It doesn't get any easier, that's for sure." She took another sip and let out a big sigh.

"I'm so sorry, Danny."

Danica returned the bottle to her drawer and leaned back to prop her feet on top of the cluttered desk.

"I'm dealing, but thanks." She didn't mention that the department was now threatening to turn the case over to the FBI. She hadn't even mentioned that to her core team. She didn't want to upset them. They were putting in long enough hours as it was.

There was a soft pause.

"You're not…drinking are you?"

Danica placed her feet on the floor and leaned forward. "That's actually no longer any of your business."

"It is though. I care about you."

Danica closed her eyes and took another hearty sip. She winced as the alcohol burned its way down her tight feeling gullet.

"Danny?"

"So, what's the news, El? I know you didn't call just to lecture me."

"I have an update on the skeletal remains."

Danica grabbed a random notebook and hurriedly flipped it open to a blank page. She sat poised, ready to write with a pen in her hand.

"Both victims had broken hyoid bones."

"Oh?"

"And victim two suffered a fracture of the left tibia, most likely as a child."

Danica scribbled. "Anything else?"

"That's it so far. Also, I need those dental records from the families that have them."

"You got it."

There was another pause.

"You going to be okay?" Eleanor asked.

Danny sipped more whiskey. "Always am."

"If you need to talk…I'm here."

Danny scowled. "Thanks, but you seem kind of busy with your new partner."

"Who, Lyra?"

"Is that her name?"

"You know that's her name."

"I musta forgot."

Eleanor sighed. "Please don't act this way."

"Gotta go, work calls."

"I mean it, Danny. I'm always here."

"Talk soon," Danica said as she hung up. She hung her head in her hands and ran her fingers through her hair. She was very much aware of her bad behavior, but at the moment she couldn't care less. She had numerous missing persons to find and two families to console once they identified the skeletal remains.

Eleanor would just have to deal for the time being. She could just go enjoy her time with Lyra. She took another drink and thought again of Lyra and her mesmerizing eyes. Was there anything between her and Eleanor? If there was, would she be okay with that?

No. Hell no.

But why?

Because I still care about El.

But that wasn't all.

Because I like Lyra as well.

She finished off the whiskey in her cup. Her body warmed as her buzz finally kicked in. Pretty soon, she'd forget all about Eleanor and Lyra. In fact, in about two seconds, she'd forget everything except the case at hand. When she needed to, she had laser-like focus, to the point of obsession. Many said it wasn't healthy, but she didn't care. It was her process and frankly, she had very little life outside the force, so her over working didn't really make a difference. Her mother, of course, would say differently, but she was the only one since she and Eleanor called it quits. And she remedied the situation with her mother every Sunday at mass.

She shuffled the files on her desk, searching for the ones she wanted. Her mind craved more liquor, but she resisted. She had to work and she couldn't drink herself into oblivion at headquarters.

She was nose deep, searching through the missing women files, looking for a reported tibia fracture, when Devereaux walked in with another detective, one of her core team members, Rita McNally. Devereaux collapsed his heavy frame into his squeaky chair.

"You go see the Givens mother?" he asked as he leaned forward to crack open a can of Pepsi.

Rita crossed her arms and leaned on his desk. She and Devereaux and some of the others had spent the day searching around the farm for evidence. Then they'd searched other nearby cane fields. They looked tired and overly sunned.

"Mm."

"Yeah? How'd that go?"

"The usual."

He sucked in some air through his clenched teeth. "That bad, eh?"

Danica glanced up. "Worse."

"Really?" Rita said.

"They're blaming me for being unable to locate her and rightfully so. I'm the one who told them I'd find her."

"Sheesh, that's rough, Danny," she said.

"I know. It was stupid. But these poor families. Their heartache. It kills me. Just kills me."

"Yeah, but you can't be stupid," Devereaux said.

She gave him a look and he held up his palms in defense. "Just sayin'."

Danica returned her focus to the file open in front of her. She flipped through the pages, searching for the notes on identifying marks. Other than freckles and tattoos, there was nothing noted.

"Shit." She ran her fingers through her hair again. "I've got to call all the families and ask about a broken left tibia."

"Want some help?" Rita asked.

"Would you mind?"

Devereaux frowned at her. "You know we don't, D."

Danica slid half the files over to his desk for them and then lifted her phone. As she dialed the first number, she longed again for more whiskey.

This was going to be a very long night.

CHAPTER NINE

The early morning sky was overcast, and a cool humidity hung in the air as he stepped outside to retrieve the newspaper. Unable to wait until he got back inside, he opened it up to the front page and gasped.

SEARCH FOR MORE REMAINS CONTINUES AT SUGAR MILL FARM

He headed back indoors and made himself comfortable at his small kitchen table. The old shotgun house was quiet, the gray light of the overcast sky filtering in through the open windows. His lovely was quietly sleeping, bound and gagged in the bedroom. They'd had a beautiful night the evening before, with dinner and a dance. He still recalled how he'd escorted her across the floor, her lithe body nearly limp in his arms. He'd loved the feel of her next to him, her ragged breath on his neck, and the curve of her delicate hip in his palm. It was an evening he'd never forget.

Pushing that from his mind, he sipped his tepid coffee and began reading the newspaper, going over each word carefully, wanting to savor the moment. Normally, he'd get up to reheat his coffee, but this article was too important. They'd found some of his lovelies, and he needed to know what was going on with the investigation.

After all, this was his doing. He wondered if they had been shocked to come across all the bones in the cane. If they'd felt grief or sadness. Or if they'd felt responsible in not having found the missing women alive. He grinned as he considered that. He hoped they'd been upset. Served them right. They were too stupid to catch him, or even scare him into stopping.

He read and reread the article. He was so proud of himself he couldn't stop grinning. Very little information had been given about the victims or the circumstances in which they'd died, but he knew that was simply because the police didn't want to jeopardize the investigation. Still, he wondered what all they'd learned. Were they on to him now? No, of course not. He hadn't even been questioned.

No, they didn't have a clue.

He glanced back down at the paper.

What's this?

He looked closer and ironed out the crease with the side of his hand. There was a photo of the investigators at the crime scene. And a woman, standing right in the center of a few cops and CSI officials, caught his eye. She was blond and beautiful, with chin length hair and a slight but still athletic physique. He didn't usually go for blondes, but he would make an exception for her.

He read the caption under the photo. It seemed her name was Lyra Aarden, and she was a bioarchaeologist helping out with the recovery of the skeletal remains.

"Lyra," he whispered. "Lyra Aarden."

He ran his fingertips across her photo, savoring her appearance. Who was she? And why was she helping? Her name hadn't been mentioned in the previous article. Only the detective working the case and the forensic anthropologist who was analyzing the bones. This was one time when he wished he had some technology. With a smart phone or a computer, he could find out all he needed to know. But technology was evil. That's what his grandmother always said, and he listened to her. To ignore her was detrimental. He could still remember the harsh punishments he'd endured for disobeying. And though she wasn't alive to punish him now, he'd learned his lessons. Enough to still heed her instructions.

So who was this Lyra Aarden? And more importantly, where could he find her? He'd have to find out on his own.

He downed the rest of his cold coffee and reached for the scissors. He cut out the article and the photo of Lyra Aarden. Then he crossed the room to the refrigerator where he stuck the article and the photo to the door with magnets. He took a step back to observe his newfound art.

Yes, Lyra was beautiful. Almost damned near perfect. And now she was on his fridge, the bull's–eye of his next target. He knew it would be dangerous to pursue her, knowing she was working very close with the law, but he had to try. And wouldn't that be the ultimate slap in the face for the police if he got her? Yes, he had to try to get close to her. For she was his new destiny. His next lovely.

CHAPTER TEN

"Don't worry, Auntie Lyra, I've got a steady hand."

"Yeah?" Lyra laughed at her oldest niece, Daphne, and handed over a small saw that came with the pumpkin decorating kit.

"You're right, you do," Lyra said. "That's why you're such a good artist."

"What about me? Am I good artist, too?" Haley asked from her perched position on the kitchen chair. She was three years younger than Daphne, having just turned four.

"Uh-huh, sure are. Your work is excellent," Lyra said as she rounded the table to help her to continue to clean out her pumpkin.

"See, Daph," Haley said. "I'm a good artist, too."

"Yeah, but you still can't carve a pumpkin. You're too little."

"Am not."

"Are so."

"Hey," Lyra said softly, "let's just focus on cleaning out this pumpkin, okay?"

"It's gooey," Haley said with a giggle.

"It is, isn't it?" Lyra said.

Haley dipped her hand inside the pumpkin and stuck out her tongue in concentration. When she brought her hand back out, it was full of pumpkin guts.

"And squishy!" she said as she squeezed the slick insides so they'd ooze between her fingers.

"That's so gross," Daphne said with a scowl.

"It's fun," Haley countered.

"Here, let me get in there with a scoop," Lyra said. She held onto the large pumpkin and began scraping the sides, clearing out what was left of the stringy remnants. Haley watched her intently, still squeezing the pumpkin goo in her hands.

"This is gonna be the bestest jack-o'-lantern ever!" she said.

"That it is," Lyra said as she finished.

"These will definitely be better than the ones we did at Grandma's," Daphne said. "Those were for babies. Grandma wouldn't even let us draw our own designs. Plus, she doesn't have a steady hand, so the pumpkins looked silly."

"I don't know, a silly pumpkin or two might be okay for Halloween," Lyra said. "After all we all look silly when we dress up, don't we?"

"Yup!" Haley said as she deposited her pumpkin guts on the designated newspaper. "Look, Auntie Lyra, I covered your picture." She pointed an orange coated finger at the paper.

Lyra took a glance. "You sure did."

"Now, you really look silly!"

Lyra chuckled and slid the cleaned out pumpkin over to her and handed her a black marker. "Go ahead and draw your pumpkin's face."

"Really?" She took the marker and snuck out her tongue again.

"Why were you in the paper, Auntie Lyra?" Daphne asked.

Lyra sat to watch the girls. "I'm helping out with an investigation," she said. "So, I was there when the newspaper photographer took the picture."

"Investigation of what?" Daphne asked, keenly carving out her pumpkin with the small saw.

"I'm just helping to try to find some missing people," she said.

"Somebody got lost?" Haley asked, glancing up from her pumpkin.

"They sure did," Lyra said. "But let's not focus on that right now, 'k? Let's concentrate on making these the best darn jack-o'-lanterns on the block."

"Yeah!" Haley said, raising a fist.

Lyra rose and crossed to the kitchen island. "Who's up for some hot chocolate while we work?"

"Yes!" Daphne said.

"Me, too!" Haley said.

Lyra began preparing the drinks and her brother, Louie, walked in with a mug of his own. "I think I'll partake, if that's okay with you."

"No, Daddy, you gotta be a pumpkin decorator first," Haley said.

"A pumpkin decorator? What if I'm the one decorating the rest of the house? Doesn't that count?"

"Yeah," Daphne said. "I guess that counts."

Louie rinsed the coffee from his mug and set it on the counter next to the others. He then got busy filling the mugs and child cups with water while Lyra opened the packages of hot chocolate.

"You doing any better?" he asked in a low voice so the girls were unable to hear.

Lyra shrugged.

"Working a murder investigation can get to anyone. You shouldn't be so hard on yourself."

"It's just so eerie, Lou. I've worked with dozens and dozens of remains and yet these are getting to me."

Louie placed a warm hand on her shoulder. "You work with bones. Study bones. Obsess over bones. *Old* bones. Not missing young women who are victims of a homicide."

"Yeah, it's been rough. I keep thinking of their families and how they must be feeling." She'd been disturbed by the new information about the hyoid bones. But she'd held herself together in front of Eleanor and the others. She wanted to continue to work the case, so she knew she had to steel herself for whatever came her way. But since then, she'd found that it was bothering her more and more. She was even having nightmares.

"Maybe you should let the police handle this," Louie said softly. He handed over a warm child cup fresh from the microwave. "Let them solve this case without you."

"I want to help," Lyra said, stirring in the hot chocolate mix. "It feels good to be back in the field."

"Maybe so, but this isn't your ordinary fieldwork, Ly. This is…" He shook his head. "Something beyond what you're used to. It could even be dangerous."

Lyra laughed, but then stopped when she saw the concerned look on his face. "Sorry," she said. "But you have nothing to worry about."

"Really? Because I feel like this is too much for you. You haven't been yourself lately. You've been quiet and distant. Even the girls have been asking what's wrong with you."

Lyra looked over at the girls. They were chatting and giggling as they worked happily on their pumpkins. How could she explain the craziness she'd been experiencing with her concerns over the case and the killer at large, as well as her fondness for Eleanor and her attraction to Detective Wallace? Louie wouldn't understand. Hell, she didn't even understand.

"I'll do better," Lyra said. "But I'm not quitting the case." She had to keep helping, now more than ever. Because now she'd seen real evil, and even though it scared the hell out of her, she knew someone had to help stop it.

She delivered the cups of hot chocolate to the girls and returned to the kitchen for her own mug. She was stirring in the mix when Louie started in again.

"You need a life, Ly. A real life. Not just one full of bones in the ground and traveling to God forbid destinations."

Lyra felt her chest tighten at his suggestion. "And what, exactly, is it that you consider a real life?"

"You know, having a partner, a family. People you can come home to at night. Love."

She spread her arms, referring to the entire room and its occupants. "Do I not have that?"

He sighed. "I mean you build a family of your own. You know damn well what I mean."

"I don't have time." It was an excuse, one she used frequently. He knew it and she knew it.

"What do you have now? Nothing but time. And yet you're out digging up more bones."

Lyra finished over-stirring her drink and took a tiny tentative sip. It was perfect.

"What can I say? I love bones."

"And history and anything else pertaining to knowledge. But, sis, come on. There's more to life. I mean, why don't you date?"

She didn't answer. She didn't have one.

"Didn't that woman you're working with take you out for lunch the other day?"

Lyra gave him a look. "I work with her, Lou."

"So? You don't *technically* work for her. You're just helping out, right? Do you not like her?"

"I like her just fine." She liked her very much. Eleanor was striking and extremely intelligent and renowned in her field. Could she see herself falling for her? Maybe. They had an awful lot in common. But more than anything, she wanted to remain on this case and keep working. An image of Detective Wallace also came to mind, and she flushed. She had to admit, she felt stronger about her than she did Eleanor, she just didn't think Detective Wallace felt the same.

How can I be attracted to anyone while working a case that is beginning to terrify me?

She guessed Louie was right. Maybe it had been too long since she'd had someone and now it was starting to affect her in her professional life.

Well, it's not every day that I get to work with two beautiful women.

"Then ask her out. I know she's a little older than you, but who cares? You've always been drawn to older women."

"How do you know she's older than me?" *Just what all did he know?*

"I saw her pic in the paper, silly. She's standing right next to you."

"Oh."

"Your cheeks are red," he said, smiling. "I've said something that's gotten to you."

She scoffed and took her mug to return to the table with the girls. She'd had enough of Louie for the moment. But to her dismay, he followed with his own mug in tow and sat down with her. His grin remained.

"You do like her."

She glared at him over the rim of her mug.

"What's it going to hurt? Just offer to buy her lunch next time. Get to know her. Open yourself up a little and let her in. You need companionship."

"I could say the same about you," she said.

Daphne piped in. "Daddy dates," she said.

They both looked at her in surprise. She'd been following the conversation and they'd been oblivious.

"Don't you, Daddy?"

"Yeah, Daddy dates real pretty ladies," Haley said. She now had black marker all over her hands. Thank God it was washable. She turned her pumpkin to face Lyra for inspection. Lyra nodded.

"Excellent job, Haley. That one ranks right up there with one of the best I've seen."

"Really?" she said with a huge smile.

"What about mine, Auntie Lyra?" Daphne asked. She also turned her pumpkin around for Lyra to see. She'd carved out the triangle eyes and had just started in on the nose.

"Wow, hon. Yours, too. Great job."

Daphne grinned a toothless grin and turned her pumpkin back around to finish.

Lyra looked at Louie who was sipping his hot chocolate with his trademark smirk.

She shook her head but said nothing. Her little brother had made his point, and damn it if there wasn't something about it that was resonating with her. She was lonely, especially late at night when she was tossing and turning in bed. It had been too long since she'd been with anyone special. But asking Eleanor out? Even to another lunch? Wouldn't that be a bit presumptuous? She wasn't sure. Eleanor seemed open to the whole thing, offering to make her dinner sometime and everything. Could she be interested? Or was it just southern hospitality?

Whatever it was, she found herself excited at the idea of going to Eleanor's for dinner. But as for asking her out to lunch? She'd let that slide for the time being and see how things played out. Her mind went to Detective Wallace and she realized that she'd very much like to have lunch with her. But that really would come off as odd asking her out. Or would it? She could offer to talk about the case.

Louie continued to smirk at her and she considered telling him all about Detective Wallace and her feelings, but she'd be damned if she was going to share that.

Nope, for the time being, Louie would just have to settle for his know-it-all smirk.

CHAPTER ELEVEN

"Mom, you here?" Eleanor asked as she entered the spacious Acadian style house in South Baton Rouge. It was Saturday and she'd just made the two-hour drive up to visit. She'd thought about canceling and going out to the crime scene instead, but she knew the technicians had the skills and they were on it, along with Lyra, and she'd made dinner plans with her mother weeks ago.

"In here, Ellie."

Eleanor walked into the kitchen where she found her mother standing at the stove, stirring something in a large steaming pot.

"It's nice to see you," her mother said. "I wasn't sure you were going to make it."

"Yeah, I've got a huge case in my lap, so this will be my last trip up for a while."

"Big case, huh? You talking about that suspected serial murder case?"

"'Fraid so." Eleanor walked up behind her. "Whatcha doing?"

"Oh, I'm just making a roux," she said, turning to give Eleanor a quick kiss on the cheek.

"Well, it sure smells good," Eleanor said, taking a big whiff from the pot. She studied the blond roux.

"Étouffée?"

"You know it." Her mother continued to stir. "Here, give a taste."

She held up the wooden spoon for Eleanor who carefully took a small sip. "Mm, yes."

"It's ready?"

"Yes."

Her mother nodded and adjusted the burner.

"You want me to clean the shrimp?" Eleanor asked, noting the bowl of shrimp sitting in the sink.

"If you want to."

Eleanor began rinsing and cleaning the shrimp while her mother added the holy trinity of green peppers, celery, and onion to her roux.

"You're making a lot," Eleanor said. "Is that so I can take some home with me?"

"Why, sure, if you want to. And because…"

Eleanor's stomach clenched. "Because…?"

"Timothy's going to join us."

Eleanor sighed at the mention of her mother's new boyfriend. Here she'd cast work aside and driven two hours to have a nice evening with her mother and she had to go and invite Mister Cheesy.

"What do you have against him? He's a very nice man."

"I'm sure he is, Mom."

"Then what's the problem? Why won't you give him a chance?"

"There's no problem."

"Could've fooled me." She turned and reached for her iced tea. Eleanor noted her trademark apron that read *Hot Stuff Coming Through (And I don't Mean the Food)*. It made her smile, however briefly.

"I just wish you'd waited a little bit longer before you started dating is all."

"Eleanor Marie," her mother said. "Your father's been gone almost two years. How long did you want me to wait?"

"I don't know. It just doesn't feel…right."

Her mother returned to the stove. "You know no one can ever replace your father."

"I know that, Mom. I do." But wasn't that really her issue? The fact that Timothy wasn't her father and yet her mother was moving on as if he were. Like they'd been together for years. It just didn't feel right to her.

"I understand your feelings, hon, but you're going to have to get over them. What would you have me do? Wait for another year? What about my happiness?"

"I'm just not ready, Mom."

"*You're* not ready?"

Her mother laughed softly. "I'm afraid it's not up to you. I'm my own person, you know."

"You hardly know him."

"I'm getting to know him. That's what dating is."

"You're moving too fast." She finished rinsing and cleaning the shrimp and washed her hands.

"You're letting your trepidations and your grief for your father influence you. If you had properly grieved, you—"

"Everyone grieves in their own way, Mom. Isn't that what you always say? You being the well-known psychiatrist and all? Author of two books on the subject?"

"Which is why I know of what I speak."

Eleanor poured herself a small glass of white wine, finishing off the already open bottle. "I don't need to hear the psychobabble, Mom. Really."

"I think you do. You've worked yourself to the bone, no pun intended, instead of allowing yourself to grieve."

"Ha. That was a good one."

"I thought so." Her mother smiled. "I just worry about you. You're all alone in that house, doing nothing but looking at bones and bodies. It has to be depressing. I don't care what you say."

"I love it. For me it's about the science, not the drab."

Her mother sipped more of her tea and eyed Eleanor's glass of wine. "I have some more in the cellar."

"This is fine."

"I hope you aren't drinking too much these days."

Eleanor brought the glass down from her lips. "I'm not."

God, is this what I sound like when I talk to Danny?

She hoped not, but the doorbell rang before she could give it much consideration.

"Will you get that?" her mother asked.

Eleanor fought sighing and headed for the front door. When she pulled it open she found Timothy standing there wearing his cheesy grin, holding a huge bouquet of yellow roses.

"Why hello, young lady," he said, removing his bulky sunglasses. "And how are you this evening?"

"Fine, thank you. And you?" She tried her best to sound friendly, but she knew her voice was still tight with indignation. She just couldn't seem to help herself. She found the man ridiculous with his usual light gray slacks and black suspenders and his oversized sunglasses and silly looking bow tie. He was a trial lawyer, her mother had said, therefore he had to look his best on a daily basis. But to Eleanor he always looked like he'd just stepped off an episode of *Matlock*.

"I'm doing alright," he said as she stepped aside and he entered the house.

He surprised her by handing over the roses. "These, my fair lady, are for you."

"Me?"

"Why, yes. Your mother told me yellow roses were your favorite."

Oh, great. He's trying to butter me up.

She took the flowers, thanked him, and turned toward the kitchen. She couldn't help but roll her eyes.

"Timothy's here," she announced.

Her mother turned and beamed. "Hello, handsome. How was your day?"

Timothy walked up and kissed her cheek. "It was just dandy, my pretty lady, just dandy."

Eleanor wanted to gag, but instead she went back to the sink and retrieved an empty vase in the cabinet below. Then she filled it with water and got busy cutting the stems on the roses. Even if she didn't want them, her mother would. So, she'd do the right thing and care for them so they'd last.

"Oh, what pretty roses," her mother said as she eyed the bouquet with big eyes. "You shouldn't have."

"I didn't," Timothy said, patting her on the backside. "Those are for Eleanor."

"Well, how nice. Isn't that nice, sweetie?"

"It's very nice, Mom." She was glad she was busy cutting the stems or else she was sure her mother would be able to see right through her just by the look on her face.

Timothy smacked his hands together and rubbed them so that they sounded like sandpaper. "What can I do to help?"

"Not a thing," her mother said. "Eleanor's doing it. You just go make yourself comfortable."

"Now, now, I'm sure there's something I can do."

"No, you're the guest. You don't lift a finger."

He sank his hands into his oversized pockets and leaned back on his heels. "Well, then, I suppose I'll just supervise."

"Yes, you just stand there and look handsome."

He grinned and his teeth, though straight, had a slight yellow hue to them in comparison to his white beard. Eleanor surmised it was from all the cigars he and his colleagues enjoyed at the country club. She wasn't sure how her mother could handle smelling the smoke. But she supposed it went well with the scent of the Sazerac cocktail he favored.

Her mind went briefly to Danny and the way her lips sometimes tasted of whiskey. Sometimes it bothered her, while other times, it just seemed to heighten the sweet sting of her passionate kiss.

I hope she's okay.

She hadn't sounded good on the phone earlier and she was almost positive she'd been drinking. She just hoped she wasn't overdoing it. Danny had a tendency to overwork and get overly obsessed with her cases. And this one, the missing women...had been her worst yet.

"You seeing anyone special, Eleanor?" her mother asked.

"Me? No. Why do you ask?"

"I'm just curious. You sounded like you had a little more life to you when we spoke the other day. And I thought that maybe, just maybe, you may have met someone."

Eleanor didn't know what conversation she was referring to, but she definitely wasn't dating. Unless one counted her lunch with Lyra Aarden, which she didn't, even if she did have a wonderful time with her. She finished with the roses and washed her hands.

"Guess I was wrong," her mother said. She came to the sink and grabbed the bowl of shrimp. "You wanna start the rice for me? The rice maker's under the cabinet behind you there."

Eleanor retrieved the rice maker and got busy preparing the rice to cook. Her mother returned to her étouffée and chatted quietly with Timothy. He stood right next to her the entire time with his hand on the small of her back. Occasionally, they'd laugh and lean into one another. It almost looked like a greeting card photo and once she even found herself looking at them with envy.

Was that her problem? She was jealous that her mother had found someone and she hadn't?

God, am I that hard up that I'd be jealous of my own mother's happiness?

She felt sick at the possibility and decided then and there to change her attitude. It was obvious that her mother was happy. More than obvious. So she was just going to go with it. It wasn't like she came up to Baton Rouge often to see her, so she needed to make the most of her time with her. Especially now that things were going to kick into high gear with this case.

Who knew when the next time she'd see her would be?

"Why don't I set the table," Eleanor said as she gathered her mother's expensive chinaware.

"Thank you, dear."

When she finished with that, she poured them both a glass of wine and then stood to lean back against the counter to watch them interact. And for the first time in as many years, she saw true happiness radiate from her mother.

That alone, she finally realized, was worth the trip up to Baton Rouge.

CHAPTER TWELVE

Danica rolled over from her haphazard position on the sofa and answered her phone.

"Wallace," she said with a groggy voice. She glanced at her wristwatch for the time. It was after eight a.m. She immediately sat up and ran her fingers through her hair. Her files were strewn across her coffee table, along with an open bottle of Sazerac straight rye whiskey. It was the last of the bottles her father had left behind, and every time she drank some it reminded her of him. She took a quick swig and grimaced as Eleanor's voice came over the line.

"I've been trying to reach you since last night."

"Really?" She pulled the phone away from her ear and eyed the screen. She'd missed four calls from her.

"Did you pass out?"

"No." She knew she sounded defensive, but she really hadn't passed out. Not from alcohol anyway. She must've simply been exhausted.

"I hadn't slept in a while. So I must've really crashed and slept through your calls."

"You're not sleeping?"

"I'm working this case, El. I don't have time. We've been out searching the rural areas for Tina Givens. It must've really worn me out. I can't believe I slept as long as I did last night."

"You need sleep," Eleanor said.

"Noted. So, what's up?"

"I don't know. You had called me."

"Right." She rubbed her temple, trying to focus her foggy thoughts. "Where were you?"

"You mean you care?"

Danica groaned. "I just meant, I had tried to reach you and you didn't get back to me."

"I was in Baton Rouge."

"Your mother's?"

"Yes."

"When we have this case to work?"

"Yes, Danny. I made sure the techs had it covered when I left and Lyra was there as well. I already had the plans with my mother, and I knew I wouldn't be able to see her again anytime soon because of the case. So, I went. Is that a problem?"

"No, no problem. I just wish you would've texted me."

"What for?"

"To let me know, El. Come on."

"Honestly, Danny, I didn't think it was a good idea."

"Why not?"

"I thought you might be drunk. It was after seven on Saturday when you called and with your track record…"

"Jesus, El."

"Well. I didn't want to deal, okay? You're not yourself when you drink."

"I was working the case."

"You're even worse when you're doing that and drinking. You get cranky. Short. Rude."

"Okay, okay, I'm an ass, I get it."

"Only when you drink."

Danica frowned and considered swiping the whiskey bottle off the coffee table. But she didn't want to risk breaking it and spilling the whiskey. So instead she sat back and took a deep breath.

"What did you need?" Eleanor asked. "That couldn't wait till today?"

Danica flipped through one of her notebooks. When she found what she was looking for she tore out the page. "I was wondering if it was possible for someone to fracture their tibia and not know it."

"You mean not get treatment for it?"

"Whatever."

"I suppose."

"Would they walk funny?"

"Depends on the fracture."

"What about the one on victim number two?"

"Mm, yes, I suppose. If she didn't get treatment for it, then she may have limped and then continued to do so even after it healed. Why? Do you have someone who fits that description?"

"Gabby Detriech."

"Did you get me her dental records? Because we have the skull and jaw for comparison, remember?"

"None on file. Family is low income and couldn't afford it."

"So reason states that they may not have treated an injured leg either."

"Correct."

"Did she walk with a limp?"

"She did. Says right here in my notes. She walked with a slight limp, favoring her left leg."

"That's gotta be her. Did you ask why she walked with a limp?"

"Her aunt said she wasn't sure exactly why, but she knew it was from an old injury."

"I'd call again and see if you can get any more specifics."

"I'm on it."

There was a long silence. Danica continued to rub her temple, feeling a powerful headache coming on. "You doing okay?" she asked, genuinely curious.

"I am, Danny, thanks."

"How's Susan?"

Eleanor chuckled. "She's the same. How's your mother?"

"Probably pissed at me. I missed eight a.m. mass."

"Uh-oh."

"Yeah. I'll make it up to her."

"Man, I'd hate to be you."

Danica walked into the kitchen. She was suddenly very thirsty. She grabbed a bottle of water out of the fridge and downed some along with two Advil.

"Tell me about it." She leaned against the counter. "I better go. Maybe I can talk her into the ten thirty."

"Good luck."

"Thanks."

"And, Danny? Please take care."

Danica's heart warmed. "Thanks, El. Talk to you soon." She ended the call and stared at the screen. Despite their noticeable differences, she often missed Eleanor and she wondered if things could've ever worked out.

No, because I couldn't stop the drinking.

She tossed the phone on the counter and headed for her bedroom for a quick shower and change of clothes. As she dressed, she thought of Eleanor and her happiness. She deserved someone better, someone who didn't need to run to the bottle to cope. She thought about Lyra Aarden and wondered what kind of person she was on an intimate level. On paper she seemed perfect for Eleanor, but Danica couldn't allow herself to go there. Her own attraction to Lyra was too strong and the thought of her with Eleanor made her stomach flip. Whatever would she do if the two of them ended up together?

She rid herself of the notion and focused instead on another woman.

One, she knew for certain, she couldn't ignore.

Her mother.

CHAPTER THIRTEEN

Forty minutes later, Danica was sitting outside her mother's weathered clapboard home, debating what to say. Her thoughts were interrupted however, by the front door opening. Her mother stepped out onto the porch and placed a hand on her hip. She was still dressed in her finest Sunday dress, wearing her little black pumps and all. And at the moment, one shoe-covered foot was tapping in an impatient manner.

"Fuck," Danica breathed.

She exited the car and said a silent prayer for her own well-being.

"Do I even want to know?" her mother asked as she waited for Danica to walk up the porch steps.

"I just overslept," Danica said. "I've been pulling some all-nighters."

"You don't want me to have to say it, do you? Because I will, if needed."

Danica stood in front of her, feeling very much a chastised child. She clenched her jaw and closed her eyes, trying for patience.

"Would you like to go to ten thirty mass with me?"

Her mother was silent. Her foot stilled.

"I've already been as you know. To the eight o'clock service."

"I know, I'm just offering to go with you this time."

"You mean since you were absent from the one earlier?"

"Yes, ma'am."

She glanced at her watch. "Will we make it on time?"

"If we leave now."

"Let me get my pocketbook." She went back inside and emerged with her purse. "Let's go then."

They headed for the car. "You know I don't like this police car you drive. Why you don't drive your own car to pick me up, I'll never know."

"I have to work after mass," Danica said. They both crawled inside, and Danica started the vehicle and pulled out of the gravel drive to head to church. She was hoping they'd ride in silence, but she wasn't that lucky.

"You're working too much," her mother said.

"I thought you weren't going to say it." It was old news and something her mother lectured her on frequently.

"I feel like it's needed."

"I'm sorry I missed mass."

"I know you are. But sorry doesn't do much good, does it?"

Danica thought of Oliver Givens and what he'd said about her sorries not meaning shit. She winced at the rising guilt.

"No, ma'am, it doesn't."

"Then do better."

"Yes, ma'am."

"Now, tell me how you are."

"I'm fine, just...busy."

"Mm-hm. So I gathered. You getting along okay otherwise?"

"Same as I was last week."

Her mother laughed. "Okay."

"Well, I don't know what else to say. You don't want to hear about work or who I date. So what else is there?"

"You're dating?" She looked at her and Danica swore she could feel her stare boring a hole into the side of her head.

"No." But would she like to be? With Lyra? Yes, she realized she would. It was a nice, warm thought to fall into and she enjoyed the comforting sensation of swimming in that fantasy. But her mother yanked her out of it like a fish on a hook.

"Then why mention it?" She shook her head. "And as for your work, you know I don't care for all that detective talk. Murders and mayhem and such. I heard enough of it from your father."

"I know. That was my point."

"You could talk about other things. Like your hobbies, and your work with the Lord."

"I haven't had time for either lately."

There was more silence and Danica regretted sharing that last bit of information.

"You didn't have to tell me, I already knew. Father O'Toole told me today that he hasn't seen you at the senior center lately. I'm going to assume that you know how I feel about that."

Danica was very much aware, but she knew she'd share it anyway so she braced herself by tightening her grip on the steering wheel.

"You shouldn't shirk your responsibilities at the center just because you're busy with work. Your volunteer work there is just as important. Those people need you. They look forward to seeing you."

More important than solving serial murders? I don't think so.

But she kept her mouth shut and kept driving.

"As for your dating, you're right, I don't want to hear about that."

"Yes, ma'am." She never had. She'd never been okay with her sexuality and she'd never approved of anyone she saw. She'd tolerated Eleanor, but Danica figured it was because she was a bit older and she was always overly friendly to her. Even when her mother didn't deserve it. Eleanor had successfully killed her with kindness on several occasions.

But what would she think of Lyra? Would she show her the same kind of semi-respect or would she see her as she had the others and treat them with hostility? She didn't like thinking about that particular scenario, regardless of how nice the fantasy of dating Lyra had been.

She slowed and pulled into the church parking lot. She dropped her mother off in front and then found a spot near the back and parked. She took her time walking up to the door where her mother stood waiting, talking softly to Father O'Toole.

"Father," Danica nodded.

"Danica. Nice to see you."

"You as well."

"Your mother tells me you've been working too much."

"I've got a murderer to catch, Father."

He clapped her shoulder. "Well, I'm glad to see you can still make time for mass."

"I try." She followed her mother inside and sat next to her in the pew. She bowed her head and stared at her hands, the bright light streaming in through the large arched windows hurting her head. She sat like that for most of the service, counting the minutes until she could leave and drop off her mother.

But she knew doing so wouldn't give her that much relief.

She had another family member to visit. An aunt. And she feared she'd be feeling much worse than this during that particular visit.

CHAPTER FOURTEEN

The morning was crisp with a heavy dew in the air. He drove with his windows down and hummed along to Connie Smith's "Burning a Hole in My Mind." He opened a snack-size Snickers bar and tossed the wrapper in the passenger seat along with the two others. Halloween was coming up and he'd stopped and bought some candy for himself. He didn't celebrate Halloween so there was no need to buy any for the kids. He'd just sit in the house with his lovely, eating by candlelight, celebrating the two of them. He hoped she'd be willing, but the way things had been going with her, he doubted it. She was just too frigid and out of it. He'd tried easing up on the sedatives, but nothing seemed to help. She was just on another planet.

At least the others had put up a fight when they could. That had made things a lot more interesting, and frankly, it had done wonders for his libido. But as soon as they got a little too rambunctious, he'd given them more drugged wine and they'd become more complacent once again. He loved having that kind of control. They were his lovelies and he could do with them as he pleased and they would act accordingly.

He swallowed the last bite of his candy bar and grabbed his single serving container of milk and took a big swig. Then he wiped his mouth with the back of his hand and tried to remain calm as he came up on the Sugar Mill Farm cane field and the dump site. But his excitement grew as he drew closer and closer. He eased his foot off the gas as he approached, and he caught sight of something. Or more like someone.

He slowed as he neared her. A woman, dressed in athletic shorts and a sweatshirt, jogging along the main road on the outskirts of the cane field. His eyes widened as he took her in. She was blond, with chin length hair, held back by a sweat band. Her legs were lithe and muscular, and she was running with a slight limp.

Could this be her? Could this be the mysterious Lyra Aarden he'd seen in the paper?

She turned to look at him as he drove by and he accelerated, not wanting to draw attention to himself. He studied her in the rearview mirror.

It was her, it had to be.

He continued to watch her as she turned down the dirt road that bisected the cane. She was running toward the dump site. The sweet place where he left all his lovelies.

Yes, it was her. It had to be.

He drove a little farther down the main road and pulled into a gas station to turn around. He got out and topped off his tank, just in case someone was watching. Then he sat in his vehicle for a moment, hoping he'd see her come out of the burnt cane. But no such luck.

A strange tightness seemed to wrap his ribs. He felt sick yet excited. He recognized the feeling for what it was. He was longing again. Longing for a new lovely. He wanted Lyra and he wanted her now.

He squeezed the steering wheel and clenched his jaw. The radio crackled to life with another song, but he ignored it. He kept watching the cane field, willing Lyra to emerge. But all he saw were more vehicles pulling in. More cops, and CSI personnel going to the dump site.

A part of him knew he should be proud, but he just couldn't get there in his mind. Lyra had overtaken him, and he was growing angry at not being able to get to her.

Beyond frustrated, he started his car and pulled back onto the main road. He wished he could sit and wait for her, in order to follow her home, but he had to work. There was no way around it. He'd already taken two days off in order to spend time with his lovely. Now, his finances were demanding he take a shift.

He drove past the cane field and cursed under his breath at his misfortune. Life was so unfair. Nothing ever seemed to go his way. Not even with his latest lovely.

"I've got to get rid of her soon."

Yes, that was the plan. Get rid of her and get ready for Lyra.

And he knew just how to get rid of her.

He looked at the cane field in his rearview mirror and smiled. The new plan made him feel better. So much better, that he decided he just might go home early and pay a visit to his lovely. Perhaps she'd be up for another dance across the house. Perhaps she'd let him kiss her. Touch her. Perhaps this time she'd perk up and realize just how good he was to her and how lucky she was to have him.

Then perhaps she could learn to love him. If even only for one night.

A few hours later, he left work behind and climbed in his car and drove toward the drug store. He had something in mind for his lovely. He hoped it would help quell his longing for Lyra for the time being. He grabbed what he needed and headed out, making it home in under ten minutes. The house was quiet when he entered, with only the faint sound of moaning coming from the bedroom.

He deposited his bags on the kitchen table and stood in the doorway to the bedroom, looking in at his lovely. She'd fallen to the floor and was scrambling to try to get out of her binds.

"Tsk, tsk," he said, as he came to her side, cut her binds, and helped her stand. "Very naughty girl." He brushed her dark hair away from her moist cheeks. "See what happens when you don't obey? You get yourself into trouble." He walked her into the kitchen and sat her at the table.

He got eye level with her and spoke. "If I remove the gag, are you going to be a good girl?" He slowly withdrew his hunting knife again and held it in front of her face. She nodded and he removed her gag. He watched her cough for a few seconds and then went to the sink to get her some water. She was not only moist from tears, but she was moist with sweat as well.

"How long were you on the floor?" he asked. "You could've really hurt yourself."

He held the water up to her mouth and helped her take a few sips. "It's best to wait for me," he said. "That way you don't get hurt." He smiled at her. "Because, remember, I'm always going to be the one who wins. You'd be wise to remember that."

He dug through the bags on the table. "Now, I've brought you some goodies from the store, although you don't really deserve them. You misbehaved and that's not okay. But...I suppose I can forgive you this time." He pulled out a snack-sized Butterfinger and opened the wrapper. He held the candy up for her to eat. "It's going to be Halloween soon," he said. "I thought you might like some chocolate."

But she turned her head and refused to look at him.

"Butterfinger, not your thing? Okay. Snickers it is." He opened a Snickers and held it up to her. "I'm rather partial to the Snickers myself." He inched it closer to her lips. "Come on, take a little bite."

But she shook her head.

"Not hungry?"

She didn't respond.

He shrugged. "Suit yourself." He dug in the bags some more. "You're not into the candy, but this next thing you're really going to be into." He held up the goods one by one. "What do you think? Exciting, right?" He smiled again. "I told you, you would love it."

He opened a box and pulled on some latex gloves.

"Now, let's get started."

CHAPTER FIFTEEN

"Please don't tell me you're going running again," Louie said as he breezed into the kitchen. He'd just returned from walking Daphne to the bus stop and he was hurrying to get Haley ready for preschool, trying to get her into her jacket. "You've been running every morning for days now."

"I feel better," Lyra said, doing her usual stretches.

"I thought for sure you'd have given that up after stumbling upon you know what."

"What?" Haley said. "What did you stumble upon, Auntie Lyra?"

"I just stumbled onto some rocks," she said. "No biggie."

"Oh, is that how you hurt your knee?"

"Yep. But it's all better now."

Louie zipped up Haley's jacket and playfully smacked her on the butt. "Go get your library books. They're due today." She took off for her room and Louie faced Lyra.

"At least tell me you're running a different route?"

"Why would I do that?"

"Really, Lyra?"

"The sugarcane farm is probably safer now than it was before. There's no way he'll be hanging out there now."

"Um, hello? He dumped his bodies there."

"Which is why he will steer clear. We're working that scene big time and the techs are probably already there starting."

He sighed and straightened his tie in the reflection of the microwave door. "If you say so."

"I do."

"I thought you were scared."

"I am."

He scowled. "You're not acting like it."

"I have to continue living life, Lou. Even if I'm afraid. Besides, I feel comfortable at the sugarcane farm now. I know everyone working the scene. They'll be there and it'll be safe. No need to worry."

"Okay," he said.

Haley ran back down the hall with her pile of books in her arms. One slid out and she tripped over it and sprawled onto the carpet.

"Oh, no." Lyra hurried to her and picked her up. "Are you okay, sweetie?"

She rubbed her eye with her fist. "Nuh-uh."

"Tell me what hurts."

Louie examined her as Lyra held her. "Looks like you got some carpet burn on your chin," he said, gently lifting her chin with a finger. "Does it hurt?"

She nodded.

"Aw. It won't hurt for long, hon. Want Daddy to put some feel good medicine on it along with a Little Mermaid Band-Aid?"

She nodded again and Louie took her and carried her back down the hall. Lyra picked up the books and placed them on the counter. She eyed the covers and smiled. Children's books were so wonderful. She loved reading them to the girls.

After stacking them carefully, she called out good-bye to Louie and Haley and exited the house. She bounced on her feet for a few seconds in the driveway and then headed out on her run.

It was a beautiful fall day, with a nice crispness to the air. The temperature had dropped the last couple of days and she could see her breath coming out in moist puffs as she ran. The cool air infiltrated her lungs and made her feel alive and alert. It was nice and she relaxed into her rhythm.

She thought about the case as she ran. She hadn't heard anything from Eleanor over the weekend, so she didn't think there had been any major news. But still she wondered how the investigation was going and what all Detective Wallace had learned, if anything.

She'd enjoyed her time in the field and felt good about the progress she and the techs made. They'd discovered more bones, which looked to belong to yet another body. They'd also found another necklace but had yet to find the charm.

She wondered about the significance of the tiny hummingbird charm and then stopped dead in her tracks.

"Wait a minute." She thought back to the books on the kitchen counter. "Oh, my God." She turned around and considered running back to the house, but then changed her mind. Louie had probably left already, taking the books with him. She faced forward and started running again. She headed straight for the sugarcane farm. She knew who would be there and she couldn't wait to share the news.

She ran harder and faster than her usual pace, and by the time she arrived at the turnoff, she was breathless, with a deep ache in her ribs. She slowed, having little choice, and walked the rest of the way up the dirt roadway.

She was waved through at the barricade by an officer that recognized her. She could see a half dozen cars or so parked along the white tents of the crime scene. They'd expanded their search grid and now had several tents erected. A policeman sat and watched the area overnight to keep guard. So far, to her knowledge, they'd had nothing to report.

She wondered if the killer was aware of the security guard at night. Surely he was. And surely he wouldn't return.

Detective Wallace's cruiser came into sight and she hurried the last few yards to where she was standing alongside a tech covered from head to toe in the white garb. She was glad to see they were already on scene, and she wondered if she'd be assigned to work alongside them again. Eleanor hadn't specified yet so her duty was still up in the air. She suspected however, that she'd be in the lab with Eleanor. They had new bones to comb over.

"Detective Wallace," she said as she stopped alongside her, still breathless. She rested her hands on her hips and tried to breathe through the pain in her side. The detective looked even more fetching today than she had previously, in pressed black slacks and a crisp white blouse, which really offset her dark mane. Her gun holster was pulled tight across her chest, making her well-rounded bust and well-muscled physique all the more noticeable.

"Lyra Aarden, what a surprise." She smiled at her, taking Lyra aback.

"I have something," she stammered. "A clue."

"A clue?"

"Yeah. You know. For the investigation."

Detective Wallace stared at her for a moment as if to decide whether or not she was serious. Then she excused the tech and led Lyra away.

"What's up?"

"I—"

"Wait a minute. Did you run here again?"

Lyra blinked at her. "What? Yes."

"Why?"

"Why not?"

She shook her head. "Never mind. What did you have for me?"

"A book."

"A book?"

"Uh-huh. A children's book."

"Okaay."

"I read them. To my nieces. And…" She swallowed.

"And?"

"There's this book. About a little hummingbird. A tiny silver hummingbird. And…"

Detective Wallace waited.

"The illustrations look just like the charms we found."

Detective Wallace was quiet. And then it seemed the message clicked and she guided her closer to her vehicle.

"How close is 'look like'?"

"Identical."

"You're positive?"

"Uh-huh."

"And it's a children's book? What's the title?" She pulled her handheld notebook from her back pocket and scribbled with her pen.

"*Flying Home.*"

"Okay. Got it."

She returned her notebook to her pocket and opened the car door for Lyra. "Get in," she said.

"What? Why?" Lyra asked.

"Because I'm taking you home."

"Good idea, but the book is no longer at the house. My brother is returning it to the library."

"I'm not worried about the book."

She rounded the vehicle and crawled inside behind the wheel. She started the engine as Lyra climbed in the passenger side.

"What are you worried about, then?" she asked as she closed the door.

Detective Wallace put the car in reverse and backed up. "You."

Lyra fought flushing. Detective Wallace was concerned about her. What did it mean?

"Me? I'm fine."

"Thankfully, yes. You currently are. But that could change in the matter of seconds."

"What do you mean?"

"I mean it only takes a second for someone to incapacitate you. And if you're running with your earbuds in you'd never know they were coming."

"Not you, too," Lyra breathed. "My brother already gives me enough grief about running this route." While she was thrilled to know that Detective Wallace was concerned for her safety, she really didn't need another nosy guardian like Louie, even though he meant well.

Detective Wallace put the car in drive and sped down the dirt road. "He's right. You shouldn't be running this route. Come to think of it, you shouldn't be running any route. Not by yourself. Not right now. Not with the killer still out there. Sugar Mill Farm just isn't a safe town for attractive young women at the moment."

She thinks I'm attractive?

"But wouldn't this route be the safest now? With all of us working it?" She hoped her voice wasn't quaking like her body was. Detective Wallace thought she was attractive. The day just kept getting better.

Detective Wallace turned onto the main road. "It could be. But are you willing to risk your life on that?"

Lyra grew serious again. She didn't like the paranoia over her runs. She was already scared enough. "I'm not even the killer's type. He likes younger than me, right? Dark hair?"

"From what we've found so far, yes. But killers have been known to change their minds, you know. Change tactics. Especially if they are following the case and they want to try to throw us."

"I didn't consider that."

"I just want you to be more careful."

Lyra glanced over at her. "Thanks. But I'm okay."

Detective Wallace didn't look at her. Just kept her eyes on the road. "I'd like to keep you that way."

"Really?" Lyra asked with a grin. "I must be growing on you, after all."

This time Detective Wallace did meet her gaze. "Possibly. A little."

Lyra chuckled. "So, you *did* dislike me?" She was teasing. Sort of.

Detective Wallace looked back through the windshield and followed Lyra's directions to Louie's. They slowed as they neared his street.

"No, I didn't dislike you," she said softly.

Lyra was touched that she'd even answered. "I'm just not your favorite person, though, am I?"

Detective Wallace pulled up alongside Louie's house and stopped the car. Her pine-scented car deodorizer swung from the rearview mirror. She looked at Lyra once again.

"What does it matter?"

Lyra shrugged. "It just does."

"But why?"

"Because I don't like it when people dislike me."

Detective Wallace laughed. "I see. Well, you don't have to worry. I like you just fine. And to prove it to you, how about you and I have lunch together some time?"

Lyra's heart skipped a beat. "Lunch?"

"You know, that meal that one tends to eat in the middle of the day?"

"Right. Lunch." She laughed nervously. It was what she had wanted but had been too afraid to ask. "Sure."

Lyra smiled and Detective Wallace returned it. "Great." She was truly very beautiful when she smiled.

"You should do that more often," Lyra said as she opened her door.

"What's that?"

She crawled from the car and leaned down to look through the window. "Smile." She closed the door. "You're pretty cute when you do."

She turned and walked toward the house.

"Hey!"

Lyra stopped and looked back.

Detective Wallace spoke. "You are, too."

Lyra grinned. She waved and then headed inside as she heard Detective Wallace pull away. The day was turning out exceptionally well. She now had a lunch date with Detective Wallace and she'd even gone out on a limb and flirted with her too. And Detective Wallace hadn't exactly shut her down.

CHAPTER SIXTEEN

Eleanor sipped her chestnut praline latte as she looked over the dental records she'd received from Danny. The odontologist would, of course, make the final determination, but she could already tell that none of the records matched those of victim number two.

It seemed as though Gabby Dietrich was more than likely victim number two and she had no dental records to speak of. They would have to run DNA to make the final determination. Doing so would take time, time they didn't really have. She held out hope that maybe somewhere, a local hospital or emergency clinic had treated her for her fractured tibia at some point and taken X-rays. It would be a huge help and they could identify her a whole lot quicker.

She took another drink and set the dental X-rays aside. She moved to the wooden container closest to the wide screen monitor and switched on the overhead camera and light. She snapped on some gloves to begin gently arranging the bones in anatomical position.

She glanced up as she heard the door open. She smiled as Lyra entered, carrying two cups of coffee.

"Aw, I see you've already got one," she said as she approached the table and set the drinks down away from the examination area.

"Don't worry, I'll still drink it," Eleanor said. "I'm a coffee fiend."

"I got you a chestnut praline latte. That's what you like, right?"

"Mm-hm."

"Perfect." Lyra shrugged out of her jacket and slipped into her lab coat. Then she snapped on some gloves and rounded the table to stand across from Eleanor.

"What have we got?"

"Well, as you know, we have a complete skull, so that's good. She's female." She continued to display the bones as they would sit in the human body.

"Right."

Lyra lifted a femur and measured it. "She was rather petite. Just like the others."

"Uh-huh."

"Any luck with those dental records?"

"Not pertaining to victim number two. But we may hit the mark with this particular set of bones. You want to get the X-rays? They're over there." She motioned with her head toward the stack of files at the end of the table.

Lyra left the bones, removed her gloves, and slid the first set of X-rays into the view box.

Eleanor carefully examined the lower jaw first, comparing them with the X-ray. No dice.

"Next one," she said.

Lyra slid in the next X-ray.

Eleanor again examined the lower set of teeth first. The three fillings matched up. She moved on to the upper set and found the chipped tooth. It matched perfectly with the X-ray.

"Bingo."

Lyra appeared surprised. "Really?"

"Yep. What's her name?"

Lyra checked.

"Carroll Reynolds."

"Beautiful."

"How many does this make?" Lyra asked.

"Three."

"And there are four missing women?"

"Five now, counting Tammy Givens."

"We've definitely found his killing field."

"Seems so. Did you happen to stop by the scene this morning?"

"I did, yes."

"Were they having any luck with the ground penetrating radar?"

Lyra shifted a little as if uncomfortable. "I'm not really sure."

"Were they not using it?"

"I didn't notice. I was busy talking with Detective Wallace."

"Really?" Eleanor stopped and focused on Lyra, more than a little surprised. "Was she polite?"

"She was." A tiny grin lifted the corner of Lyra's mouth.

"What?"

Lyra blinked. "What, what?"

"You grinned."

"Oh. No reason really. It's just that...Detective Wallace was actually kind of funny today."

"Funny?" Eleanor dropped the piece of bone she was handling. Thankfully, it didn't have far to fall and it landed in the box. She picked it up once again, embarrassed at being so frazzled. "What exactly do you mean by funny?"

"Nothing. Never mind. What's important is what I discovered."

"You discovered something?"

"You know the silver hummingbird charms we're finding with the victims? Well, I discovered a children's book about a little silver hummingbird with illustrations that are identical in appearance to the necklaces."

"Identical?"

"To a T."

"What's the book about? You know, the plot?"

"It's about a baby hummingbird looking for a new home."

"Unbelievable."

"My brother returned the book to the library this morning, but I told Detective Wallace all about it. Hopefully, she'll look into it."

"Oh, she will. She's probably already got her hands on it." Though that was most likely true, knowing Danny like she did, it wasn't what was on the forefront of her mind. "So, is that all you two discussed?"

"Sorry?"

"Or did you have something else to discuss?"

Lyra pressed her lips together. "No, that was it."

Eleanor felt her muscles soften in relief. She even laughed a little at her own ridiculous reaction. She knew it shouldn't, but the thought of her and Danny together was causing some jealousy to rise like bile in her throat. Lyra spoke again.

"Well, she did tell me to be careful on my runs. What she actually said was that I shouldn't be running at all with this killer still on the loose. And she wanted me to be more careful."

"Oh," Eleanor tucked her hair behind her ear. "She said that, did she?" She felt heat flushing her face. She spoke again to hopefully distract from it. "She's right, of course. You really should be more careful."

"I appreciate everyone's concern, but I'm okay."

"Yeah?"

"Uh-huh."

"But you will be more careful, won't you?"

Lyra smiled. "I will."

"Good." *That wasn't so bad, was it? Everything is fine. Danny and Lyra are colleagues, just like she and I are. Nothing to worry about. And even if they were more than that, it's none of my business. Right?* She swallowed, somehow not the least bit convinced. *Right.*

She finished arranging the bones and the door to the lab opened again and Dr. Ray Mecum entered, a sour look upon his face.

Dr. Mecum was one hell of an odontologist, but the man had an awful disposition. Especially when he got called in at a time he considered to be inconvenient. And it seemed that the current time was not exactly okay with him.

"I had two root canals scheduled today. One of them this morning. And then I get the call to come in. Said it can't wait." He placed his leather bag on the table and scowled as he snapped on a pair of gloves. Then he slid on his specialty eyeglasses and retrieved his instruments. "So what do you have for me?" He looked directly at Eleanor. She burned under his irritated gaze.

"Caucasian female. Early to mid twenties. Petite in stature." Eleanor motioned toward the skull and jaw. "Skull is intact, along with both lower mandibles."

"Did you do a preliminary?"

"I did."

"And?"

"They appear to match the dental records for one of our missing women. A Carroll Reynolds, twenty-two."

"Hmph." He carefully picked up the lower jaw and began to examine it, holding it up in front of his face. "We'll see about that." He peered up over his glasses. "You going to show me the X-rays, or what?"

Eleanor looked to Lyra, who jerked into motion. Her eyes were large like a deer caught in headlights. Apparently, she wasn't used to someone being so blatantly rude. Eleanor understood her disbelief and she wished she could comfort her somehow. She chose to do what she could. "Dr. Mecum, this is Dr. Lyra Aarden. She's joining us from Arizona State."

"Arizona, huh?"

Lyra slid in the first X-ray. "Yes."

"What, are you a grad student there, or something?"

Lyra looked to Eleanor in disbelief again. As if she thought maybe he was joking.

"Dr. Aarden is a bioarchaeologist. The top in her field. We're very lucky to have her," Eleanor said. *There. Take that, you grumpy old bastard.* She felt good in having said it. So good she almost puffed up her chest in rebellious indignation, but she refrained.

"Sun Devils," he scoffed as he began meticulously measuring the teeth. "I'm an LSU man myself. Tigers eat Sun Devils, you know."

Lyra continued to stare at him with wide eyes. But then they narrowed and Eleanor braced herself.

"Tigers eat a lot of things that aren't good for them."

Dr. Mecum glanced up at her. Then he did something that truly shocked Eleanor. He laughed.

"I'm sure they probably do, don't they?"

Eleanor breathed easy as they all shared a laugh. Then she continued, making sure Dr. Mecum knew just whom he was working with. "Dr. Aarden actually comes to us highly recommended from ASU. I couldn't be happier with her."

Lyra took a quick glance at her. She smiled as though a bit embarrassed by her praise.

"Well, it seems I'm quite lucky, then," Dr. Mecum said as he continued to examine the teeth and compare them to the X-Rays and dental records. "I've got not one, but two intelligent women helping me out." He smiled and Eleanor about fell over in shock. She'd never even seen his teeth before.

"But now, I need to concentrate," he said by way of dismissal. "If you don't mind."

Eleanor took her cue. "Of course." She led Lyra by the elbow into her office and quietly closed the door. "He likes to talk to himself as he works," she said as Lyra watched him through the office window.

"Interesting," she said.

"That's a new word for him," Eleanor said as she rearranged the papers on her desk and eased into her chair. She sipped her latte and tried to breathe easy. They most likely had another identification. She was relieved.

"Yeah, I could see how one would have some choice words to describe him," Lyra said as she turned and sank into the chair across from the desk. "How long have you been working with him?"

"Ray? Oh, Lord. Maybe twelve, thirteen years?"

"Wow. And he's always been this way?"

"No. He's never friendly like he was today." She chuckled and Lyra joined her. "I think you brought out the best in him."

"I don't think it was me."

"I do."

Lyra shifted her gaze at the obvious compliment. Then she shifted her body position. She seemed nervous.

"What's wrong?" Eleanor asked. "Something bothering you?"

"No, that's not it." She paused and then met Eleanor's gaze once again. "I was just thinking about lunch the other day. It was nice."

"It was, wasn't it?" Eleanor studied her and then decided to take a chance. "What about dinner tonight? Your choice of restaurant."

"My choice?"

"It's only fair, don't you think? Since I subjected you to my favorite Cajun cuisine."

Lyra didn't answer right away. She seemed to be thinking over the proposition rather hard.

"You don't have to say yes, of course," Eleanor said, feeling more than disappointment. "I just thought since we'd be working late anyway—"

"No, I think it sounds great."

Eleanor's heart lifted despite her trying to control it. "Wonderful."

Lyra seemed pleased, but then her face clouded. "You think they're going to find more remains?"

Eleanor understood her sudden change in mood. "Highly likely. Especially with the ground penetrating radar. They're also supposed to use the cadaver dogs again."

Lyra grew quiet and again seemed to be mulling over something of great importance. "What do you think Detective Wallace is doing today? Other than finding the book?"

Eleanor's elated heart dropped. "I'm not sure." She cocked her head. "Why so curious about Detective Wallace?"

"I'm not," she said, shaking her head in defiance. Eleanor wondered who it was she was trying to convince.

"There's no shame in it."

"I'm not—I—just—"

"I'll call her and ask."

"Oh, no, no need to do that. I just—"

"It's no problem. We need to touch base anyhow."

Eleanor lifted the phone and dialed Danny. Funny how she still knew her number by heart. As she listened to the line ring, she watched Lyra and wondered just how curious Lyra really was about Danny. Just how curious, indeed.

CHAPTER SEVENTEEN

Ms. Francine Broussard lived outside of town just beyond the old abandoned sawmill on Sweet Magnolia Lane. Her home was weather-worn and in dire straits with faded clapboards, a patched roof, and an old tattered swing on the front porch. It swayed slightly in the wind as Danica stood at the front door, waiting for someone to answer her polite knock.

After a few long moments, Danica was just about to turn to leave when she heard the door creak open. A wrinkled face peered out.

"What you want?"

"Miss Francine? It's me, Detective Danica Wallace. Remember? I'm the one investigating your niece's disappearance."

Ms. Broussard stared at her for what seemed like an eternity. Then, finally, and with a grunt of sorts, she pulled open the door.

"I remember," she said, turning her back on Danica for her to follow her inside. "I'll ask you again though. What you want?"

"I've come to talk about Gabby."

"What about her?" She settled down on an ancient-looking recliner and grabbed the television remote. She thumbed down a daytime soap and sat and waited for Danica to speak.

Danica eased down on the plaid couch and clutched her hands together. "I'm wondering if you have any of her old medical records? You know, from doctor's visits, things like that?"

Ms. Broussard gave a laugh that led into a deep-sounding cough. It rattled her frail-looking body. Danica waited until she'd finished.

"Anything you have would be really helpful."

"Child, just what makes you think I've got such things?"

"I wasn't sure, but I—"

"I ain't got no such thing."

"Do you happen to remember the names or places where she was taken for treatment? Perhaps when she was a child?"

Again, she laughed and coughed. But this time she scowled, as if irritated.

"No," she said flatly. "Gabby didn't go to no doctors. We took care of her here."

Danica glanced around the tiny shabby living area. Noted the old television set, the worn floorboards and faded peeling wallpaper. The strong scent of cat urine was burning her nose, but she saw no cats.

Danica tried a different question. "Do you ever remember Gabby taking a fall? Maybe hurting her leg?"

"I already told you about that."

Danica froze. "Come again?"

"You asked about her limp. I told you I don't rightly know. I just heard she'd hurt her leg and that she walks funny. Always has."

"Do you recall which leg she limped on?"

"She favors her left leg. Has since she was itty-bitty. Since her Mama done up and left her with me."

Danica pulled her notebook out and began to take notes. "That's another thing? Do you happen to know where her mother is?"

"I don't have any idea where that woman is and I don't care to."

Danica spoke softer, sensing her growing irritability. "Miss Francine, is there anyone I can speak to who might know about how she injured her leg?"

Ms. Broussard looked off toward the wall. "Virginia."

"Virginia?"

"Virginia Broussard. Her half sister. She lives over on Vernon Street, next to the gas station. Has four little ones running around. Can't miss 'em. She might remember how Gabby hurt her leg."

Danica scribbled furiously. "Do you remember Gabby wearing a sterling silver necklace? One like this with a hummingbird charm?" She held out her phone with the picture of the necklace and Ms. Broussard narrowed her eyes at it.

"No."

"One last question, Miss Francine. Do you have anything of Gabby's that might have her DNA on it? Such as a hairbrush or a toothbrush? Something like that?"

"I've got both. In the bathroom down the hall. Her stuff's in the top drawer."

Danica stood. "Down here?"

"Mm-hm."

Danica headed down the hall and into the bathroom. A fat cat darted out as she entered. She carefully put on some gloves and opened the top drawer. She plucked out a hairbrush and a toothbrush and bagged them. She labeled them quickly and then returned to Ms. Broussard who was sitting in silence.

"Why do you want that stuff?"

Danica eased back down onto the couch. Another cat emerged from the hallway and began rubbing up against her legs.

"We use it to help identify victims."

Ms. Broussard didn't speak for a long moment.

"You think you found her?"

"We're not yet sure."

"But you found something that could be." She shook her head. "That's what Anita said down the way. That y'all been finding bones and such."

"Yes, ma'am."

She wiped at her cheek as if an errant tear had fallen and angered her. "I told her not to walk at night. Told her a thousand times."

"She liked to walk at night?"

"That child walks everywhere. Can't afford no car. Works over at the Dollar Store."

"Yes, ma'am, I remember."

"She walks home from work no matter what time of night. Walks everywhere like nothing in this world could hurt her. Now she—now she—" She coughed again and this time grabbed a tissue and spit something up. Danica could see that the fluid was red. Blood. Ms. Broussard was not well.

"I won't take up any more of your time," Danica said as she stood. "Is there anything I can get for you before I go?"

"Nah."

The cat darted toward the door and beat Danica to it. It ran out as Danica pulled the door open. "Thank you, very much for your time. I'll be in touch."

Ms. Broussard didn't respond. She just raised the remote control and thumbed up the volume to her soap opera. Danica left her in peace and headed back for her vehicle.

❖

An hour later, Danica watched through the wet glass as Devereaux ran through the rain.

"Here we go," he said as he opened the passenger door and slid inside. He dug inside a grease-stained white paper sack and handed over a big wrapped sandwich and a large Styrofoam drink cup. "One ragin' Cajun po'boy just as you ordered. With smoked sausage, boudin, and jalapeños."

"Thanks," she said, taking the sandwich and drink. She unwrapped the po'boy and sank into a good-sized bite. "Mm, so good."

"Those jalapeños make it," he said, doing the same to his sandwich. He groaned as he chewed and then sipped on his soda.

Danica swallowed and took a drink of her sweet tea. The windshield wipers moaned as they swept the falling rain droplets away. She watched half-hypnotized as she ate. There was just something about a good, spicy po'boy on a rainy day that did it for her.

"I've been jonesin' for some boudin," Devereaux said.

"Mm, you and me both."

They chewed on in silence for a while before Devereaux spoke again.

"How long should we give her?"

Danica eyed her watch. "'Nother half hour or so."

"Wonder where she is. Neighbor said she doesn't have a job, so…"

"She's probably just out and about."

They had been waiting on Virginia Broussard for over an hour and Devereaux's patience was wearing thin. The man hated stakeouts.

"Won't be too much longer," Danica said, trying to relax him. At least he had the food now to distract him. That should buy her another fifteen minutes at least.

"You really think she's gonna be able to help?"

"Hard to know. But it doesn't hurt trying."

"I guess. But I think our best bet is going the DNA route."

Danica took another sip of her tea. "We're doing that regardless. But it would be nice to know before then."

"Mm," he said by way of a nod.

"I just don't know why Miss Francine didn't mention her before," Danica said.

"Who knows?"

"Probably could've helped us a long time ago."

"Wonder why Virginia didn't come forward on her own? Surely she knows her sister is missing."

Danica shook her head. "I got the impression that the family isn't close."

"Ah."

"Yeah, so don't be surprised if we get a chilly reception." Danica chewed and then spoke with her mouth half-full. "Mm, here we go, I think that's her." She re-wrapped her sandwich and took another sip of tea to help her swallow. Then she grabbed her notebook and pen and stepped out of the car and into the rain.

Devereaux followed suit with a grunt and joined her in a light jog up to the woman emerging from an old Ford station wagon.

Virginia Broussard looked at them with a furrowed brow as she retrieved a small child from a car seat.

"Who are you?" she asked. Three other children emerged from the car and raced around in the rain.

"Shane! Toby! Lyle! Get your asses inside the house, now!" She heaved the heavy-looking toddler up into her arms. "God dammit! I said now!"

All three boys stopped dead in their tracks and turned to look at her. She pointed toward the house and they marched one by one up the porch steps and in the front door.

Virginia then hurried toward the steps herself as the toddler began to cry. "I ain't got time for no games," she said as she moved along.

Danica and Devereaux followed, unwilling to let her get out of their sight.

"Ms. Broussard, please," Danica said. "We just need a moment of your time."

They all hurried up the steps and stood soaking wet on the front porch. Danica could smell the cigarette smoke wafting out of the house through the open door. Someone was home and that someone had ignored their knocks.

Virginia affirmed that suspicion by turning to yell inside the house.

"Henry! Get your ass out here to get these groceries!"

She faced them once again, brow still furrowed. Sound came from the house. First the screams and giggles of the boys, and then a deep baritone.

"Alright, alright, woman, I'm coming." A large man, bigger than Devereaux and twice as strong looking, appeared in the doorway behind the screen. He shoved open the door and stepped outside. He, too, gave Danica and Devereaux a firm look.

"Who the hell are you?"

"Detectives," Devereaux said, sticking out his chest. "Devereaux and Wallace. Louisiana State Police."

"We're here to ask you a few questions about Gabby Dietrich," Danica said to Virginia. "Your sister."

Virginia didn't speak, just scoffed as if she were disgusted.

"I ain't got nothing to say," she said, readjusting the crying child. When the child kept crying, she seemed to grow even more frustrated, and she set the child down and smacked it on the rear. "Get inside," she said.

The toddler ran inside and let the screen slam behind him. Henry, meanwhile, eyed them cautiously as he walked down the steps to the car to unload the groceries.

"Please, we just need to know if you have any information on how Gabby hurt her leg?"

"Her leg? What you wanna know about that for?" She looked genuinely perplexed.

"It could help with identification," Danica said.

Virginia narrowed her eyes. "Ah, so you found her. She dead then?"

"We're not sure," Devereaux said.

"Right," Virginia said. "So, you need to know about the leg." She grumbled and then spoke. "She fell out of a tree when she was little. Near about four or so."

"And she never went to the doctor or hospital for it?"

"You really think my mama would ever take us to a doctor or hospital? Hell woulda likely froze over first."

"Do you think she broke her leg?"

"Most likely."

"And she limped from then on?"

"Like a gimp."

"And it was her left leg?"

"As far as I can remember."

Danica was surprised at how willingly she was giving them information. She tried for more.

"Do you know anyone who would want to hurt Gabby?"

She let out a laugh. "Now you're getting ahead of yourselves. I ain't got no more for you."

"Why not?" Devereaux asked. Henry returned to the porch with bags of groceries. "You didn't like her?"

Danica gave him a look letting him know he needed to cool it.

"I didn't know her," Virginia said. "Didn't care to."

"So, you don't know anything about her social life?" Danica said.

"No, ma'am. She wasn't nothing to me."

"What about her habits? Did you know anything about her walking late at night or anything like that?"

"I done told y'all. I didn't know her. Now, if you'll kindly get the hell off my porch, I'd appreciate it." Henry emerged from the house and glared at them. Devereaux puffed up his chest again but started heading down the steps.

Danica thanked Virginia for her time and followed Devereaux back out into the cold rain. They climbed in the vehicle and dried off as best they could with a towel.

"She was real helpful," Devereaux said.

"At least she knew about the leg."

"Doesn't help us find who killed her," he said.

"She walked with a limp, right?"

"Yeah, so?"

"Well, think about it. If I ask you if you saw a woman walking down the road late at night, you might not remember, right? But if I asked you if you saw a woman walking with a limp, it might ring a bell."

"Hm. Yeah, I think you might be on to something there."

"See?" She tapped her temple. "It's not all full of cotton."

He chuckled. "No. Just boudin."

She laughed. "Just wish I'd thought of it sooner." She started the car. It was time to head to State Street.

CHAPTER EIGHTEEN

He walked in the door with a fresh bouquet of flowers and headed for the bedroom. He'd worked a five-hour shift and he expected to find her fast asleep on the bed, having drugged her considerably over breakfast, just as he had the others. But to his shock, she wasn't in her place on the bed.

Panicked, he dropped the flowers and searched the bedroom and the other side of the bed. She was nowhere to be found. He straightened and thought for a moment. Then he went across the hall to the bathroom. He found her on the floor next to the toilet, head bleeding, still bound and gagged. She'd somehow managed to hop her way across the bedroom, the hall, and into the bathroom. Once there, she must've fallen and hit her head on the counter or the toilet.

"That's what I get for not tying you to the bed."

He lifted her and tried to stand her on her feet. She went limp in his arms and nearly fell again.

"Jesus, Mary, and Joseph," he said as he hoisted her up again. He dragged her into the bedroom and sat her on the bed. He carefully removed her gag and brushed her hair back from her face. He held her jaw and snapped his fingers in front of her.

"Look at me," he said. Her eyes opened but rolled back in her head. He snapped his fingers again and held her face with both hands. "Focus," he said. But she closed her eyes again and fell to the side. He left her and crossed to the bathroom where he retrieved a wet washcloth. He reentered the bedroom and cleaned her wound. The cut was deep and near her hairline.

"You've gone and hurt yourself," he said. "How many times have I told you to wait for me?" She flinched as he dabbed the washcloth on the cut. The blood was dry and he surmised she'd been on the bathroom floor for a while. "You must've had to go to the bathroom," he said. "That's understandable." He stood and lifted her again. He cut loose her binds and led her back into the bathroom. Once there, he pulled down her leggings and panties and eased her onto the commode. He held her steady so she wouldn't fall over.

"Go ahead and go."

Her eyes rolled again and she struggled to focus.

"That's it, come around now and pee. I've got you."

She moaned and tried to speak. It came out garbled.

"Go ahead," he said.

She urinated, though not much. He cleaned her, pulled up her pants and helped her to her feet. "We've got to get more fluids in you. Even if you don't want it." He gently touched her lips. They were dry. "You're getting dehydrated."

She swayed once again.

"Come on." He led her down the hallway to the kitchen. He sat her in a chair and went to the fridge to retrieve some juice. He came back to the table and poured her a glass. "Drink," he said. He held the glass to her mouth and tilted it. The orange liquid touched her lips and she reacted. She opened her mouth and swallowed the juice heartily.

"That's it," he said. "Good, girl." She took hold of the glass and gulped, spilling the juice down her chin and neck. He sat back and smiled. "Somebody's thirsty." She finished the drink and he took the glass and set it on the table. "More?"

She managed to look at him but said nothing. But her gaze shifted over to the carton of orange juice.

"Ah, you do." He poured her another glass. "Here." He slid it to her but held fast to it. She tried to take it, but he wouldn't let her. "How 'bout a little kiss, first?"

She stared at him with dead eyes. Drool slipped down the side of her mouth. He cleaned her with a paper napkin, wiping away the drool and the juice.

"What do you say?" he said. He leaned toward her. She didn't move. Just kept looking at him with those lifeless eyes. He leaned in and placed a kiss on her open mouth. She didn't respond. He tried again. Nothing.

He sat back and sighed. He released the glass and she lifted it and gulped down the small amount of juice, once again dripping it on herself. "You messed yourself, again," he said. He wiped her clean slowly, and she shifted her eyes away from him. He brushed back her hair. Loose strands were falling over her brow and cheeks. He had to admit she wasn't looking good. Not like she had when he'd first laid eyes on her. Now she was...different. Part of it was his doing. He'd had a plan and it hadn't exactly worked. She didn't look good. And she wasn't acting right. She was listless and misbehaving, the drugs not working properly.

He wasn't sure what to do. Drugging her was making her limp and lifeless. To the point of drooling. And yet, she was able to get up and get to the bathroom. What was he to do? An increase in dosage and she'd likely die.

Was he ready for that?

"What to do, what to do?" he said. "I suppose I could always let you go."

No response.

He laughed. "You can't even react to that, can you? What's it going to take?"

No response.

His smile faltered and he slammed his hand on the table.

She flinched ever so slightly.

"Is that what it takes?" he said. "Me, losing my temper?"

Nothing.

He rubbed his jaw. "I just don't know what to do here. I've done so much for you and you give me nothing. Absolutely nothing." He leaned forward and grabbed her. "Damn it, look at me!" Her gaze drifted toward him but didn't focus on his face. "Jesus!" He leaned back and released her.

"Look at all I've done for you? The dinners, the flowers, the special treatment." He caught sight of the handheld mirror on the table that he'd used previously and held it up to her. "Look. Look at yourself. Look what I did for you and nothing. Absolutely nothing."

She looked in the mirror but didn't react. A single tear streamed down her face. He slammed the mirror down and was surprised when it only cracked but didn't break.

"You know what, you're not what I expected." He stood and began to pace. "Not at all. Not at all like the others. You're—I don't know. Driving me crazy." He stopped and stared at her.

No reaction.

He sighed. "I've got to face the truth. You're not who I want. Not anymore. Perhaps Grandmother was right. You're all worthless."

More drool dripped down her chin. He massaged his forehead, struggling to control his temper. When she continued to stare into oblivion, he marched over to the counter and grabbed the bottle of sedatives. He opened two capsules and poured them into more juice. Then he grabbed the glass and yanked her head back by the hair and forced the juice down her throat. She choked and coughed but he got most of it down.

"There," he said, breathless. He cleaned her face and forced her into a stand. "Come on," he said. He led her back down the hallway with a new plan in mind. He smiled as it took hold in his mind.

CHAPTER NINETEEN

So, this is your idea of excellent cuisine?" Eleanor asked from the passenger seat of Lyra's Jeep Renegade as they pulled into the Thai restaurant and parked.

"Sure is," Lyra said with a smile. "You okay with it?"

"I'm willing to try anything once."

Lyra killed the engine. "You mean you've never had Thai food?"

"This'll be a first."

"Holy shit," Lyra said. "You've got to get out more."

Eleanor laughed. "So, I've heard."

They exited the vehicle and headed inside. The hostess led them to a small table in the corner with a maroon tablecloth and handed them the menus. She left them with a polite smile and then promptly delivered their water.

"What's good here?" Eleanor asked.

"Everything."

"You've had everything?"

"Pretty much. I eat here all the time."

"Wow, you must really have a thing for Thai food."

"I do."

Eleanor glanced up from her menu. "Any particular reason why?"

"I recently spent a few months in Thailand and it's safe to say I got addicted."

"Thailand, really? How fascinating. I'm assuming it was for work?"

"I was helping out a colleague."

"You'll have to tell me all about it."

"I would love to. It'll be nice to talk to someone who can appreciate all that I did and saw."

"I know exactly what you mean. It's not every day that I meet someone who's happy to talk about bones." Eleanor smiled at her and then refocused on the menu. "So, what about the red chili chicken? That any good?"

"It is."

"Spicy?"

"Mm-hm."

"That's what I'll have then."

Lyra laughed. "You and your spicy food."

"I know, I'm hopeless." She slid her menu to the side and sat quietly while Lyra looked over the menu.

"I don't even know why I'm looking, I know the whole thing by heart." She tossed the menu aside. "I'm going to take your lead and go for the pad ka prao."

"That spicy?"

"Yep."

"Wow, I'm impressed."

Lyra laughed. "Shut up."

"No, seriously. You're a lot more open-minded than I gave you credit for."

"I'm not some stick-in-the-mud," Lyra said.

"I guess not."

"I'm a little offended that you thought so."

Eleanor shrugged. "You came off as a little soft-spoken. So I thought you might be a little reserved."

Lyra scoffed and sipped her water. "Hardly."

Eleanor folded her hands beneath her chin. "Really? Do tell."

Lyra shook her head. "You're bad."

"I know, isn't it fun?"

Lyra angled her head. "Come to think of it, I kind of thought the same about you. I figured you were some high-strung professional. Especially the way Detective Wallace seems to interact with you."

"I'm very professional with the detective," she said. "I have to be. It helps keep our boundaries clear while we work."

"Makes sense."

"But I'm not a stick-in-the-mud either," she said with a smile. "I can be fun."

"So, I'm discovering."

The waitress approached and took their order. She welcomed Lyra personally and called her by name.

"Wow, you really do come here a lot," Eleanor said.

Lyra chuckled. "I wasn't exaggerating."

Eleanor's eyes sparkled as she smiled. "So, tell me a little more about yourself, Lyra Aarden. Do you have someone special back in that desert of yours? Let me guess, she's a goddess, all beautifully tanned and exotic looking. And she spends her time playing golf in all that beautiful weather."

Lyra cracked up. "I'm afraid to disappoint, but no."

"No, you don't have a girlfriend, or no she's not all tanned and into golf?"

"I don't have anyone special."

"Why on earth not?"

"I could ask the same of you."

Eleanor waved her off. "Cher, girl, I'm too busy for love." But her eyes glimmered a little, leading Lyra to believe that maybe there was more to the story there. However, she didn't press, wanting Eleanor to only share what she was comfortable with.

"So am I. Up until recently, I wasn't even in the country."

"You travel a lot then?"

"I do and I love it. However, my superior at Arizona State is asking me to focus more on fieldwork around home when I return. We've recently discovered a site with ancient pottery at a construction site outside of Phoenix and we're waiting on the clearance to excavate."

"Native American?"

"We think it's Hohokam. Should be very interesting."

"Sounds like it."

"You don't travel?"

"You mean abroad? I don't really have the time," Eleanor said. "With my caseload here lately, I mostly spend my time in and around Louisiana."

"There's plenty of work here?" Lyra said.

"Mm. And occasionally I get called out to different counties and sometimes, Mississippi and Alabama and the like."

"But you love it," Lyra said.

"I do."

"I hear ya."

The waitress brought their drinks and Lyra watched as Eleanor sipped her Diet Coke. She caught herself staring at her lips. They were the perfect shade of rose and full and she wondered, for the briefest of moments, what they would feel like to kiss. She chastised herself for the thought, but then relaxed, knowing it was a natural curiosity when spending time with such a beautiful woman. She knew she'd wonder the same about Detective Wallace, given the opportunity, and she considered it now, as she recalled her perfectly bow shaped lips and the way they curled upward when she smiled.

"What?" Eleanor said, snapping Lyra out of her trance.

"Hm? Nothing."

"No, that wasn't nothing," Eleanor said. "That was definitely something."

"I—" She shook her head.

"You're blushing." Eleanor smiled devilishly. "Now you really must tell me."

Oh, God, I can't. "I—it was nothing really."

"Chicken."

Lyra almost spit out her drink in laughter. "Am not."

"Are so."

"I'm just—I don't know. I'm not sure it would be appropriate to say."

"Oh, my God. Now you absolutely have to tell me."

Lyra blushed harder. "I can't."

"You must."

Eleanor looked at her expectantly. She blinked her green eyes at her and Lyra was at a loss, with Detective Wallace temporarily forgotten. Eleanor was so striking with her stylishly short salt-and-pepper hair and penetrating gaze. And those damn rose-colored lips.

Fuck.

"I'm waiting," she teased her.

Lyra took a sip of her tea. She took a deep breath. "I was just thinking…"

"Yes?"

"That you—you have nice lips."

Eleanor stared at her. Then she blinked a few times rapidly. "I—thank you." This time she reddened.

"Now who's blushing," Lyra said.

Eleanor laughed. "Touché."

"You wanted to know," Lyra said. *And I can't believe I told you. What is going on with me?*

"I did."

"Be careful what you ask for."

"I'm not regretting it," she said. "Not in the least."

"No?"

"Nope." She fanned herself. "But boy, it got hot in here, didn't it?"

Lyra laughed. "A little bit."

"We haven't even had the spicy food yet."

"I'm not sure we need it," Lyra said and then clamped her mouth shut. *My God, I'm losing my mind.* She closed her eyes and tried to get control of herself. She felt guilty even though she wasn't sure why. She wasn't involved with Detective Wallace, nor Eleanor for that matter. Still, she shouldn't be flirting with her. Not when she had feelings for Danny.

"I'm not sure we need it either," Eleanor said softly, adding to the heaviness of the moment. She studied her and obviously noticed her change in demeanor.

"You okay?"

Lyra blinked. "Fine."

"You don't seem fine."

"I just shouldn't have said that. It was inappropriate and I'm sorry."

"You don't need to apologize, Lyra. You were just being honest."

"Yes, but if I'm being honest, I—" She couldn't finish her sentence. She didn't want to hurt Eleanor by telling her about her feelings toward Detective Wallace.

The waitress returned just then and broke the tension. Eleanor hastily unfolded her napkin and placed it on her lap and Lyra did the same. They both smiled and thanked the waitress.

"This looks wonderful," Eleanor said. "Smells divine as well."

"Sure does," Lyra said, glad to have been interrupted. She took a forkful of chicken and blew on it. Then she took a bite. "Mm."

Eleanor did the same. "Mm, is right. This is really good."

"I'm glad you like it."

"Like it? I may be their new regular. This is fabulous. Just the right amount of heat."

Lyra beamed. "It's nice seeing you so relaxed and enjoying yourself."

"Is it? I suppose with work I am rather serious, aren't I?"

"You have to be. You can't exactly be joking around with human remains."

"No, I suppose not. Just please don't tell me I'm as bad as Dr. Ray."

"Oh, hell no."

"Thank God."

"He's something else, isn't he?"

"That's an understatement for sure."

They both laughed and Lyra ate more of her vegetables. Eleanor was right, there was just the right amount of heat. "Would you like to try a bite of mine?"

Eleanor perked up. "You don't mind?"

"Not at all." She pushed her plate closer to Eleanor and waited as she forked a bite. She chewed slowly and her face lit up.

"Wow, that's excellent."

"Right?"

"Would you like some of mine?"

Lyra nodded. "Please."

"Wait, you've had it, haven't you? So, it's no mystery to you."

"Doesn't mean I don't want a bite." She grinned sheepishly.

Eleanor eased her plate toward her. "Then by all means, help yourself."

Lyra took a bite and groaned. "Yep, just as I remembered."

"Seriously good, right?"

"Mm-hm." Lyra sipped more of her tea and relaxed as they chitchatted the rest of the meal.

By the time the check came, Lyra had all but forgotten the guilt she'd felt. She'd thoroughly enjoyed their conversation and the meal.

Lyra reached for the bill but Eleanor beat her to it. "No, it's my treat," Eleanor said.

"I can't let you do that. You got the last one."

"So?" She slid the bill toward her and eyed the amount. Then she pulled out her wallet and counted out some cash. She left more than enough for a hefty tip and closed her purse. "Shall we?"

Lyra sighed. "You shouldn't have done that." She stood alongside Eleanor and headed for the door with her. "But thank you nonetheless." Eleanor was an incredibly generous and kind woman.

"You're welcome nonetheless," she said. She placed her hand on the small of Lyra's back and escorted her through the door. They walked out into a steady drizzle.

"Oh, no," Lyra said, ducking. The raindrops were cool on her skin and they hurried to her Jeep and crawled inside.

"Shoo," Eleanor said as they settled in, both of them slightly wet. "That rain is a bit cold." She ran her hands through her hair and checked her makeup in the fold down mirror.

"You still look good," Lyra said. "No worries there." She meant it as a sincere compliment, but it came out sounding raspy and passionate. Eleanor, it seemed, had picked up on it as well.

She looked at her in obvious surprise. "You think?"

Lyra swallowed. "Uh-huh."

"Thank you." Her eyes drifted down Lyra's face to her mouth. "You do as well. In fact, you look really good. Good enough to taste."

Lyra heated under her heavy gaze. Her head began to spin and the sound of the raindrops ticking on the windshield seemed to be luring her to her but a car horn sounded behind them and they both jerked.

"What the hell?" Eleanor said, obviously frustrated. She touched her fingers to her mouth and looked in the mirror. "What does he want?"

"I don't know," Lyra said. But she was glad for the distraction. She'd almost done something she'd possibly regret. She eyed the sedan. "He probably wants this spot."

"What an asshole."

Lyra started the engine and backed out of the parking space. Then she drove from the lot and headed toward Eleanor's.

"I had a nice time tonight," Eleanor said. "Thank you for choosing the restaurant, and for driving."

Lyra, despite feeling relieved, was still heated from their intimate moment and her heart rate had yet to slow. "It was my pleasure."

"We must do it again, sometime."

"Yes," Lyra said. "I...agree." But did she? Another meal would no doubt lead to more intimate moments. Was she ready for that? She couldn't help but wonder if nearly kissing Detective Wallace would leave her feeling just as excited and torn.

They both watched the road and listened to the whine of the wipers.

Eleanor took her hand as she continued to drive, making her feel guilty once again.

"When we get to my house, would you like to come in for a night cap?"

Oh God. Really? "Are you sure?"

"I've never been more sure."

What should I do? She thought of Louie and how he'd said she'd needed to date, that she was putting work before her personal life and true happiness. But she really honestly didn't know if she should. Not when she was so torn over Detective Wallace.

Lyra pulled into Eleanor's gated community and waited as Eleanor opened the entrance with her remote. Then she drove in and eased alongside her home, parking along the curb.

"You can park in the driveway," Eleanor said.

Lyra pointed. "Someone's there. It looks like Detective Wallace's car."

Eleanor looked up from digging in her purse. "It is."

Just then Detective Wallace emerged from the awning at the front door. She jogged to the Jeep. Eleanor opened the door.

Detective Wallace stopped dead in her tracks when she saw Lyra. "Oh," she said. "I didn't realize." Lyra could tell by the shocked look on her face that she wasn't happy and her stomach sank, knowing she was the cause.

"We just returned from dinner," Eleanor said.

"Well, don't let me interrupt," Detective Wallace said.

Lyra wanted desperately to help the situation, to somehow explain. But what could she do? Tell the truth? That she and Eleanor had had a wonderful time and almost shared a passionate kiss with maybe the promise of more?

Shit.

Detective Wallace turned to go.

"Danny, wait." Eleanor faced Lyra. "I'm sorry," she said. "But I should see what she needs."

Lyra nodded. "It's okay."

"Rain check?"

Lyra smiled softly, even though she felt uneasy as hell. "Sure."

"Okay then. Have a nice night."

"You, too."

Eleanor closed the door and hurried after Detective Wallace. Lyra turned her Jeep around and didn't wait to see whether or not they went inside.

Because now, a new feeling emerged and she was just too damn jealous to stomach the sight.

CHAPTER TWENTY

"Danny, will you please stop," Eleanor said as she hurried after her.

Danny yanked open the door to her unmarked cruiser. "No, you don't have to worry, I'm going." She tried to climb inside, but Eleanor held on to the door, not allowing her to pull it closed.

Danny halted. "It's no problem. We can talk later."

But there was a problem. She sounded like hell, looked even worse. "No, we talk now," Eleanor demanded. She walked toward the house. "Come on, let's get out of this rain."

She paused at the front door, waiting as Danny slowly closed her car door and followed. Eleanor then unlocked the front door and stepped inside, allowing Danny to enter behind her.

"I really didn't mean to interrupt. I didn't know...you know...you and Lyra Aarden."

"It's quite alright." She deposited her purse on the counter and dug in the fridge for a couple of bottles of Smartwater. She handed one to Danny and then headed for the couch where she motioned for Danny to follow as she switched on the gas fireplace. "I told you, we'd just returned from dinner." She left out how she'd proposed that the night continue. She didn't think Danny could handle it by the look of things, and it was really none of her business either. Plus she couldn't believe she'd actually done it. What happened to keeping things professional? That had obviously gone right out the window. Perhaps it was a good thing that they were interrupted.

"Yes, well, I'm sure you would've liked to have said a proper good-bye." Danny was watching her, as if waiting for her to confirm that that was indeed what they were planning on doing. Saying good-bye.

Eleanor didn't rise to the bait. "So, what brings you by?" She opened the Smartwater and encouraged Danny to do the same. She looked like she needed some minerals and electrolytes. "Have you eaten? I can reheat something if you like? Won't take but a minute."

Danny sipped her drink. She rubbed her forehead. "I—shit. I actually can't even remember why I came by."

"Oh?" Were things worse than she thought?

But then Danny seemed to come around. She straightened. "Oh, I remember. Sorry, it's been a day."

"I understand."

"I wanted to tell you I went by Gabby Dietrich's sister's house today. And I've got some news. It seems that Gabby fell out of a tree when she was little, and she limped from that day forward."

"And she wasn't treated for it?"

"Not according to her sister."

"Her left leg?"

"Yes."

"This is good news."

"I thought so."

Eleanor set her drink down on the coffee table. "Anything else?"

Danny seemed to think a moment.

"You could've told me that over the phone," Eleanor said softly.

"I know. I just thought—I wanted to see you."

"Why?"

Danny looked incredulous. "Do I have to have a reason? I thought we were friends."

"We are. But…it would be nice if you called before you came by."

Danny stood. "I should go."

"Danny, no, don't."

"I really should. I've intruded and you're right. I should've called first. I'm sorry, El." A deep sadness seemed to overcome her and Eleanor rose to stand alongside her. She lightly touched her arm.

"Please, stay," she said. "Stay and talk to me."

Danny shuddered. "You really shouldn't touch me, El. It's been too long since I've been touched."

Eleanor saw the stirring in her eyes and she let her hand fall. "Let me make you something to eat. You look like death warmed over."

"I guess you would know better than anyone what that looks like," Danny said.

Eleanor laughed. "Still a smart-ass, aren't you?"

"Guilty as charged."

"Come on," Eleanor took her by the hand and led her to the bar. "Sit." She guided her to a barstool and got busy plucking leftovers from the fridge. "I've got some gumbo in here," she said. "That sound good?"

"I guess. I do need to eat."

Eleanor removed the lid to the Pyrex bowl and spooned some into a serving bowl.

Danny spoke. "You too full from your dinner to eat with me?"

Eleanor chuckled. "Um, yes. More than full."

"Where did ya'll go?"

"We went to a Thai restaurant."

"Thai food?"

"Mm-hm."

"That's a little unusual for you, isn't it?"

"It is."

"Did you enjoy it?"

Eleanor met her gaze. "I did." She placed the bowl in the microwave and covered it with a paper towel.

"Lyra, she's…good company?"

Eleanor busied herself at the sink. "She is."

"You like her."

"Mm. She's nice."

"She's more than nice. She's…very attractive. Not to mention intelligent."

"She is, yes."

"Your interest in her is…. more than professional?"

"Does it really matter?" *Why are you asking, Danny? Are you as interested in Lyra as Lyra seems to be in you?*

Danny grew quiet and the microwave beeped. Eleanor retrieved the bowl with a potholder and stirred the contents. She carefully tasted it and returned it to the microwave. She wondered where Danny was going with the questions.

"It matters," Danny said.

Eleanor wiped down the counter, wishing she'd drop the whole Lyra topic. "And why is that?"

"Because," Danny said. "You're—"

"Yes?" She stopped wiping. Waiting.

"Working with her."

Eleanor laughed softly. "Not officially. And that didn't stop us now, did it?"

Danny seemed to stumble over her reply. "Yes, but we—it was—we were different."

"How so?"

"We—I don't know. It just seems different, okay?"

Eleanor finally met her gaze. "I don't need your permission, do I? Because if I do, then that's news to me. Last I knew we were over and have been for some time now."

Danny blinked at her as if she were at a loss for words. As if her statement had totally left her flabbergasted. Maybe it had.

"I—we still have feelings. You can't deny that. I see it in you sometimes."

Eleanor ignored the beeping microwave and went to her. She took her hands in hers. "Danny, I do sometimes still have feelings of attraction for you but…they can't go anywhere. And they never can again. It wouldn't be good," she said. "We'd just end up right where we left off and it wasn't good in the end. Not for either of us."

Danny closed her eyes and breathed deeply. "You're right. About all of it. I'm just—so tired, so stressed and so—"

"Confused?"

She looked at her. "Confused?"

"About your own attraction to Lyra."

Danny's breath hitched. "Is it that obvious?"

"'Fraid so."

"Does it upset you?"

Eleanor drew away, needing to put some distance between them.

"Your gumbo's ready," she said, walking to the microwave. She'd suspected Danny's interest in Lyra, but hearing confirmation of it felt like a slap to the face and she scolded herself for that, wishing she had better control of her emotions. After all, Lyra was beautiful and fun and intelligent. It should come as no surprise that Danny would find her attractive as well. She needed to get a grip.

"Fuck the gumbo," Danny said.

"No, not fuck the gumbo," she said as she retrieved it. "You need to eat."

"I'm fine," Danny said. "Really, El. I just want you to answer the question."

"You look like hell, Danny. Seriously. Stop arguing with me and eat something, for God's sake."

"I'm not trying to argue with you," she said. "I just think we should talk about this."

Eleanor stirred the gumbo and brought it to her. She set it in front of her and handed over a spoon.

"Only if you answer the question," Danny said softly. She offered a tired-looking smile.

Eleanor couldn't deny her the right to know. Danny deserved the truth. "I'm not upset, I'm—I don't know, worried."

"About?"

"The problems this might cause with Lyra and the case. We can't all be in some sick love triangle."

"We aren't, are we?"

"I don't know. How does Lyra feel about you?"

Danny seemed to squirm in her seat. "I thought she felt the same. Why? Has she said something?"

"She talks about you a lot, like she has an interest."

"She does?"

"Yes." She seemed happy to hear that, even if she was trying her best to hide it.

"So, what do we do?"

Eleanor picked at the dish rag she'd been using to wipe down the counters. She thought about the good times she'd had with Lyra, and about how much they had in common. But she also thought about all the times Lyra had asked about Danny, and how she'd seemed hesitant when Eleanor had suggested they continue their evening in the house. It seemed there was only one thing to do. It was obvious to her now even if it did hurt. She had to allow Lyra and Danny to explore their feelings without having her in the middle. It was the right thing to do. The mature thing to do. But fucking A if it didn't suck.

Danny slid the bowl closer and stirred the gumbo.

Eleanor reached across the bar and squeezed her hand. "You need to find happiness, Danny, and it isn't with me, that's obvious. And I'd like to say that it may lie with Lyra, but that wouldn't be the truth either. Happiness, true happiness, it lies within."

Danny swallowed.

"But," Eleanor continued. "I'm willing to step back, so you and Lyra can explore your feelings for each other, because I think you need to see where things can go with her. She's a good person and she seems to really care about you."

Danny lowered her spoon. "El," she said, her eyes filling with tears.

"Don't." Eleanor released her hand and wiped her own eyes. "I don't want to cry."

"Too late," Danny said. She stood and came around the counter to embrace her. She held her tight and whispered in her ear. "I love you," she said. "And I thank you."

Eleanor felt the warm tears slide down her face. She inhaled Danny's woodsy scent and rested in her strong arms, knowing for certain now that she'd never get to call her her own again. Not only that, but it was unlikely she'd ever get to call Lyra hers either and somehow, someway, even though it hurt so badly she felt like her heart was being crushed, she knew it was right. This was how it had to be done.

Danny drew away and smoothed away Eleanor's tears with her thumbs.

"I mean it, I love you, El."

Eleanor fought for her voice, her throat tight with pain. "I love you, too." She sniffled and gently pushed her away. "Now go eat your food."

"You won't stop until I do eat, will you?"

"Absolutely not."

Danny walked slowly back to the barstool and sat. She took a spoonful of gumbo, blew on it, and chewed. She pointed at the bowl with her spoon. "It's really good."

Eleanor felt herself smile, but her heart still felt like it was in the vice grip of a most cruel hand. "I'm glad you like it." She'd just lost the two most dynamic women she'd ever met in her life. And somehow she had to be okay with that.

"I've always loved your cooking." Danny said, watching her closely.

"I'll send the rest with you. You can finish it off at home." She turned away from her, feeling too much of her concerned gaze. She busied herself at the kitchen sink and composed herself while watching Danny in her peripheral vision.

"Thanks," Danny said. She took another bite and then shoved the bowl away. "I should really take off. I've got to meet Devereaux to question more witnesses. We're hoping someone might remember seeing Gabby Dietrich walking home the night she went missing."

"Haven't you already questioned people?"

"We have. But we're hoping someone might remember her limp. I guess it was considerable. Something people would definitely notice."

"Ah. Good idea."

Eleanor replaced the lid on the gumbo and handed it over. "I really wish you'd stay and finish your meal."

Danny took the Pyrex bowl. "I would like that very much, El. Only…I think we both need some time and I really need to get back to work."

Eleanor closed her eyes. She was right of course. She wanted nothing more than to lie down and have a good cry. "Okay."

"I hope you understand."

"I do." She opened her arms and embraced her.

They stood like that for a long while, holding one another. Eleanor again inhaled her woodsy scent. Another tear escaped her eye. "I want nothing more than for you to be happy, Danny."

"I want the same for you."

They drew apart. Danny gently wiped Eleanor's tear away. "I hope you know that."

"I do."

"Go home and eat. Get some rest. Devereaux can wait."

"It could wait, but it shouldn't. Tina's out there somewhere."

Eleanor sighed. "There's no way I can change your mind, is there?"

"No."

"Okay, then. Go. But be safe. Promise me you'll be safe."

Danny touched her cheek. "Ever the worrier." She leaned in and kissed her cheek. "I promise." She headed for the door. Eleanor watched her go as another tear escaped and fell down her face.

Take care of you, Danny.

Please. Take care of you.

CHAPTER TWENTY-ONE

"Come on, big guy, I need you," Danica said into her cell phone as she exited Eleanor's neighborhood. "I want to question that guy at the gas station again and he works the evening shift."

"I can't," Devereaux said. "Molly will kill me if I leave tonight."

"We have a case to work," Danica said.

"Yeah, and we've been working it. For three days straight. Sheesh, you're about to kill me, Danny. Take a fucking break."

"No time for breaks," she said. "You know that."

"Well, you're just going to have to question that witness without me tonight."

"Fine." Danica ended the call and tossed the phone on the passenger seat. She could do it without him. No problemo. Things might even go better without him.

She sped toward State Street, ready to question one of the remaining businesses they hadn't hit yet, ignoring the texts coming in. She knew it was Devereaux, telling her to go home. Lecturing her about rest, etc. He often sounded a lot like Eleanor when it came to her overworking. She rubbed her eyes and slowed as she pulled into Mike's Buy and Go. She was tired. Beyond tired. But she kept thinking about Tina Givens. If they could find out what happened to Gabby Dietrich, it might lead them to Tina.

She crawled from her car and entered the store with a ding from an overhead bell. She headed straight for the drink cooler and got herself two Monsters. She cracked one open as she headed for the checkout counter. To her relief, Mike was working the evening shift, just as she'd hoped.

"Remember me?" she asked as she set the drinks down in front of him.

"Kinda hard to forget a cop," he said. "Even a woman one."

Danica ignored his attitude and paid for her drinks. "I've got some more questions for you."

"I told you I don't know anything."

"I know. I, too, remember. But I'm hoping this time around something might jog your memory."

"Yeah? What's that?"

"Seems our victim walked with a considerable limp." She pulled Gabby's photo out from her back pocket. It wasn't a great picture. It had been taken candidly and Gabby wasn't completely facing the camera. But it was all Francine Broussard had, so it would have to work.

She showed him the picture.

"Yeah, I'm still not sure. Lots of girls come in here."

"Again, she walked with a considerable limp. And she would've been walking home from the Dollar Store. Maybe she stopped in here for a late-night snack, or something to drink?"

Mike took the photo and studied it closer. "What did you say her name was again?"

"Gabby. Gabby Dietrich."

"Gabby," he said softly, more to himself. He tapped the picture. "Yeah, come to think of it…"

"What?" Danny asked, hopeful.

"A girl came in sometimes asking to use the restroom. And she walked funny. Kind of had her foot turning in some. But she looked different than this. Had different hair. It was longer than this last time I saw her with a green stripe in the front."

Danica whipped out her notebook and took notes. No one had told her about the dyed hair. What in the hell was her family thinking in not telling her these things? Miss Francine especially. Maybe she just really didn't understand the importance.

"When did you last see her?"

"Shoot, I don't know. It's been a long while now."

"She went missing six months ago," Danica said. "The night of April fourth. She was last seen leaving the Dollar Store on foot."

"I don't know what day it was, but yeah that sounds about right. About six months ago or so."

"And your cameras don't work, right?"

"Nah. It just hasn't been a priority to fix them."

Danica finished scribbling and glanced up at him. "Do you remember if she was with someone the last time you saw her? A man?"

He seemed to think for a moment. "No, there was no one. She came in, used the restroom, and then left."

"Did you see her at all after she left?"

He thought again. "You know I think it was raining that night. Off and on."

Danica nodded. "It was."

"Seems to me she was complaining about it. About having to walk in the rain."

"But you didn't see her again after she walked out the door?"

"How do you mean?"

"Like maybe she got in a car or something? Got a ride from someone?"

He shook his head. "Nah, nothing like that that I can remember."

Danica sighed. "You're sure?"

He held up his hands. "Hey, I told you all I know."

Danica put away her notebook. "Yeah, alright. I appreciate it."

She handed him her card. "Please, call if you think of anything else." She took her drinks and headed back to her car. She drove home quietly, without music, thinking about the case. She sipped her Monster and rubbed her eyes. They were growing heavier and heavier.

She refocused on the road and tightened her hands on the steering wheel. She accelerated, wanting to get home quickly. She needed a drink. A good stiff one. And some more Monster to help keep her awake.

She wanted to look over Gabby's file again and go over the other witness statements they'd taken back in April when she'd first gone missing. She didn't have time for sleep, and she didn't have time to think about Eleanor, or their conversation about Lyra.

She blinked, forcing her eyes open, but they wouldn't cooperate. They drifted closed again and she jerked, opening them quickly. Her car crossed the yellow line, and she yanked her steering wheel hard to the right and over-corrected. Her vehicle spun out of control and she slammed into something hard. Something that stopped the momentum of the car. Something that hurt her terribly.

And then…there was nothing.

"Wha?"

"Detective Wallace, can you hear me?" A siren-like female voice asked.

Danica opened her heavy eyelids and tried to focus. But the world was blurry and it was so hard to keep her eyes open.

"Detective?"

"Yeah?" She turned her head toward the voice.

Oh, God, her head. How it hurt. She winced.

"Detective, can you hear me?"

"I…wha?"

"Detective, focus. Open your eyes. I'm right here."

Danica opened her eyes again. Slowly, a form came into focus. It was a woman. A familiar-looking woman.

"There you are," she said.

Danica squinted against the flashing red and blue lights. "What happened?"

"You've been in an accident," the woman said. "We're going to try to get you out of the vehicle, okay? Just sit tight and try to stay awake. You've got a pretty bad head injury there."

Danica blinked and tried to place the woman. Her face kept coming in and out of focus. And then suddenly, she remembered. "Joy?"

"That's me," she said.

Danica licked her lips. They tasted of blood.

"Haven't seen you in a while," Danica said. She hadn't worked a scene with Joy in a long time. But then again, all the people she'd found lately had been dead awhile, hardly the scene for a paramedic. She winced again as she touched her head. More blood stained her fingertips.

"Hang tight, okay? I'm going to go on the passenger side and stay with you while they pry open your door."

Danica tried to nod. It hurt too badly. Joy disappeared and then reappeared at the passenger window.

"Stay with me, Detective," she said.

Danica fought to keep her eyes open.

"Devereaux," Danica said. "You call him?"

"I did, he's on his way."

She touched her head again. "What happened? I can't…remember."

"You drove off the road and slammed into a tree," Joy said. "But you're okay. You're going to be okay."

"I need to get out," she said. "Gotta…Tina. Tina Givens." But her head pounded and it felt heavy on her shoulders. She kept nodding off, the urge to sleep overwhelming.

"Hang in there," Joy said.

Danica heard more voices coming from outside the driver's side door. Then she heard other noises. A generator. They were going to use the Jaws of Life to get her out. She clenched her eyes closed, the noise too much to bear. She drowned everything out, even Joy, and tried to remain calm. She was suddenly becoming very aware of her position, stuck in the tight, crushed space of her vehicle.

"I need to get out," she kept saying. "Gotta get out."

The next thing she knew, the door was removed and the firefighters, some she recognized, were stabilizing her head and neck as others used the ram to push the dash back. They did their best to comfort her as they removed her from the car and placed her on a backboard. From there she was carried to a stretcher and placed inside an ambulance where Joy was right by her side, gripping her hand.

"You're okay," Joy said. "You're out and you're all good. Dustin's gonna put a line in you, okay?"

"Yeah." She glanced to her right and saw Dustin, a young EMT she didn't know.

But it didn't seem to matter because she didn't feel a thing. Only her pounding head. Then there was a knock on the ambulance doors and Devereaux was suddenly inside and next to Joy.

"Holy, fuck, Danny," he said as he looked down at her. "What the hell happened?"

"Good to see you, too," she said. And then, seemingly from out of nowhere she began to tear up.

"Hey, it's alright," Devereaux said. He patted her hand. "They got you now."

But Danica could only think of one thing.

Of only one person.

"Tina," she said. "Gotta find Tina."

Then she closed her eyes and didn't open them again.

Chapter Twenty-two

Ｈow is she?" Lyra asked as she hurried down the hospital hall toward Eleanor. Her heart lurched and she felt sick to her stomach, she was so worried for Detective Wallace.

"She's...conscious. But barely," Eleanor said, looking tired.

It had been hours since the accident, but Eleanor hadn't called Lyra until morning. And by the look of things, Eleanor had been at the hospital with Detective Wallace that entire time.

"How are you?" Lyra asked, gently caressing Eleanor's arm. "Do you need to go home to get some rest?"

"I don't know. Maybe." She scooted away from her touch and rubbed her temple. "I'm just so worried about her. I don't really want to leave her alone."

Lyra wasn't sure what her moving away meant, but she knew now was not the time to ask. She looked beyond her into the hospital room. She couldn't make out Detective Wallace, just the foot of her bed. But she did see another detective sitting with her. The same man that she'd seen that first day at the crime scene.

"She's not alone right now," Lyra said.

"Devereaux's with her, but he can't stay. She won't let him. She wants him to continue to work the case."

"Wow, she's still talking about the case, huh?"

"Mm-hm. She won't ever stop."

"Is that why you're worried?"

Eleanor glanced back into the room and then lowered her voice some more. "I'm worried for many reasons."

And sad. You look so sad, Eleanor.

Lyra nodded. "Yeah, I get it."

"I'm afraid you don't," Eleanor said. "You couldn't possibly, because there are things you don't know."

"Such as?"

She sighed. "She overworks, Lyra. And she never, ever stops."

"Ever?"

"Very rarely. Her work is her life. She brings it home with her. That's one of the reasons we stopped seeing each other. And…"

"And…?"

She shook her head. "Nothing."

Lyra could tell there was something more, but she didn't push it.

"Well, she's going to have to take it easy."

"She won't do it."

"She's not going to have a choice now." A thought came to Lyra and she furrowed her brow. "What exactly caused the accident?"

"They think she fell asleep behind the wheel."

Oh, my God.

This was bad. Really bad. It seemed that Eleanor wasn't exaggerating when she said she overworked.

Just then Detective Devereaux appeared behind them in the doorway. He looked as tired and concerned as Eleanor.

"Hey," he said, rubbing his eye behind his glasses. "She's asleep for now."

"Okay," Eleanor said. "I'll keep an eye on her."

"No," he said. "You need to go home. You've been here almost as long as I have."

"I don't want to leave her alone," Eleanor said. "She's…not in a good way."

"Yeah, I noticed that, too." Sadness washed over his ruddy face. "But you need to rest, El. Danny would insist."

"I can stay with her," Lyra said. She wanted to help, but more than that she wanted, needed to see Detective Wallace first hand. She needed to make sure she was okay.

They both looked at her.

"For a little while. If it'll help," she added quickly.

"That'll be a big help," he said.

"Are you sure?" Eleanor asked. "She's not in a pleasant mood."

"I don't mind," Lyra said, a little unsure what she meant by that. But she really didn't mind.

"Go home," Detective Devereaux said to Eleanor. "I'll even escort you out."

"Okay, okay. Call me if you need to," Eleanor said, speaking to Lyra. "I'll be back a little later."

Lyra agreed and after saying good-bye to them both, she entered Detective Wallace's room and sat in a chair near the bed. She was as quiet as she could be, settling in to look at the detective as she slept. Her head was wrapped with thick gauze near her hairline. Some blood had soaked through the gauze, tainting it a dark red. Her face appeared to be bruised and burnt from the air bag. Her lip was swollen. Dried blood was there as well, and Lyra wondered if she'd bitten her lip or just slammed it against the air bag.

Thankfully, she didn't seem to have any broken bones or any further bandages or casts. Lyra recalled her own accident all too well, and the detective's fortune wasn't lost on her. She just hoped her head injury wasn't too severe.

As she was sitting there thinking of her own injuries after her own accident, the detective began to stir. She moved ever so slightly and moaned as if she were in pain. Her eyes shifted beneath her eyelids and Lyra realized she was dreaming.

She gripped her hand. "It's okay," she said. "You're just dreaming."

The detective's eyes fluttered open.

Lyra inched forward, straightening her back. "Hey," she said. "How do you feel?"

Detective Wallace blinked at her. "Where am I?" Her voice sounded rough, as if she'd swallowed gravel.

"You're in the hospital."

She licked her dry, bloody lips. "Why?"

Lyra squeezed her hand. "You were in a car accident."

Her eyes glazed over and she seemed lost in thought. "Right," she said. "Now I remember. Where's Eleanor?"

"She just left. She said she'd be back in a bit."

She was quiet again. Then, "You're…here?"

Lyra smiled. "I am. In the flesh. Is that okay?"

"No."

"No?"

"I don't want you to see me like this."

Lyra patted her hand. "Don't be silly. You should've seen me after my car accident."

"You were…in a wreck?"

"I was and it took me a long time to recover. But you look like you'll recover a lot quicker than I did."

"I will." She sounded determined. "In fact," She stripped off her covers and tried to swing her legs off the bed.

"What are you doing?" Lyra stood and grab her shoulders, trying to stop her. The detective only pulled against her for a second and then she grabbed her bandaged head and fell back against the pillows.

"Don't worry," she grumbled, wincing. "My head's not letting me go anywhere." She licked her lips. "Water?"

Lyra quickly poured her some from a small plastic pitcher. She handed her the cup and Detective Wallace took it and sipped. She winced again and Lyra felt for her, knowing her mouth must be just as sore as her head.

"More?" she asked as Detective Wallace returned the cup to her.

"No." She moved, trying to get comfortable. "How long have I been here?"

"Since last night," she said.

Detective Wallace looked down and seemed to be examining herself. When she touched her head, she looked concerned.

"My head," she said. "How bad?"

"According to Eleanor you have a minor cut and a concussion. But she didn't say anything else."

"Hurts like hell," she said.

"Do you want me to get the doctor?"

"No." She shifted again. "Devereaux here?"

"He just left as well."

"Is he working the case?"

"I'm not sure." She had assumed he was going home as exhausted as he'd looked, but she didn't want to worry the detective about it.

"We have more witnesses to question about Tina Givens," she said. "I need to know some things about the night she went missing."

"Like what?" Lyra asked. "Maybe I can help." She didn't want her trying to climb out of the bed again.

"I don't think so."

"Why not try me? It's worth a shot, right? We've got nothing else to do." When she didn't respond, Lyra spoke again. "Come on, Detective."

She started to laugh but stopped herself, as if fearing it would hurt her head. "Call me Danny," she said.

"You sure?"

"All my friends call me Danny." She smiled, ever so slightly.

Lyra returned it. "So, we're friends now, eh?"

"Apparently."

Lyra patted her hand. "Don't get so excited."

"Stop making me laugh," Danny said. "It hurts."

Lyra held up her palm. "Okay, I'll try. But you're going to have to tell me what you're thinking as far as Tina Givens goes. To see if I can help."

Danny studied her closely. "Okay," she said. "For starters, I need to know what the weather was like the night she disappeared."

"Easy," Lyra said, and she whipped out her phone and asked for the date. Danny gave it and she searched for the weather on that particular evening.

"Light showers," she said. "Balmy seventy-six degrees."

"Rain," Danny said softly.

"Some, yes."

"And she was near a gas station on State Street." She looked off in the distance. "I wonder if there's a connection."

Lyra thought for a moment. "You could always check the security cameras at the gas station if that's what you're wondering about."

"We did," she said. "We saw Tina walk by on the street but that was it."

"No vehicles?"

"At the gas station? There were some of course. We looked into all of them. Nothing significant."

"What about the cars going by?"

"Couldn't get license plates, so it was difficult to identify them."

Lyra thought back to some of the security footage she'd seen throughout her lifetime. The quality of the picture was rarely good enough to make out details.

"What about the tip line I've been seeing on television? Has anyone called in with any info about that night? Or about the cars?"

"We've had hundreds of leads," she said. "A lot of people have come forward to identify themselves, letting us know that they were in a specific car. But they've all been cleared."

"All of them?"

"Uh-huh."

"Well, how would you know for sure?"

"We can't. Not for sure. But we checked backgrounds and arrest records, and they were all cleared."

Lyra considered this. "Maybe you should go back over the footage again."

"That's what I want to do. I want to re-examine the footage from near where the girls went missing. I also need to look into the other victims and see if it was raining on the nights they disappeared."

"You think the rain plays a part in this?"

"It could. If it was raining, they'd be more likely to get into a vehicle, wouldn't you say? If someone offered them a ride?"

"You've got a point."

"Only thing is, these women were street smart. Their families say they wouldn't get in a car with a stranger. So, I'm either way off base or..."

"They knew the guy."

"Yes."

"Wow. That's a scary thought."

"Oh, he's here," she said. "He's close. He knows this community. He's a part of it."

Lyra rubbed her arms. She had the chills. "You're freaking me out."

"It's true."

"So he's here, lurking."

"Watching. And waiting. It's my belief that he stalks his victims first. Plans the whole thing before he strikes. He's got a rich fantasy life and he tries to play out those fantasies."

"How creepy."

"See why I don't like the idea of you running alone right now?"

"I get it," she said.

"But you're still doing it, aren't you?"

"For the time being. But I'm only running during the day and always on a route I'm familiar with."

"I'm sure these victims would tell you that they thought they were being safe too if they could."

"I have to exercise," she said. "I get cranky if I don't."

"So, go to the gym."

"I'll think about it," she said.

Danny visibly swallowed and held her head.

"Still hurts?" Lyra asked.

"Like a bitch."

"I'll get the nurse," she said, standing.

"No, don't. I don't want any painkillers."

"Why not?"

"Because I…" She turned her head to look out the window.

"Danny?"

"I…think I have a problem."

"Okay," Lyra said quietly, easing back down. "Would you like to talk about it?"

"I…" She closed her eyes. "I think everyone's right. I need to change my life."

"In what way?" She knew very little about Danny, but some of the things she did know were concerning. Though very beautiful, she always looked tired, like she hadn't slept. And her pallor was often times pale, despite being outside at the crime scene. And then there was what Eleanor had said. About her never taking time to stop.

"I think I need to take some time off work." She turned back to face her. "But not until after this case."

"But you may need to do it now," Lyra said. "You're in pretty bad shape, Danny."

"I know." She touched her head again. "I just meant that I can't go on a vacation or anything anytime soon. Not until I solve this case."

"What about an extended hospital stay? Does that count as vacation time? Because you're pretty beat up and concussions take time to heal."

"I'll be fine," she said.

Lyra cocked her head. "What does time off have to do with not wanting painkillers?"

Danny began examining her hands. "Nothing. I…have another issue."

"Another issue?"

"I drink, Lyra." She looked at her. "A lot."

"Oh."

"You surprised?"

Lyra fought for the right thing to say. "Yes, actually. I'm quite surprised."

"Guess I hide it well."

"Well, you don't drink at work, do you?"

"I didn't used to, but lately…"

"I see."

"I need to quit. And if I do that, I don't want to take any pain killers either. I don't want to rely on substances."

Lyra was silent, soaking in all that she'd shared. "That's hard to do," she said. "Quitting."

"Tell me about it. I'm already dreading it."

"You don't feel sick when you don't drink, do you?"

"No, nothing like that. God even right now, I just want a damn drink to relax."

"How about something else? Something to take your mind off things."

"Like what? I don't think there's much I can do to relax here. Hospitals make me nervous in general."

"How about a massage?"

"A massage?" She laughed again and winced. "Ow, fuck. You really gotta stop cracking me up."

"I just meant that maybe I could call a nurse and they'd give you a massage."

"I seriously doubt it. I don't think that's part of their job."

Lyra thought. "Well, I could do it."

"Are you serious?"

"Sure, why not." It wasn't something she'd thought through and now, with Danny's reaction, she wondered if she'd gone too far. Too late to back out now.

"Because just the thought of anyone rubbing my shoulders makes me tense up."

Lyra scooted forward and searched her mind for a way to right things. "How about this?" She gently took her hand and began to massage her palm, with no intention of doing anything other than helping her relax. But it quickly became apparent that her gesture was doing far more.

Danny sharply inhaled and then froze.

"Is this okay?" Lyra asked, her own heart thudding in her chest.

"I don't know," she said.

"It's supposed to be relaxing. You look like you're about to bolt." *Or throw up. Oh, God. Should I be doing this?*

"It feels weird. It feels..."

"Good?" she asked, hope against hope.

Danny pressed her lips together. "Yeah," she croaked.

"Because I can stop. If you want me to."

Danny held her gaze. "No. I don't want you to stop."

Lyra kept massaging, pressing deeply into the palm of her hand. She was very much aware of the way her body was reacting to the feel of Danny beneath her fingertips, but she wasn't about to say anything. Especially, if Danny didn't feel the same. But by the look of her, with the pulse racing at the base of her neck, and the intense gaze she was giving her, she was sure she did. Either that or she was really about to take off and run.

"I don't want you to ever stop." Her eyes drifted closed.

Lyra struggled for something to say. There was a heaviness in the air between them now. It was palpable and much stronger than it had been between them in the car, even if it was unspoken. Finally, Danny broke it and opened her eyes.

"It feels really good, Lyra. You feel really good."

"So do you."

Danny's hazel blue eyes glinted with what looked like a spark of desire. "I'm not the only one feeling this then?"

Lyra shook her head and rasped, "No, you're not."

"I didn't think so," she said. "But I wasn't so sure when I saw you with Eleanor at her house…"

"I know. I—Eleanor is incredible. I really like her, but…"

"Yes?"

"I can't deny my feelings for you. So it would be wrong to start something with her when I'm attracted to you."

"Are you sure? Especially after what I just shared with you? You don't think I'm some big loser now that you know my downfalls?" She chuckled at herself, but Lyra didn't find it humorous. She didn't think Danny insulting herself was funny. She had too much respect for her for that.

"Of course not."

"Yeah, well, a lot of people would."

"Not me. I don't judge."

"Ah. One of those."

"One of those, what?"

"Good people."

This time Lyra laughed, unable to help it. "I'd like to think so."

"You are," Danny said. "I can tell." She held her gaze for a long moment, as if she were truly taking her in for the first time. "You're very beautiful, Lyra Aarden. Do you know that?"

"I do now."

Danny smiled. "I'll be sure to remind you of it often."

"Does that mean you want to spend more time with me then?"

"Oh, absolutely. If that's okay with you."

"It's more than okay."

"You sure? Even though I'm stuck in this hospital for the time being?"

"I'm sure."

Danny relaxed further into her pillows with a hopeful look on her face. She focused on their hands and entwined her fingers with Lyra's.

"Is that a bad thing?" Lyra asked, wondering what all she was thinking.

"No, not at all." She managed to smile. "But it's going to take some getting used to. I haven't had someone want to spend time with me in a long while."

"Well then, you better buckle up. Because I plan on sticking around."

Danny grinned and squeezed her hand. "I look forward to it."

CHAPTER TWENTY-THREE

H e didn't like it, didn't like it one bit.
She had been about to kiss a woman. When she was in her Jeep the other night, he was sure of it.

And now, he was in his car at the gas station waiting for her. He stared down the road at the entrance to the cane farm. A quick glance at his wristwatch pissed him off even more. It was getting late and she had yet to go for her run today. He'd waited for her earlier that morning and she hadn't showed. So, he'd come back tonight to wait again and nothing. It had been a few days now since she'd run.

Where was she? What was going on?

Not only was she absent, but she was most likely a homosexual. Something he hadn't ever experienced before, as far as his lovelies went. What would it mean, if anything?

"It means she'll be even harder to convince to love and appreciate me."

He opened his bottle of milk he'd bought from the gas station and drank heartily. Then he tossed the empty container on his seat.

"I'll just have to change her mind." But he thought of his current lovely and how difficult she'd been thus far. Could he really change Lyra Aarden and get her to love and appreciate him?

He wasn't sure. But he knew he'd give anything to try.

After a few more minutes and a few curious looks from people pulling into the station, he decided he'd better leave. He drove onto the main road and headed home. He didn't feel like working tonight, so he'd just have to tighten his purse strings a little. He had more important things to do. Like get his lovely ready for her big reveal. It was going to be monumental and he could afford no mistakes.

He also had Lyra Aarden front and foremost on his mind, and he knew he couldn't shake her anytime soon. He was obsessed now, and realizing that she was gay was only adding fuel to the fire. He'd been so angry at her the night before in seeing her lean in to kiss that woman, that he'd almost jumped out of his car and approached her. And then, as they'd left, something else happened. He'd become aroused. Highly aroused.

It had confused him and he'd fantasized the whole way home about how he'd force her to change her mind. How she'd change and she'd love *him*. It was such an exciting thought, he hadn't even slept. Not a wink. And he'd been almost disgusted with his current lovely lying next to him.

He'd hated the way she'd sounded as she breathed. He was so ready to get rid of her. She was nothing to him now. Not even worthy of his final fantasy. No, she would be different and he had just the plan for her.

He slowed and pulled into his gravel drive. Then he hurried into the house to the bedroom. His lovely was on the bed, tied to the headboard, waiting for him. But he had no feelings toward her other than contempt.

He slid his big knife from his back pocket and cut her loose. He loved doing it that way, loved seeing her eyes widen with fright as he brandished the knife. "Get up," he said. He pulled her up by the arm and led her into the kitchen. "Sit," he said, returning his knife to his back pocket. He crossed to the fridge and got out some leftover Raising Cane's chicken fingers. He no longer felt like cooking for her. She could just have fast food.

"You gotta eat," he said. "I'm not giving you to them malnourished. Oh, no. You're going to be presentable in every way."

He opened the box of chicken and grabbed a finger. He plopped it on a paper plate and then scooped out some coleslaw for her. He then slid the plate to her and gave her a spoon.

"Eat," he said. He sat down across from her and stared, waiting.

She didn't move. Didn't respond.

"It's your last day here," he said. "Now eat."

She shifted her dead eyes over to him. "Last day?" she said with a raspy voice.

"Yes." He pointed at the plate. "Eat."

She didn't move.

"What's the matter? You want some sauce?" He opened a small container of sauce and put it on her plate.

Tears slid down her face.

"Oh, don't start that again," he said. He reached in the box and grabbed a smaller finger. He threw it at her and it bounced off her chest and fell onto the table. "Eat! For God's sake!"

She full on cried then. Tears and sobs. Her cheeks reddened, along with her eyes. Her body shook as she wailed.

"Jesus Christ," he said as he stood. "Am I going to have to shove it down your throat? Because I will. Just like your drinks."

She shook her head vehemently.

"Then, eat."

Slowly, she picked up the finger and took a bite. He sank back down into his chair and watched her.

"There, that's better," he said. "Eat up."

He pulled the box closer to him and retrieved his own chicken finger and took a bite. "Mm, nothing like cold chicken, right?"

She didn't answer. But she was eating, however slowly.

"We've got to get you bathed and then dressed," he said, thinking aloud. "And I need to wash and blow dry your hair."

She stopped chewing. "I..." she croaked. "Don't hurt...me."

He stared at her. "Don't worry," he said. "You won't feel a thing."

Fear clouded her eyes, and she began to cry again and shake.

"Jesus," he let out. "I said you won't feel a thing. Is that not good enough?"

"Don't...want to die," she said.

But he'd had enough. The only time she'd spoken and it was to boss him around. "Damned whore," he said as he stood and grabbed the sedatives off the counter. He broke the capsules open and poured the contents into her glass of milk.

"No," she said as she started to shake her head. "No."

"You don't get a say," he said as he stirred the medication in. "Because you're not the boss." He took the milk and came to stand at her side. He grabbed a fist full of hair and yanked her head back. She yelped and cried, but he forced the milk down her gullet, causing her to choke and gurgle.

"Drink," he said with a clenched jaw.

She fought him, more so than usual, but he managed to get most of it down. He released her. "Now, get up." He yanked her up by the arm and led her down the hallway. Then he shoved her into the bathroom.

"Get undressed," he said.

She stood cowering in the corner near the clawfoot tub.

"Now!" he said. He turned on the bath faucet. He felt the water, adjusted the temperature, and turned to face her. "I'll give you a nice, warm bath. No need to thank me."

She trembled as she undressed. He lost his patience and helped her, tearing off her blouse and yanking down her leggings and panties. She no longer stank since he'd been bathing her, but she still looked bad. She'd lost a lot of weight and she looked almost skeletal standing there all pale and skinny.

"Get in," he said, holding her hand. She stepped into the water and sank down, still shaking. "The water's nice, so stop the damn shaking. Got it?"

She nodded but didn't stop. She just hugged herself, bringing her knees up to her chest.

"Jesus," he whispered as he began to bathe her. He couldn't trust her to do it. She wouldn't get clean enough. No, he needed to do it real good. Real good. Like the way his grandmother used to bathe him.

He lathered the washcloth and rubbed her down firmly, furiously. Then he rinsed her and did it again. Next, he scrubbed her hair with anti-dandruff shampoo. He had to get rid of her flakes and dry scalp. Then he wiped down her face and took the nail brush to scrub under her nails. He'd trim them short when she got out and scrub them again at the sink.

She was going to be sparkling clean if he had anything to say about it.

He pulled the stopper from the drain and held out a towel for her. "Get out."

She carefully stepped out of the tub and into the towel. He wrapped her and then rubbed her dry much like he'd washed her.

She made a noise of pain and disapproval.

"Be quiet," he said. He finished and looked at her. Now she was skinny and flushed red from the vigorous cleaning and drying. He grabbed her hand and pushed her down onto the closed toilet. He combed her hair out, in too much of a hurry to do it slowly and carefully so it wouldn't hurt. She made noises like she had before, but he ignored them and blew her hair dry with the old hair dryer. Then he grabbed her hand again. "Bedroom," he said. They entered the bedroom, and he shoved her down onto the bed.

"Wait," he said. He dug in his closet, scraping the hangers along the rod as he searched. "Here we go." He found the dress in the clear plastic cover and laid it on the bed. He unzipped the cover and pulled out the dress. He examined it carefully.

"Perfect." He looked to her again. "Stand up."

She stood and he helped her into the dress. "Don't touch it," he said. "I don't want you to wrinkle it or ruin it."

He carefully eased her back down to the bed to sit. "Don't move," he said. Then he opened his dresser drawer and retrieved a small red velvet box. He opened it and took out the sterling silver chain with the hummingbird charm. He smiled, thinking of his grandmother.

She looked nothing like his grandmother now, since the change, but she looked good enough with the dress and charm. He wondered what the police would think.

He slipped the necklace around her neck and fastened the clasp.

Her eyes started to drift closed. He didn't have much time before the drugs fully kicked in. Quickly, he changed his clothes and gave himself a once-over in the mirror.

"Come on," he said, helping her stand. He guided her back down the hall to the front door. He pulled aside the curtain and glanced outside. Darkness had fallen and he was good to go.

He opened the door and pulled his knife from his back pocket once again and brandished it in front of her face.

"Not a peep," he said.

She stared at him, dumbfounded. He smacked her cheeks. "I mean it," he said.

Then, with one last glance, he led her out to the car.

It was time.

❖

He turned down the back road and drove slowly, keeping an eye out for any police presence. He was coming onto the cane farm, and he hoped it would be covert enough to avoid anyone nearby. He knew there shouldn't be, save for the security guard at the front of the other road, but still, he wanted to be careful. He drove onward and killed his headlights. He kept his eyes peeled as Patsy Cline crooned "Walkin' After Midnight," setting the mood just right, just as she always did.

He smiled and spoke to his passenger. "Beautiful night, isn't it?" he said.

She didn't respond. "Well, it is," he continued. "And you look much better in the moonlight."

He reached for her hand. It was cool and listless, but it didn't matter.

This was it.

Finally.

He'd kept her for days, just like the others, caring for her, feeding her home cooked meals, bathing her in his old clawfoot bathtub. Keeping her drugged so she was mellow, pliable. So he could hold her and dance with her across the worn wooden floor. Usually he cherished those moments, but with her it had been different. Now, however, he felt like he could forgive her. She was, after all, going to be his ultimate gift to the police.

"I love you," he whispered as he smoothed down his starched dress shirt and tie. "I'll always love you." He squeezed her hand and hummed along as he slowed the car at the clearing. Crime scene tape was still up, along with a few white tents. According to the news, they were in the process of looking for more of his lovelies. Well, he was about to give them quite a show.

"Now, they won't have to look so hard."

He killed the engine and sat for a long moment, waiting, making sure they were alone. When he was satisfied, he crawled from the vehicle and crossed to the passenger door. He opened it carefully and took his most prized possession to date from the seat and into his arms.

"Careful," he said as he better positioned her against his body. "We don't want to mess up your makeup. Or your pretty dress. Grandmother had that made special, you know. But you know what? It looks better on you."

He lifted her and walked to the edge of the burnt cane. He knelt there near a tent and laid her down like a limp doll. "But don't tell her that. No, she must never know, you understand?"

She nodded. "Good."

"I'm going to miss you," he said. "Believe it or not."

He held her hand as he glanced around. "I'm going to leave you right here, in the clearing. So that means I won't be able to come back and visit you because they'll find you soon."

"But you don't mind, do you?" He kissed the back of her perfectly painted fingers. "I knew you wouldn't. Know why? Because you're my girl, aren't you? My lovely. Forever and always."

He carefully rested her hand on her stomach and maneuvered the necklace on her neck. He made sure the charm, the small hummingbird, was facing forward and then sat back on his knees to examine her.

"There," he said. "Now you can fly. Fly far away home."

He smiled at her and smoothed his tie again. Some of her makeup had gotten on the shoulder of his shirt, but he had enough experience to know that he could get it out. He knew he probably shouldn't wear his fanciest clothes to take his lovelies to their sweet fields of cane, but he always obeyed his elders.

"You must wear your Sunday best to do your best," he said, once again appraising her appearance.

The makeup he'd applied to her was perfect, leaving her lips looking as full and as colorful as they had in life, before she'd let herself wither away. The blue shades of her eye shadow accented her eyes perfectly, along with the eyeliner and mascara that accompanied it. She looked almost like she had when he'd first seen her.

Leaning down, he skimmed her soft as silk skin with the backs of his fingers. Then he placed a gentle kiss on the hollow of her cheek. He stroked her hair and studied her face, imprinting it into memory. Unable to hold back, he placed his hands around her neck and squeezed. Her eyes lolled a little, but she didn't wake. He squeezed as hard as he could until he needed a breath. Then, ready once again, he tightened his hands around her throat. She moaned, her eyes fluttered. But she was still too drugged to wake. He squeezed harder.

The noise of a car passing on the main road broke the spell, and he straightened and brushed her bangs back from her forehead.

"I have to go now," he said, wiping some sweat from his brow. He leaned in again and this time kissed her cool lips. "You still taste sweet," he said as he drew away. He stood and looked down upon her. "My lovely," he said. "Good-bye."

He backed away to his car. "I don't want to leave," he said, wanting some more time with her, needing to finish, but it was too risky. "But I have to."

He climbed inside and pulled the door closed. He eased down the window. "Good-bye, my lovely. Good-bye."

He started his car and turned around. With his gaze fixed on the dark cane in his rearview mirror, he drove slowly from the cane field and back into the world he despised.

CHAPTER TWENTY-FOUR

Danica sat in her unmarked cruiser with her hands on the steering wheel. Ahead of her, through the windshield, a handful of police personnel, as well as paramedics, moved around the crime scene like a swarm of bees. The scene was familiar, since she'd been there on an almost daily basis. Only today the temperature had dropped a good twenty degrees and a slight breeze was blowing. And well, *she* was different. She gently touched her forehead where her bandage was. Her headache had eased a little but not much. The dark sunglasses helped, but not quite enough. She was still squinting against the oncoming winter sun. And then there were her other injuries. Though minor, mostly scrapes and bruises on her legs and forearms, and strain on her muscles, she found that she was still sore and slow going. But there was no way she could've stayed in the hospital. She would've gone crazy thinking about the case and all that needed to be done. So, she'd left against doctor's orders and returned to work, much to everyone's concern.

She was glad she had left early, though. Because there was something else different at the cane farm today.

A body. A female from what she could see, resting outside an erected tent in the supine position with her hands on her abdomen. She looked like she was resting peacefully. She hoped for her sake she really was.

She looked at the photo of Tina Givens on her instrument panel. She touched the picture and prayed. If this was Tina Givens, she hoped her passing was quick and painless.

She extinguished her engine and climbed from the car, photo in hand. She slipped off her sunglasses and walked up to the scene. She had to maneuver slowly due to some dizziness and stiffness, but she made it without incident. Devereaux was already there, and she knew, right away, that the deceased was indeed Tina Givens. She could tell by the sorrowful look on his droopy face.

"Hey," he said as he came to stand next to her.

"It's her?" she said, not yet able to bring herself to look at the body. The paramedics were still around her. She wondered why. She didn't want them screwing up any trace evidence.

"It is."

"Fuck."

"Yeah. But—"

"But what?"

Danica looked again at the paramedics. She didn't know this particular pair, but from what she could see they were definitely screwing with her crime scene. Devereaux tightened his grip on her arm.

"Danny. She's alive."

Danica swayed. "Come again?"

"She's *alive.*"

Danica blinked at him in disbelief and then shoved him aside to hurry to the body.

"She's drugged or something, but she's definitely alive," Devereaux said as he followed her.

Danica stared down at the body, incredulous.

"She's alive?" Danica asked.

One of the paramedics glanced up at her. "We got a pulse. It's faint but steady."

Danica slipped into a pair of gloves and knelt. She studied the serene face, the well-placed makeup and the pretty dress. It wasn't how Tina normally looked, based upon the photos she'd seen, but there was no mistaking it was her. Even with the change to her hair.

She slid the photo into her back pocket, no longer needing it for comparison, as a technician moved around Tina snapping photos. The sun glinted off her hair and reflected off something on her neck.

Danica gently fingered the necklace with the hummingbird charm.

"Recognize it?" Devereaux asked, kneeling down next to her.

"It's the same as the ones found in the surface scatter."

"His calling card," Devereaux said.

He swore and Danica's heart pounded as guilt tried to infiltrate. She felt responsible for Tina Givens. She'd promised her mother she'd do everything she could to find her alive. She was indeed alive, but would she survive whatever was done to her? Just what kind of road lay ahead?

"He's taunting us," she said. "He knew we weren't done investigating here."

"He's a tricky fucker, ain't he?"

"He's confident. That's not good."

"Looks like he strangled her." Devereaux pointed at her neck. "See the marks?"

"Mm-hm."

The paramedic nodded his agreement as well.

"She stable?" Danica asked.

He pulled the stethoscope from his ears. "For now."

"You better get her to the hospital."

"Yes, ma'am."

She lifted Tina's hand and examined the perfectly painted nails. "He sure took his time with her. Got her all dolled up and everything."

"How could this have happened?" she asked Devereaux as the paramedics loaded her up on a gurney.

"Looks like he came in from the back on that old abandoned road. Security at the front entrance didn't hear or see anything. Not even headlights."

"Unbelievable," she said. "He's making us look like a bunch of fools."

"You got that right." Devereaux turned as they heard another car approach from behind.

"Looks like the good doctor has just arrived."

Danica craned her neck and then winced as a stab of pain washed over her. She saw both Eleanor and Lyra emerge from Eleanor's Audi, just as the paramedics loaded Tina Givens into the ambulance.

"Wonderful." She knew Eleanor would give her a hard time about working while still suffering with a concussion and well, she really didn't like seeing her with Lyra even though she was now certain that nothing was going on between them. It still stung and reminded her of that night at Eleanor's when she'd stumbled upon them together in Lyra's Jeep after they'd been out to dinner.

Devereaux squinted in the early morning sunlight. "Isn't that—"

"Yes."

"Lyra something or other?"

Danica gave him a stern look.

"Damn, it must suck to be you."

"Lyra's not an issue." She almost explained further about how she was actually looking forward to seeing Lyra, but she decided not to get into it. At the moment, they had more important things to contend with. "Can we just focus on Tina Givens, please?"

"Hey, sure. Whatever you say. I'll just ignore the fact that you like this woman."

Danica narrowed her eyes at him.

"I've known you for a long time, Danny. And I can tell when you like someone."

"Oh, you cannot."

"Detectives," Eleanor said as she and Lyra approached.

"Doc," Devereaux greeted her with his best shit-eating grin. He gave a nod to Lyra.

"Detective," Lyra said in response.

"We thought we'd come by and see if what we heard is true."

"It's true alright," Devereaux said. "She ain't a corpse."

"How did they know and I didn't?" Danica asked, more than pissed off.

Devereaux shrugged. "I told you what I knew. Someone called in a woman's body."

Danica pulled her keys from her pocket wanting to get to the hospital as soon as possible in case Tina woke.

"Who is it?" Eleanor asked.

"It's my latest missing girl," Danica said. "Tina Givens."

"And she's alive?" Lyra asked.

"So far," Devereaux said.

"She appears to have been strangled," Danica said. "So he either meant to kill her or he got off on torturing her."

"And how are you?" Eleanor asked Danica.

Danica could see the unspoken concern she had for her. Eleanor definitely still cared. Knowing that pierced her heart.

"I'm okay."

"She shouldn't be here," Devereaux said. "But you try and stop her."

"I'm really fine," she said, slipping on her dark shades. "I just have a headache." She smiled at Lyra who returned one of her own. Words, it seemed weren't needed.

"That's because you have a concussion," Eleanor said. "Which means you should be home, resting."

"I can't now. I need to get to the hospital."

"The hospital can wait," Eleanor said, lightly gripping her arm to stop her from going.

"It can't," Danica said. "Really."

"First, tell me about Tina. What did you find?"

Danica saw the concern on Eleanor's face and gave in. "From what we can tell, she hasn't been here all that long."

"She's been cared for," Devereaux said.

"She appears to have been well dressed and even bathed. She's lost some weight and she looks different, but overall she looks okay," Danica said.

"How does she look different?" Lyra asked.

"Her hair. It's changed. It's now short and blond. A lot like...yours," Danica said.

Lyra scrunched her brow. "Mine?"

"Holy shit, you're right," Devereaux said. "I wonder what the hell that means."

"It doesn't mean anything," Lyra said.

"It means something," Danica said. "He wouldn't have done that to her otherwise."

"Yeah, but it has nothing to do with me," Lyra said, a look of fear washing over her.

"It could," Danica said. "Or it couldn't. Bottom line is, when he took her she had long, dark hair. All of them did."

"So, he's keeping them alive after he takes them," Eleanor said. "I wonder why."

"So he can pretend," Danica said softly, recalling Tina's flawless skin and new hair style.

"Pretend?" Lyra asked.

"Yes," Danica said. "He dolled her up. The bathing, the makeup, the nice dress. He's living out some sort of fantasy with them. Then, when he's done with them, he leaves them here. In the sugarcane."

"Ballsy motherfucker," Devereaux said. "Coming here and leaving her."

"He's taunting us," Danica said. "He wants us to pay attention to him now."

"What took him so long?" Eleanor asked.

Danica spoke. "It's because we finally found his killing field. He's letting us know that he's aware and that he's still in control."

"Tell me about her appearance," Lyra said.

"Well, the dress appeared new but it was old-fashioned. Like something out of the mid-century."

"Yeah, it looked like it needed an apron tied over it," Devereaux said.

"Her makeup looked the same," Danica said. "Very nineteen fifties."

"Interesting," Eleanor said.

"She was barefoot," Devereaux said.

"What do you make of that?" Lyra asked.

Danica shook her head. "I'm not sure. Other than he obviously carried her to this spot. No mud or dirt on her suggesting otherwise."

"So, he strangled her somewhere else and dropped her here," Devereaux said.

"Either that or she was drugged enough for him to handle easily." She glanced behind her. "Only one set of footprints leading to the body and back again."

A CSI tech was taking photos of the footprints while another was taking a cast.

"We have a lot of work to do," Eleanor said.

Danica nodded. "I should get going."

"You should go home," Eleanor said.

Danica studied her, debating what to say next. Eleanor was older and more seasoned when it came to winning disagreements, and there was something sexy about her stern jaw and fiery eyes that usually left Danica helpless. But not this time. Eleanor was questioning her ability to work with Lyra there watching the whole thing. She didn't want Lyra thinking anything bad about her. Especially when it came to doing her job effectively.

Danica walked back to her cruiser, upset. She couldn't let Eleanor see her like this. She'd read right through her.

A soft voice came from behind her. "Danny?"

It was Lyra. She hurried up to her. "You sure you're okay?"

Danica pressed her lips together. "Honestly, I've been better. But I'm fine enough to work, if that's what you mean."

"I just want to make sure you're okay. Work aside." She lightly grazed her arm. "If you need anything, you know where to find me."

"I do," Danica said softly. "How about today, say one? We still have that lunch date, remember?"

Lyra seemed surprised. "I—okay."

Danica checked her watch. "Ralphael's okay?"

"Sure." Lyra grazed her arm again, causing goose flesh to rise on her skin.

Danica almost shuddered it felt so good. "Thanks, you know, for checking on me."

Lyra dropped her hand, seemingly aware of the feelings her touch had elicited. She gave her another smile and nodded, before walking away.

Devereaux came ambling over, giving Lyra a long look as he passed her by. "You want some company?"

Danica crawled behind the wheel and waited for him to climb in the passenger side. When he did, she started the car and turned around to head back out of the cane field. She aimed for the main road and thought again of Tina Givens.

She hoped with all her might that she would awaken and remember. And then she realized just what it was she was hoping for.

CHAPTER TWENTY-FIVE

I think he originally placed the bodies in the cane knowing they'd be burned, eradicating almost all evidence," Lyra said as she and Danica sat down for lunch at Raphael's, a local Italian eatery.

Danica had just returned from the hospital where Tina Givens was still in and out of consciousness, after apparently being drugged by a strong sedative. She wasn't well enough to talk yet, so Danica and Devereaux had left, leaving Tina to recover some more with her family by her bedside.

"Agreed," Danica said as she studied the menu. "Mm, let's start with the toasted focaccia. Sound good?"

"Absolutely." Lyra glanced up from the menu. "But then he left this body right under our noses. Wanting her to be discovered."

"And what do you think about that?" Danica asked, enjoying their conversation. She was so glad Lyra had been able to meet up today. She'd been wanting to see her, but with the case, her injury, and her crazy schedule, it had been difficult to do so.

"I think it's like you said. He's taunting us."

"And the body?" Danica handed over the photos from the scene she'd just picked up from the station. Lyra studied them carefully.

"Well, she was immaculate. Clearly bathed and carefully dressed and made up. It was almost as if he were presenting her as a…gift."

"Good observation," Danica said. "But do you agree with my assessment on that?"

"What? That he was pretending with them? Living out some fantasy?"

"Mm-hm."

"It's possible. I don't know much about serial killers, but I know that they all have fantasies about their kills."

"True."

Lyra raised an eyebrow. "How is it that you seem to know so much? I mean, you seem to know things that aren't obvious to the naked eye."

Danica set down her Coke. She'd been afraid this question would come. It usually did when she discussed a case. But sharing the answer with Lyra…she had to take more things into consideration first. Like how Lyra would react for starters.

Lyra blinked. "I'm sorry. I shouldn't have asked."

"No, it's fine. It's just…"

"There's just something about you that's…special."

Danica cleared her throat. Lyra was correct, but she was still hesitant. Sharing her past was never easy, but she wanted to get to know Lyra, so she decided to open up and share a bit.

"When I was little, I saw something that no child should see. And—my father was a cop. A detective, like me. So, I learned pretty early on the ins and outs of an investigation. He would share some things with me, and then question me, teaching me. You could say it was too much for a child. But then again, what I'd seen…"

Lyra waited.

"I'm sorry, I don't think I should say anymore. We are, after all, trying to have an enjoyable lunch." *And I don't want to scare you off with my past trauma. I already come across as flawed with my drinking.*

"I understand."

"I know we're discussing the investigation and some rather disturbing aspects of it, but it's different when talking about your own personal experiences."

Lyra nodded. "You're right."

There was a brief silence and then Lyra returned her focus to the photos. "What about the dress? It's so dated. What do you think the meaning is behind that?"

"That's a really good question. One that I'm still thinking on." She'd done nothing but think about it. So much so, that she'd been up all night and now she was fighting like hell not to doze off in her chair, which would look really bad in front of Lyra. She'd think it was her fault, that Danica wasn't into their lunch date, and that couldn't be further from the truth. She swallowed more tea, hoping the caffeine would kick in and give her a much-needed boost.

Lyra returned the photos and read over the menu once again. "What are you gonna have?"

Danica breathed easy, glad that Lyra was choosing to move on from her past. "Well, I'm torn between the Bolognese lasagna and the chicken parmesan. What about you?"

"The eggplant parmesan."

"Ah, a no-brainer for you. You must promise me a bite."

She smiled. "Will do."

The waiter came and took their orders. Danica chose the lasagna, and the waiter quickly refilled their drinks and left them alone once again.

"This place is nice," Lyra said, smoothing her palm along the white tablecloth.

"It's always very quiet at lunch, too. Something I appreciate."

"You come here often?"

"I come to relax and clear my head."

"Really? I thought for sure you were going to say you took working lunches."

Danica chuckled. "Not always."

"I thought you were just taking a lunch to be polite to me."

"Nope."

"You ever have lunch with Eleanor?"

She felt her eyebrows shoot up at the question. Eleanor? Why mention her? "Not recently. I've been very busy with this case."

"Right."

"Why do you ask?"

Lyra shrugged. "Just curious."

"Are you sure?"

"Yes."

Why had she asked? Was she trying to find out just how close the two still were? Could she be into Eleanor even though Eleanor had said she wasn't?

Her phone beeped, interrupting, and Lyra watched as she pulled it from her waist and checked it. She furrowed her brow.

"Something wrong?" Lyra asked.

"Tina Givens has yet to wake up fully. Her family is hysterical with worry."

"Oh, no."

"Yeah, it's gotta be hard on them."

Lyra seemed to consider her comment. "What about you?"

Danica put her phone away. "Me?"

"It's hard on you, too. I can tell."

Danica plucked at the tablecloth. She wanted to share her personal life with Lyra, she really did. But she wasn't used to doing so and she was finding the task more difficult than she'd imagined. It had been way too long since she'd allowed herself to be vulnerable. "It never gets any easier. Cases like these."

"I can't even imagine the stress you're under."

Danica smiled. "Well, let's not talk about that."

"Okay. How about we go back to Eleanor?"

"El?"

"Mm-hm. Why didn't it work out between you two?"

"Why do you ask?"

Lyra shrugged. "Just curious. You're both beautiful, intelligent women and I just wonder what could've possibly gone wrong."

"She's a very special person, Eleanor is. It just—we weren't right for each other."

"No?"

"As she says, I fly by the seat of my pants and she's too uptight. With our jobs, that works, but in a relationship, it didn't."

"I can understand that."

"Really? Because we didn't." She laughed. "Took us a while to figure it out."

"I think that happens to everyone. Especially women. We want things to work out."

"Mm. Is that what it is?"

"That's been my experience."

"What *is* your experience?" Danica asked. "You haven't really discussed your relationship history."

"There's not much to say. I've been traveling."

"Any relationships at all?"

"Two."

Danica smiled. "And?"

"Well, what do you want to know?"

"Everything."

Lyra laughed. The waiter returned with their appetizer. They both took a piece of the toasted bread and dipped it in olive oil.

"Mm, so good," Danica said.

"It is."

"So, do tell. I wanna know."

"Let's see. I've had two serious relationships. The first was with a fellow graduate student. Her name was April. We were together for two years. Then after her there was Jamie. She was a librarian. Total book nerd. Had my heart immediately."

"You like the studious type, eh? And those of the female persuasion?"

"Oh, yes." She blushed.

Danica let her off the hook a bit. "Anyway, you were saying you like the studious type?"

"Honestly, I think that's the type that prefers me. I'm such a nerd. I always have my nose in a book, most of the time about bones."

Danica smirked and took another bite of bread. "So, you wouldn't ever consider someone less studious? Maybe someone who's all about intrigue?"

She smiled and lifted a shoulder. "I might consider it."

"Depends on who the woman is?"

"Yes."

Danica's heart rate kicked up. They were flirting again and it felt so right, so natural. She was feeling so good, she was almost light-headed. Which, considering her headaches of late, was a good thing.

"So, how long were you with Jamie?"

"Three years. Then I got offered an opportunity to go to Egypt and she didn't want to leave her job and go with. And, well, we were already growing apart by that time anyway. So, it wasn't difficult to end it."

"I'm sorry to hear that."

"Don't be. It is what it is. No one's fault."

"Are you still in touch?"

"We still email. But we don't do that much."

"And April?"

"I think she moved to England to study. So, no, we lost touch. What about you? Anyone other than Eleanor?"

"Not too many, no."

"Why is that?"

"I think I've just been okay with being alone."

"Wow, I don't hear that too often. But I understand it."

Lyra sipped her tea and the waiter returned with their lunch. They thanked him and dug in. They ate in silence for a while before Danica spoke again.

"We're going to have to try the DNA match to be sure, but I think our victim number two is Gabby Dietrich."

"You think so?"

"Her family confirmed the broken left tibia."

"That's good."

"Mm. I just don't have a lot of confidence in the DNA testing."

"Because of the burnt remains?"

"Mm-hm."

"Guess we'll have to wait and see. We still have a lot of work to do with the rest of the remains. Hopefully, we can identify those more readily."

They continued to eat and talk, spending most of the time discussing the case. Time flew, and Danica was disappointed when she eyed her watch.

"As much as I hate for this to end, we should probably get back to it, don't you think?"

"Probably. But I don't want it to end, either."

Danica's heart warmed. She'd had such a good time. She could understand why Eleanor liked her so much, because she was growing very fond of her as well. "We'll have to get together again sometime."

"I'd like that."

Danica smiled at her, and for a moment she wasn't sure what else to say. She almost felt bashful, something she hadn't experienced since high school when she'd dated the first girl she'd liked. "Thank you for joining me and thank you for staying with me in the hospital. It really meant a lot."

"It was my pleasure."

They took each other in for a moment and then Lyra stood. She hurried to the waiter and got the bill and proceeded to pay it in full. She returned to the table with a devious smile and set some cash down for a hefty tip. "Okay, we can go now."

"I saw all that, you know," Danica said.

"Yeah, well, Eleanor never lets me pay, so I didn't want to risk it with you."

They laughed and walked together toward the door.

Danica had the urge to hold her hand, but she refrained. She just wanted to touch her somehow. Be close to her. Know her. Inside and out.

But that would have to wait.

As they stepped into the bright sunshine and Danica slipped on her glasses, she realized she was calmer than she had been the last few years. More at ease with everything going on around her. Suddenly the case and all the current madness didn't seem as harrowing or impossible to solve. It seemed Lyra was good for her anxiety.

She'd have to let her know that at some point. Maybe when they saw each again. She couldn't wait for that day to come.

CHAPTER TWENTY-SIX

Back at the lab, dressed in her protective gear, Lyra opened the box containing the latest discovered remains. Charred bones and fragments were nestled beneath a plastic cover and Lyra noticed that there weren't near as many as there had been with the previous collections.

"Not a whole lot to work with here," she said.

"The surface scatter is becoming more and more sparse the farther back they go," Eleanor said.

"The remains were there longer," Lyra said. "More time for scavengers and such."

They pulled open the plastic and carefully retrieved the cleaned bones. They laid them out anatomically correctly on a white sheet on the table. The skull was obviously missing, but the lower mandible was present, with teeth intact.

They first examined the pubic bone to determine sex. She was female. Then they moved on to age and height.

"Hand me that osteometric board?" Eleanor asked.

Lyra handed her the measuring scale. She watched as she began measuring the femur. She relayed the measurement and Lyra wrote it down and entered it into the computer. As they continued measuring, one of the graduate students, Allison, entered the lab.

"Dr. Stafford?"

"Uh-huh," Eleanor said as she eyed a humerus.

"We got the results back from the CT scan on victim number one."

"And?"

"Something interesting. Significant signs of osteoporosis."

Eleanor lowered the bone. "Really?"

"We're positive. The cortical layers are thin with the trabecular structure more open."

Eleanor locked eyes with Lyra. "Well, what do you know? A rather interesting clue to say the least. What do you make of it, Dr. Aarden?"

Lyra considered her options. "I'm thinking malnutrition. Possibly from an eating disorder."

"Mm. Anorexia nervosa."

"That's the one."

"Looks like I need to make another call to Detective Wallace."

"That you do."

She looked to her grad student. "Thank you. Please let me know ASAP if you find anything else."

Allison nodded and left them.

Eleanor refocused on the bones at hand. "I'd say she stood about five foot four. Would you agree?"

"I do."

"As for her age," Eleanor said. "What do you think?"

"Her third molars are fully formed, suggesting she's at least over eighteen."

"Uh-huh. Also notice the caps on the ends of long bones are fused completely. Suggesting she's at least twenty."

"Right," Lyra said. She continued looking over the remains. "The skull is missing so we can't readily identify race."

"No." Eleanor sighed. "We need to get these under the stereo-zoom microscope to see what else she has to tell us about herself. But first I'm going to go call Detective Wallace with our latest discovery." She stared off as if in deep thought.

"What's wrong?" Lyra asked.

"I was just thinking about Detective Wallace. I'm still worried about her with that concussion."

"I'm a little worried about her as well," Lyra confessed.

"She didn't look good today."

"No, not at all." Lyra had noticed her tired eyes and listless posture at lunch. And she'd kept touching the wound on her head as if she were in pain. Yes, she was worried about her, but she didn't share the extent of her concerns with Eleanor. She sensed that bringing up lunch with Danny might upset her.

They grew quiet and Lyra carefully lifted the lower mandible and examined the teeth. "I'll use the SEM on these teeth. Hopefully, I can discern diet and nutrition, etc."

"Great."

"Do you want me to have one of the grad students assist you?"

"Hm?" Lyra was already lost in thought. "No thanks, I got it."

"You sure?"

"Yes, I'll be fine."

She took the mandible over to the scanning electron microscope and sat. She was lost in thought again when Eleanor returned from her office.

"Anything good?" she asked as she leaned down next to Lyra. Her voice was raspy and soft, tickling Lyra's ear.

"She's taken antibiotics," Lyra said. Turning her head slightly toward her. Eleanor's breathing changed, and for a second, a very long second, they were still, taking in each other's close proximity.

Lyra thought about Danny and how she'd heated when they'd hugged goodbye. She wasn't feeling quite the same way with Eleanor's closeness.

"Often?" Eleanor asked.

Another grad student entered the room, interrupting. "Dr. Stafford, you wanted to see me?"

Eleanor straightened and cleared her throat. "Mitchell, yes. I'll meet you in my office."

He headed for the room in the back and Eleanor leaned in again. "Did she take them often?" she asked, again referring to the antibiotics.

"Yes, see the striations?" Lyra scooted to the side and allowed Eleanor to take a peek into the microscope.

"Hm. Anything else?"

"Not so far." Lyra pushed away from the microscope. "How did the phone call go?"

"Detective Wallace was very interested."

"Did any of the missing victims exhibit signs of an eating disorder?"

"Not offhand. But one of them could've suffered from anorexia earlier in life and then recovered some. She's going to check on it."

"That's a pretty good clue to have. I hope she's able to find something out."

Eleanor nodded. "Me, too." She motioned with her thumb. "I better go talk to Mitchell."

"Okay. I'll be here."

Eleanor looked at her for a long moment, her stare drifting down to her mouth. "Right. Okay." She backed away and Lyra watched her go, thinking about the kiss that almost happened in her Jeep. She was glad now that it hadn't happened. It would've made things a lot more complicated between the three of them. Then her mind left Eleanor and went once again to Danny. She hoped Danny would find something out in regards to their clue sooner rather than later. Because they had a killer to catch.

Sooner rather than later.

CHAPTER TWENTY-SEVEN

Eleanor sat in her car thinking twice about going up to the front door. She was parked in Danny's driveway and next to her was Danny's mother's vehicle.

The last time she'd seen her things hadn't gone well, with Linda Wallace chastising her about their breakup, initially blaming her for their separation. Apparently, according to Danny, Miss Linda had halfway tolerated their relationship. So, she'd been upset when Danny had told her they had parted ways.

Eleanor contemplated leaving, but then thought of Danny and her current condition. She hadn't sounded well on the phone and Eleanor had been bothered by her state of mind. She could only imagine how awful she must be feeling, and that was probably intensified by the critical nature of her mother's presence. It was with that in mind, that Eleanor decided to risk more insults and go knock on the door.

She rapped softly and waited patiently, holding a container of chicken, rice, and red gravy. Miss Linda finally answered, and Eleanor put on her best smile.

"Miss Linda, hello."

"Hello," she said, scowl already on her face.

Eleanor paused, thinking she would say more, but she didn't speak.

"I came to check on Danny," Eleanor said. Miss Linda remained silent, so Eleanor continued. "And I brought her some dinner." She held out the container of food.

"Oh. Well, Danica is as good as can be expected. And I'm already making her dinner."

"Mom? Who is it?" Danny came to the door and pulled it farther open. "El. Hey."

"Hi. I brought you some dinner."

"Well, please, come in." She stepped back to allow her entry. Miss Linda wiped her hands on a dishtowel with the scowl still on her face.

"I told her I'm already cooking for you."

"It sure smells good," Eleanor said, trying to play nice. "What are you making, Miss Linda?"

"She's baking a chicken with shrimp dressing."

"Oh, wow. Well, that explains why it smells so good in here."

"Why don't you stay for dinner?" Danny said. She took Eleanor's container and headed for the fridge. "I'll save this for later."

"It's chicken with rice and red gravy," Eleanor said.

"Yum," Danny said with a small smile. She looked tired. Dreadfully tired. Dark circles were under her eyes, and her posture appeared limp, like she was merely a sack of bones. She no longer wore the bandage, but the cut on her forehead was still visible, along with a few contusions and scrapes along her arms, and all of them looked painful. Eleanor wondered if she had been sleeping at all.

"What do you say?" Danny said, crossing back to her to offer her a seat on the couch. "You want to stay for dinner?"

Her gaze was a silent plea and Eleanor couldn't refuse. She knew Danny wanted her to stay and she couldn't blame her. Miss Linda's attitude was palpable, even as she stood at the oven, stirring what Eleanor guessed to be greens.

"Sure, I could do that," Eleanor said.

"Great." Danny touched her hand. She mouthed the words "thank you."

Eleanor nodded. "So, how are you feeling?"

"She's miserable," Miss Linda called out from the kitchen. "That's how she's feeling. God damned department is working her to the bone, even while she's hurt. She ought to sue, is what she should do."

Danny rubbed her forehead in obvious distress. "I'm working because it needs to be done, Mom. Someone has to solve this case."

"The missing girl's been found. The rest of them are being dug up in that cane field. End of story. Wipe your hands of it and move on."

"You know she's not all wrong," Eleanor said softly. "You really should just let Devereaux take over now that Tina Givens has been found."

Danny groaned. "I can't, El. You know I can't. It's just not in me to give up."

"Who says you're giving up? You're just passing the torch temporarily."

"Maybe you can talk some sense into her," Miss Linda said. "Do some good for a change, instead of just digging up bodies."

Danny closed her eyes as if ashamed by her mother's words.

Eleanor patted her hand, letting her know it was okay. The insult didn't even penetrate, and she just chalked it up to Miss Linda's usual banter. It no longer affected her.

"I'm sorry," Danny said, looking at her with profound sadness. "She's been on a tangent today."

"Don't worry about it."

"Maybe you can talk her into eating, too. She looks like she's going to blow away in the wind. Stubborn child. Just like her father. Head of stone. Solid stone."

Eleanor covered her mouth as she stifled a laugh and Danny rolled her eyes.

"Again, she's not all wrong," Eleanor said. "You are stubborn."

Danny smacked her arm. "Don't you start on me."

Eleanor laughed.

"God, let's just eat already, so she'll leave," she whispered.

"You're not that lucky," Eleanor said. "She'll probably insist on staying the night."

"What? No."

"You look like hell, Danny. I'm not the only one who's worried. Your mother obviously is, too. And so is Devereaux and Lyra."

"Lyra?"

"Yes, of course. We all are, Danny. You have a head injury. That's serious."

She touched her wound. "I'm doing okay."

"Bullshit."

"I am. I'm, you know, getting by."

"If you keep it up, you'll be worse off than you are now. You need rest. Rest and relaxation. That means zero stress."

"I'm taking this evening off. I promised Mom I would go to church with her."

Eleanor squeezed her hand. "I wish I could say that would do you some good, but I'm afraid more time spent with your mother might be worse than work."

"I hear that," she said. "But you try and tell her no."

"Someday you're going to have to, you know that, don't you? You're going to have to stop letting her walk all over you." They'd had this conversation before, many times. But Danny had never heeded her advice.

Danny drew away and leaned back on the couch. "It's not that simple. You know how she's been since my father died."

It was a familiar response. One she understood but didn't necessarily approve of. Danny was going to have to stand up to Miss Linda if she ever wanted a healthy mentality.

"I do. But that's no excuse for the way she treats you."

"I know," she said, pushing out a long breath. "God, I want a drink." She eyed the bottle of expensive whiskey on the coffee table. It was almost empty. Eleanor waited for her to fill the nearby glass. But she didn't.

"Don't let me stop you," Eleanor said.

"It's not you," she said. "I've stopped."

Eleanor wasn't sure she heard her correctly. "I'm sorry? Did you say you've stopped?"

"I haven't had a drink since the day of the accident."

"Danny, that's wonderful. But don't you think you should get rid of this so it doesn't tempt you?"

She shook her head and then winced. "I don't want it to have that kind of control over me. I need to have mastery over it. So, every time I want a drink I look at it and say no. Plus, it…it belonged to my father."

"I see. But Jesus, that's more than most people can do, Danny. Bravo to you. Seriously."

"Don't sing my praises yet."

"Still, you're doing it. I'm proud of you." Eleanor cocked an eyebrow. "What made you decide to quit?"

Danny touched her wound again. "I—the accident scared me. I wasn't drinking while driving, but still. I was thinking about drinking when I got home. I mean I was really wanting it. And then…the accident. It really shook me up. Had I been drinking…it could've been so much worse. I could've died, or worse, hurt someone else. And, well, Lyra really helped."

"Lyra?"

"We had a good conversation in the hospital."

Eleanor had almost forgotten that Lyra had stayed with her. She wondered what all they'd talked about.

"She's smart." Danny said.

"Yes, she is." She recalled how she'd briefly longed to kiss her in both her Jeep and the lab. Shortly after both instances, Lyra had seemed a little more distant. She supposed that was a good thing, considering how she herself had decided to back off.

"And funny." A smile crossed Danny's face as she stared off into the distance.

Eleanor palmed her heart, and then worried about her reaction. *Why am I feeling this...this jealousy? I've got to let this go.*

"That's interesting," she said. "Lyra said the same thing about you."

"What's that?"

"That you're funny."

The smile remained. "Really?"

"Uh-huh. Maybe you two should spend more time together." *What? What the hell am I saying? You're being a good person, Eleanor. Encouraging the two of them to get together. Their attraction is more than obvious, so you just have to let the pieces fall where they may.*

"Well, we did have a nice lunch."

Eleanor cocked an eyebrow, wanting to know more. But they were interrupted.

"Eleanor?" Miss Linda called. "You want to make yourself useful and help me in the kitchen?"

"Duty calls," Eleanor said as she stood.

Danny smiled wistfully.

Eleanor entered the kitchen and found Miss Linda standing there with her hands on her hips.

"You want to mash the potatoes while I tend to the greens and the chicken?"

"Yes, ma'am." She took the bowl of potatoes and retrieved the milk and butter from the fridge. Danny joined them, sitting on a stool across from Eleanor.

"Did you have any luck with the latest lead from the remains?" Eleanor asked.

"No cop talk," Miss Linda said sternly.

Eleanor shirked. "Tell me later."

Danny nodded.

"I can't stand that cop talk," Miss Linda continued. "It's disturbing and I can't understand why two perfectly good, beautiful women like yourselves do that for work." She mumbled some more as she slipped on an oven glove and opened the hinged door to pull out the chicken. It was a whole chicken stuffed with Cajun shrimp dressing, and she set the pan on the stovetop and inspected Eleanor's progress with the potatoes.

Eleanor kicked in again and grabbed the mixer from the cupboard.

"Better hurry up," Miss Linda said. "This bird's gonna get cold."

"Yes, ma'am," Eleanor said. She lifted her shoulders at Danny. "Guess I better get on it."

Danny slid off the stool and came around to stand next to her.

"Here, let me help." She grabbed the last whole potato and began dicing it as Eleanor added the milk and butter to the bowl.

"No," Miss Linda said, swooping in to take the knife from her. "No work for you, missy. You sit." She pointed with the knife back at the stool.

Danny again mouthed an apology to Eleanor and returned to the stool. She sat and watched Eleanor in silence.

Eleanor was at a loss as to what to say. It seemed that nothing would be safe around Miss Linda, so she chose to remain quiet while she finished the potatoes. And when they sat down to dinner, the silence hung uncomfortably in the air until Miss Linda spoke, sharing her stories about attending church and Danny helping out at the senior center.

"I told her, I think that would be good for her right now," she said. "For her to spend some more time there at the center." She looked at Danny expectantly. Danny said nothing but Eleanor spoke up, feeling the need to cover for her.

"Danny needs rest. Here at home. I'm afraid even the senior center would be too much for her right now. She needs rest, relaxation, and dim lighting."

Miss Linda sneered. "A little visit here and there with some old people won't kill her," she said. "Besides, she's still going to work, so the senior center won't hurt her any worse than that would."

Eleanor swallowed her bite of chicken. "You're absolutely right, Miss Linda. Work is not good for Danny right now, either. Which is why I'm advocating for her to stay home."

"Well, maybe she'll listen to you. God knows she doesn't listen to me."

Eleanor glanced at Danny. She decided to drop the matter. They ate the rest of the meal in silence. And when Eleanor left, she was afraid that she'd left Danny no better off than the way she'd found her.

And that was not a good feeling. Not a good feeling at all.

CHAPTER TWENTY-EIGHT

Danica stood outside the hospital room and looked in on Tina Givens. She was sleeping peacefully, with her mother sitting next to her holding her hand. Danica thought about going in, but chose to remain outside, hoping to talk to Mrs. Givens when she left the room.

"What are you doing here?" a voice next to her said.

Danica turned and found Oliver, Tina's brother, standing there with a frown on his face. "Haven't you people done enough? Or I'm sorry, not *near* enough?"

Danica chose to let the dig slide. "I understand you're upset, Mr. Givens."

"You understand? Well, how PC of you, Detective. Your understanding just makes everything all better now, doesn't it?" He gave a sarcastic laugh.

"I'm sorry," she said. "I know I should've done more for you. For Tina."

"Damn right, you should've. Look at her. Lying there. Doped up like a vegetable. Who knows what all he did to her."

Danica knew what the doctors were saying, and what the tests showed. Tina had been malnourished and had lost a considerable amount of weight. She'd also been dehydrated and drugged with a powerful sedative. One that was no longer on the market. She'd just awakened fully the day before, but the doctors hadn't allowed Danica and Devereaux to question her yet. Which was why Danica stopped by today. She really needed to talk to her. But since she couldn't yet, not with Oliver standing guard like he was, she decided to pivot and question him.

"Maybe you can help me in that regard," she said.

"How so?"

"I was hoping you could help fill me in on some things."

"Like what?"

"When she was found, she had on a considerable amount of makeup. Was Tina fond of heavy makeup?"

Oliver looked as though he was debating whether or not to answer her. Finally, he shook his head sternly. "No way. She hated the stuff. And when she did wear it, she made sure it was the kind that didn't test on animals. And she wore very little of that. Maybe some eyeliner and lip gloss. That's it."

Danica hurriedly scribbled down the notes in her notepad. *So the killer put the make up on himself. Why?* "What about—"

"What else?" Oliver demanded.

Danica hesitated. "She, uh, like I said, was found with heavy makeup on. She also appeared to have been thoroughly cleaned and bathed, with her nails freshly painted."

"She hated nail polish. Never wore it. Couldn't stand the smell," Oliver said.

Danica made a note.

"What does that mean?" Mrs. Givens asked as she emerged from the room. "The dress and the makeup? What does that mean?"

"We're not yet sure, Mrs. Givens."

"But you got an idea," Oliver said.

"I have some theories." Like maybe he truly cared for them in some way. Or he wanted to present them like a gift. Or he could be wanting to emulate someone he knew. The dated dress suggested the latter. "But I'm not at liberty to discuss them just yet. I have more investigating to do."

"You mean you don't want to be wrong again," Oliver said.

Danica stopped writing. She met his steely gaze. "I want to look into some things further."

"Yeah, well, you better. You damn well better."

"Rest assured, that I will." She touched the cut on her forehead. A headache was coming on and she needed to question Tina before she left. But she still had one more question for the two of them. "What about the dress she was found in? Any significance there?"

Mrs. Givens shook her head. "Tina wouldn't ever wear something like that."

Danica finished her notes and nodded. *So it's all him. The whole presentation.* "Okay, then. Thank you very much for your time. I need to go ask Tina a few questions now." She made a move toward the doorway to her room but stopped when Oliver spoke again.

"What do you mean by 'questions'?" he asked.

"I need to know how much she can recall." They both appeared concerned. "Don't worry, I've already asked her doctor and he gave me his approval."

"Just be sure you take it easy on her," Oliver said.

"I will." She pressed her lips together and nodded again for reassurance before entering the hospital room. Tina was lying quietly with her eyes half open. She became fully alert however, when she saw Danica approach.

"Ms. Givens," Danica said softly. "My name is Detective Danica Wallace. I'm the one assigned to your case. Do you mind if I sit for a moment and ask you a few questions?"

Tina shifted her eyes to hers. "You can sit," she said with a weak voice. She halfheartedly ran her hand through her bleached blond locks, trying, it seemed, to tame it. She was still pale, with prominent dark smears beneath her eyes. Her lips appeared dry and chapped, and she had angry looking marks around her wrists and some on her cheeks as well. As if she'd been gagged.

A chill ran through Danica as she took a seat. She'd seen some pretty terrible things in her line of work, but this case was getting to her in ways she'd never experienced before. And briefly, she wondered if Eleanor was right. That maybe she took this case too personally, held it and the victims too close to her heart.

She looked at Tina, so thin and pale, lying there looking completely helpless.

How can I not?

She shook the thought away and cleared her throat.

"How are you feeling?" she asked and then glanced at her watch. Devereaux was supposed to be there with her, but he was late. Or was she early? She glanced at her watch again and realized that she was indeed, early.

Tina studied her closely. "Are you in a hurry?" she asked.

"Uh, no. I'm just waiting on my partner."

"There's someone else?"

"My partner, Detective Devereaux. He should be here any moment now. Is that okay? If the two of us ask you some questions?"

She looked back toward the door. Her mother and brother were still standing outside. "Will they be in here, too?"

"Only if you want them to be."

She looked back to Danica. "I don't."

"Okay. It'll just be us then." Danica smiled softly at her. "You're feeling okay, today?"

"I'm okay," she said, glancing down at her hands. She fingered the nail polish. "I guess."

Just then there was noise outside the room and Danica saw Devereaux talking to Mrs. Givens and Oliver. He spoke to them briefly and then entered the room. He gave Danica a look, one of disappointment. She quickly explained.

"We haven't started yet," she said. "We were waiting for you."

Devereaux crossed to the bed and extended his hand. "I'm Detective Gary Devereaux, Ms. Givens. Pleasure to meet you."

She gave him her hand and he took it gently in his. When he released it he sat in the chair opposite Danica.

"How are you?" he said. "You doing okay?"

"I'm okay," she said again.

Devereaux looked to Danica, signaling her to begin, as he shifted his heavy frame to take out his notebook.

"Ms. Givens," Danica said. "Can you remember anything at all about your experience? For instance, can you recall who took you? Who did this to you?"

Danica waited on pins and needles. Tina stared straight ahead and then refocused on her hands. She sat like that for a long moment before she spoke.

"I remember him," she said.

Danica sat up straighter. "Can you tell us about him?"

She gave a shrug. "What do you want to know?"

"Do you know his name?" Devereaux asked.

She closed her eyes. "No." She took a big breath in and then released it. "But I can tell you what he looks like. What he sounds like, what he smells like." She opened her eyes. "I can tell you everything else about him, but I don't know his name."

Devereaux trained his eyes on Danica. "Okay," he said. "What does he look like?"

"He looks like an everyday guy. Average height, average build, average looks. Mousy brown hair, pale skin, blue eyes. Creepy blue eyes," she said. "Real light but wild. Like he was about to strike out at any moment. I hated his eyes." She choked up and Devereaux quickly moved to offer her a drink from a plastic cup with a straw. She took it and sipped.

"Ms. Givens," Danica said, still speaking softly. "Do you know where you were? Or where we can find him?"

She shook her head. "I don't know. I just know that it was an old shotgun house. And that there were a lot of dogs around. I always heard them barking. Hound dogs. The kind that bay."

"Good," Danica said, scribbling. "What else can you tell us? Were there any other noises?"

She seemed to think, narrowing her eyes and touching her temple. "There was a train. Not close but close enough to hear. And there was music. He liked old music. Always had it playing."

"So, he had some way to listen to music?" Devereaux asked as he wrote in his notebook.

"Just an old radio. With one of those long silver things coming out the back of it."

"An antenna?" Danica asked.

"Yes."

"What else? What about what he drove?"

Again, she shrugged. "I really can't remember. I just know that it was raining. Raining really bad and he pulled up and offered me a ride."

"And you said yes?"

"No, I didn't say anything. I just kept walking. Next thing I know, something hits me on the head from behind. It went black after that. Then the next memory I have is of being in his bedroom. His tiny little bedroom that smelled liked aftershave. Really cheap, bad aftershave."

"And he had you tied up?" Danica asked, as she pointed to her wrists.

Tina stared at the marks and she trembled.

Danica quickly reassured her. "It's okay. You're safe now. Just tell us what you can. Take your time."

"You're doing really well," Devereaux said. "Really well."

"He liked to leave me tied up."

"With rope?" Danica asked, thinking that the marks resembled rope burns.

"Yes. And he gagged me. Every time he left. He would only untie me when he was home and he…drugged me. Kept me drugged a lot.

Sometimes all I could do was sleep. I couldn't hardly walk most times. I couldn't...get away." She began to cry, her limp, delicate-looking shoulders shaking as she did.

Danica covered her hand with hers. "It's okay," she whispered. "It's okay now."

But it was obvious that Tina didn't believe it was. She was reliving her terrifying experience and Danica felt for her. She wished she could make it all better, but she knew she'd never be able to do that. Not until she caught the bastard. That, in itself, might bring Tina at least some comfort, knowing that he could never hurt her or anyone else ever again.

"Are you okay to continue?" Danica asked. "Or would you like us to come back another time?"

She wiped her eyes and shook her head. "No, I want to get it over with. Let's do it now."

Danica squeezed her hand. "You're very brave," she said. "For doing this."

"I don't feel brave," she said. "Not in any way."

"You are," Devereaux said, adjusting his glasses. "You really are."

She sniffled. "Thank you for saying that."

Danica patted her hand and it took another moment before Tina could continue. When she did, however, she sounded stronger.

"Go ahead," she said. "Ask me whatever you need to."

Danica waited a moment. What she had to ask next might be very difficult for her to face and answer. But they needed to know. She spoke slowly and softly. "Other than tying you up and drugging you, did he do anything else to you? Did he hurt you in any other manner?"

Tina visibly swallowed. She shook her head and rang her hands.

"You're sure?" Devereaux asked just as softly.

"Yes," she whispered. "I—I could sense that he wanted to sometimes. Like he would get really mad at me and lose his temper. He would force the pills down me, force me to drink, stuff like that. But—sexually—like what you mean—no, he didn't. He—" She swallowed again. "At first I thought he was going to. But then, right around the time he..." she touched her hair, "did this to my hair, he started to....I don't know. Hate me."

"How do you mean?" Devereaux asked.

"He would lose his temper, throw things, curse me. He complained about me. Said he couldn't wait to be rid of me."

Danica scribbled in her notes. "Anything else?"

"Hm?" She seemed to be lost in her thoughts.

"Did he ever talk about anything else? Or anyone else? Anything that might give us a clue as to who he is?"

She stared at her hands. "His grandmother," she said. "He often spoke of his grandmother."

"Is she alive? Did he give her name?" Danica asked.

"I never saw her and no, he never mentioned her name. He had pictures of her though. When she was younger. He would often talk to the pictures."

"What would he say?" Devereaux asked.

"Everything," she said. "He would talk to her as if she were there. About how she liked this and that and how everything had to be a certain way because of her. It was creepy. Like she was in the house with us, but there was no one else with us."

Danica made her notes and thought about what she'd said. She retrieved her phone from her back pocket and pulled up a photo.

"What about this?" she asked. "It's a tiny hummingbird necklace and you were found wearing it."

She glanced away quickly and Danica put the phone away. Tina teared up.

"Take your time," Devereaux said.

Danica handed her a box of tissues.

Tina dabbed her eyes and blew her nose. "I remember it," she finally said. "He put it on me the last night."

"What about this book?"

Again she initially averted her eyes. When she could bring herself to look at it again, she looked defeated. "I would wake up sometimes and he'd be reading it to me."

"Did he say anything about it?" Danica asked.

"He would insist I pay attention, but honestly, I was so drugged I just couldn't. And well, I think self-preservation insisted that I drown him out most of the time."

She touched her neck. "They told me he strangled me." She looked to Danica. "More than once, based on the marks. Is that true?"

"Yes."

She began to cry. Danica rested her hand on her shoulder and spoke softly to her. The interview was over. Tina had reached her threshold. Devereaux stood and handed her her water cup. She finally settled down enough to sip some of it.

"You okay?" Danica asked.

She nodded. "I will be."

"Thank you very much for your help."

"Did I help at all?"

"You did," Danica said.

"You gave us a lot to work with," Devereaux said. He squeezed her hand and eyed Danica who stood. They bid her farewell and left her their card should she need them or think of anything else.

Danica was relieved to find that Oliver and Mrs. Givens were gone. She and Devereaux headed for the elevator in silence.

Then, as they stepped inside the empty elevator, Devereaux looked at her and said exactly what she'd been thinking.

"This motherfucker is one messed up dude."

The doors closed, along with Danica's eyes.

Devereaux didn't know how right he was.

CHAPTER TWENTY-NINE

He paced in his kitchen, waiting impatiently for the newspaper. It was six o'clock in the morning and he hadn't been able to sleep since he'd left his last lovely in the cane field. He'd left her alive, he was sure of it. So, why hadn't it been reported yet? What was going on? Did he mess it up? Had he actually killed her without realizing it? Had he strangled her too hard that last time?

A rush of heat came over him as he remembered squeezing her again and again. He grew hard but ignored it, too worked up to entertain it. He needed news. Any news.

He hurriedly switched on the radio. Nothing but the old country his grandmother had loved. Even that couldn't comfort him. He switched it off and heard a soft thump. He crossed the kitchen to the front door. A quick peek from behind the curtain showed him what he needed to know. He yanked open the door and threw open the screen. He quickly snatched the newspaper and brought it back inside, closing the doors behind him. He sat at the kitchen table and opened the paper. And there it was, finally.

MISSING WOMAN FOUND ALIVE AT SUGAR MILL FARM

He hurriedly glanced over the article. They'd found her. She'd lived. He hadn't messed it up. And best of all, they still had no suspects.

He pounded the paper. "Yes!" He stood and whooped, causing the dogs next door to bay. He marched proudly around the kitchen, thrilled beyond belief. He was the ultimate killer now. Evading the police. Dumping his lovely right under their noses. The newspaper article had even questioned the police and their abilities. He loved it. Ate it up.

Yes, this was the perfect crime and he was the perfect killer. A true master.

They would write books about him.

They would revere him.

Worship him.

Hell, yes.

But wait. He returned to his seat at the table.

In order for him to get the ultimate credit, they'd have to know who he was.

How was he going to work that out? He didn't want to turn himself in. No way. He couldn't go to prison. He wouldn't make it.

But then again, the fellow prisoners would idolize him. They would praise his technique and his ability to evade the police.

But no. He couldn't do prison. Nuh-uh.

He smoothed his hands over the newspaper. So, how to let them know without getting caught? Maybe he would have to settle for the anonymity.

He would have to think on that. In the meantime, he had things to do. He needed to scrub the house and get it ready for his new lovely. He had to sweep and shine the old wood floors, beat the dust from the rugs, scrub the kitchen and bathroom, wash his linens and polish all the furniture. The house had to be in tip-top shape for her. He wanted to impress this one. More so than the other ones.

He smiled as he thought of her. Her short blond hair, her lithe, athletic body. The way she moved when she ran. Yes, he had to impress this one. Romance the hell out of her. Surely she would come around to love him. She was the one. He was sure of it.

He reread the article and stared at his last lovely's picture. It was an old photo where her hair was long and dark. She looked so different and didn't resemble his new lovely at all. He didn't like it. It made him sick. She made him sick. He knew what he wanted and it was no longer her or her type. He swiped the paper off the table and held his head in his hands.

But how was he going to get his new lovely? She wasn't a cop, but she was working closely with them. It would be tricky. Maybe too tricky.

But he was the master, right? He could do it.

He scrambled for the paper and picked it up off the floor. He needed to see her. Needed his fix. But there was no photo of her this time around.

He walked to his fridge and grabbed the old clipping off the door. He took it to his bedroom and closed the door. He extinguished the lights and reclined on his bed. When the dim light of dawn began to seep more in through his windows, he unzipped his pants and did what his grandmother said was the bad deed.

But she wasn't there anymore.

No, she was gone.

Now it was just him.

Just him and the dream of his new lovely.

Lyra Aarden.

CHAPTER THIRTY

L yra danced in her seat, singing to ABC's "Be Near Me" as she pulled into Eleanor's driveway. The sun was setting, casting a beautiful orange into the oncoming dark blue, bringing with it a slight chill. She zipped up her hoodie and sat singing, allowing the song to finish before she turned off the engine and exited the car. She had a smile on her face as she carried the bottle of wine to the door and rang the elaborate sounding chime.

Eleanor's home was beautiful. The architecture was similar to the other nearby homes. Acadian style with a steep, sloping roof with gables. It was cottage-like with red brick and a pale yellow exterior. Eleanor had flowers planted along the front walkway, adding to the cottage-like feel. A white wooden rocking chair sat near the door beneath the awning.

"Hey, you," Eleanor said as she pulled open the door.

"Hey. This is for you," she said, handing over the wine.

"Why, thank you."

"Sorry, I don't know wine."

"It's fine," she said, eyeing the label. "Come on in."

Lyra entered her home and immediately felt like she needed to remove her shoes. The place was spotless. Immaculate. Decorated in whites and yellows and grays, it was both bright and soothing at the same time.

"Should I remove my shoes?" she asked.

"What?" She chuckled. "No, that's not necessary."

"It's just so clean, I don't want to mess it up." She looked around at the open floorplan and noticed the modern gray furniture and light beige and yellow rugs and throw pillows. The art on the wall was equally modern. Large off-white roses painted in heavy strokes and thick colors. She imagined settling down on the sofa and snuggling up in a throw at the end of a hard day, taking in the art as she began to relax next to the gas fireplace. Who needed television when you had a room like this?

"Well, thank you. But no, don't worry. You won't mess it up." She walked ahead of her, wine in hand. She glanced back at her. "You look exceedingly happy this evening."

"You ever hear an old song and it just sets your mood?"

"Yes, sure."

"That happened."

"Oh, nice." They entered the kitchen and Eleanor set the wine on the counter and searched through a drawer. "I'm glad you're happy." She smiled and seemed to genuinely mean it.

"Thanks. And how are you this evening?" Lyra asked as she noted her pressed chinos and lavender Polo button-up shirt. It looked as though she'd just arrived home from work. She made the outfit look good, despite how long she may have been wearing it.

"I'm well, thank you. Just waiting on dinner." She looked to the Instant Pot on the counter.

"Gosh, what is it? It smells terrific."

"Just my signature jambalaya."

"Oh, right. Just."

Eleanor found the corkscrew and closed the drawer. "Mm-hm. Just." She winked at her.

"I have a feeling it's beyond good."

"I hope you think so. I did promise you some real, homemade, authentic Cajun cooking, didn't I?"

"You did." She had looked forward to this evening for a while now, despite her growing feelings for Danny. She hoped she and Eleanor could remain good friends and work colleagues. She really enjoyed her friendship and company.

"Well, there ya go then."

She struggled with the wine bottle for a few moments and then managed to pop the cork on the Ménage à Trois California Red. "We'll let that breathe for a moment."

"Like I said, I don't know if it's any good. I'm afraid I'm not an expert on wine."

Eleanor eyed the label. "Well, it is an interesting choice."

"How so?"

"Ménage à trois?" She lifted her brow.

Lyra blushed. "Oh. That. I meant nothing by it."

"You sure?" She smirked. "I'm kidding. God, you are so red. Relax Aarden, I'm teasing."

Lyra released the breath she was holding. "Okay. Phew. I thought you were going to call Detective Wallace over or something."

Eleanor stopped laughing. "Danny? Why would you mention her?"

"I—no reason."

"Oh, wow, you're blushing even harder now. I think I touched on something, didn't I?"

"No. There's nothing. I mean, I meant nothing by it. She was just the first person I thought of, you know, because she's...." She palmed her forehead. "I'm going to shut up now."

Eleanor poured them both a glass of wine. She took a few hearty sips. "You don't have to be embarrassed. Danny is a very beautiful woman."

"I know, I mean, she is, yes. But—" She sighed. "Never mind."

"I know you're very fond of her, Lyra. There's nothing wrong with that. Danny's quite a catch."

Lyra continued to blush. She grabbed her wine and nearly gulped. Eleanor watched her closely. Lyra set the glass down and met her gaze. She didn't speak, wasn't sure what to say. She was relieved when Eleanor went to check on their dinner.

She stirred the jambalaya and then checked on what smelled like cornbread in the oven. When she returned she was smiling as if they'd never had the conversation regarding Danny in the first place.

"You ready to eat?" she asked as she flipped a dish towel onto her shoulder. "Because it's ready."

"I'm starved," Lyra said and hopped down off the barstool. She followed Eleanor to the stovetop where she handed her a bowl. "So what's in this?" Lyra asked as she scooped her out a hearty helping and then handed her a piece of cornbread.

"Oh, lots of things. Chicken, sausage, shrimp, rice, my special Cajun seasoning, along with other things like onion and parsley, oregano, celery, and peppers."

"Your special Cajun seasoning?"

"Mm-hm. Among other things. But don't even try. I'm not sharing those."

Lyra laughed. "I wouldn't dare."

They sat at the table and sipped their wine as the jambalaya cooled. Lyra wanted to ask about the case. About whether or not Danny had found anything out about one of their victims having an eating disorder. But she was hesitant in mentioning her again.

"What?" Eleanor asked. "You look like you were about to say something."

"No." She hurriedly took a small bite and winced as it burned her mouth.

"Careful. It's hot."

"Mm, yes." She brought up another bite and this time blew on it. But Eleanor was still pinning her with her green-eyed gaze.

"You were. About to say something. I can tell."

"I just—" But she had nothing. Nothing other than the case.

"Are you wondering about Danny? Because I spoke to her today."

Lyra stared at her spoon.

"It's okay. You can ask." She sighed. "She's not doing well."

Lyra glanced back up at her, her concern, she knew, was evident. She'd briefly texted with her, but Danny had only told her she was doing okay and that she was working on the case at all hours of the day and night. She'd apologized for being so busy, but Lyra had assured her that she understood.

Eleanor continued. "In fact, I'm really worried about her. She's not taking any time off to rest. And she looks like death warmed over."

"Is she drinking?" Lyra asked.

Eleanor seemed a little surprised at the question. "That I don't know. I don't think she is, but honestly, I haven't spoken to her a whole lot." She cocked her eyebrow. "Do you…suspect otherwise?"

"Me? No. I was just curious."

"Well, last I knew, she hadn't. But she was spending time with her mother and if you knew her, you'd know how that can lead her to drink."

Lyra carefully took a bite. She pointed at the bowl with her spoon. "Wow. This is outstanding. Really. It's very, very good."

Eleanor smiled but it seemed pensive, like she was covering up her sad feelings. "Thank you. I'm glad you like it."

"What is it? What's wrong?" Lyra asked.

"Nothing. Just worried about Danny is all."

Lyra chewed. "How's the lead on that victim? The one with osteoporosis?" She hadn't heard anything more at the lab.

"Danny thinks she may have a good lead on that. But she didn't have time to go into detail. She was very busy."

Lyra nodded. "Danny does seem very busy." She forked a bite of shrimp.

"Danny?" Eleanor said.

Lyra glanced up at her. "Hm?"

"You called her Danny."

"I did?"

"You usually call her Detective Wallace."

"Oh." She felt herself begin to panic. She felt guilt, but she had no idea why. "She told me to call her that while we were at the hospital. I just—"

"Oh, of course." Eleanor said, refocusing on her food. "Of course she did. I just wasn't aware."

"And then at lunch with her I—it's not a problem is it?" Her heart was pounding. What was happening? Why was she freaking out? More so, why was *Eleanor* freaking out?

"No, silly. It's not a problem. Why would it be a problem?" She took another bite. "So, you had lunch with her?"

Lyra swallowed. The bite had been too hot, and her throat burned. She nervously coughed into her napkin. What should she do? Say?

"I did, yes."

"Well, it sounds like you two are getting along very well and spending some time together."

"Would that be an issue if we were?" She was so confused. She'd thought the relationship between Eleanor and Danny had ended long ago. But the way she was acting was saying otherwise, which she'd secretly feared.

"Don't be ridiculous." She stabbed a bite and ate, refusing to look at Lyra as she chewed.

Lyra set down her fork. She picked up her napkin and wiped her mouth. Then she set it on the table. The Danny issue was a problem. A big problem. And that was now more than obvious.

"What are you doing?" Eleanor asked as she took notice.

"I think I'd better go."

"Go? Why?"

"Because there obviously is a problem, and somehow I've caused it." She'd been right when she joked earlier that three lesbians couldn't work together. Oh, how right she'd been. And it seemed it was all her doing.

"No," Eleanor tossed her own napkin on the table. "I told you—"

"I know what you said, Eleanor. But obviously, you feel otherwise."

"I feel otherwise?"

"Yes." She stood and looked deep into her eyes. And she saw it then. Saw what was always there but she'd refused to see. "I think you still have feelings for Danny—er, Detective Wallace. And I've come in the middle of that somehow. I didn't mean to. I just—I like you both so very much…"

Eleanor blinked rapidly. Then she laughed. "I think you're mistaken. I don't have feelings for Danny. I—"

"I think I'm right. And I think I should go."

"You don't need to leave, Lyra. For goodness sake." She stood.

"I do. It's now very apparent that you love Danny."

"I do—" She stopped herself.

"See?"

"Lyra, what I feel for Danny—"

"Is still profound. I can see it in your eyes."

She opened her mouth but then clamped it shut.

"It's written all over you. And that's okay."

"No, it's not. Lyra, listen. There will never be anything between Danny and me again."

"But your feelings remain."

"What I'm upset about is…"

Lyra waited for her to finish.

Her gaze dropped down to the table. "I'm afraid I'm jealous, Lyra. I—had feelings for you that I thought I had reconciled. But tonight, that jealousy reared its ugly head again and I'm sorry."

Lyra closed her eyes.

She opened them and found Eleanor staring at her. "I can clearly see the feelings you and Danny have for each other and that got to me, though I had vowed to let my feelings go. I'm so very sorry. Please accept my apology. And please don't leave."

"I don't know what to say," Lyra said. She was relieved to hear the truth from Eleanor, but it was obvious that Eleanor was still disheartened over the whole thing.

"I'm sorry, too" Lyra said. "For all this."

"You can't help how you feel. And I adore you both and want you to be happy."

"Are you—sure? I don't want to upset you, Eleanor. You mean a lot to me, too."

"I'm sure." She smiled softly. "Now, please, sit and eat with me. I'd be heartbroken if you left."

The tightness in Lyra's chest loosened. She eased back down into her chair.

"Thank you," Eleanor said.

"No, thank you. This meal is incredible."

"So are you. My dear friend."

Lyra reached across the table to squeeze her hand. "You are, too, Eleanor. You are, too."

CHAPTER THIRTY-ONE

*C*ome on, Danny," her daddy said. "Cast it out like this, now." He slung his arm back over his head to toss out his fishing line. Danny did as instructed, but her line didn't go out near as far as her daddy's.

"That's okay. Try again."

She reeled in her line and tried again, but still didn't succeed. She slumped her shoulders, defeated. Her daddy smiled at her and reeled his line in. Then he stood behind her and knelt down to talk in her ear.

"It's alright, darlin.' I'll help you this time, okay?"

She nodded as tears threatened to fall from her eyes. She wanted, more than anything, to be like her daddy. To be as good as him in every way possible.

"Do it with me, now," he said. He reached for her pole and drew it back over her shoulder. Danny allowed him to lead and they cast the line out, farther than she'd ever been able to cast on her own. She hopped up and down in excitement.

"Be still now," her daddy said, laughing. "You don't want to scare the fish away."

Danny stilled and her daddy went back to his own rod, but he didn't cast it out. Instead, he sat in his folding chair and opened up the cooler for a can of beer. He sighed as he relaxed and sipped it.

"I'm doing it, Daddy," she said, so proud she could burst.

"I know, darlin.' You're doing great."

"I'm gonna catch a big one, I can feel it."

He chuckled softly. "I have no doubt that you will."

"And Mama can cook it up for supper tonight."

"You catch a big one and we're going to clean it and cook it up right here."

She turned to look at him. "Really?"

"You bet."

She hopped up and down again but then remembered what he'd said about scaring the fish. She calmed and stared hard at the line where it disappeared into the water. Waiting, just waiting for that big fish to come along and take a bite.

"When's it gonna happen, Daddy?" she asked.

"It takes time," he said.

"But how long?"

"Sometimes it takes a long time."

"But I want it now," she said.

"Well, sometimes it helps if you reel your line back in and cast it out again.

"Really?"

"Go on, now," he said. "Reel yourself back in."

She started to reel her line back in, but her line stuck and her rod bent. She yelled, "Daddy, I got one, I got one!"

He hurriedly came to her. "Reel it in," he said.

She tried but her line wouldn't budge. "I can't."

He set his beer down and took her pole. "Here, let me try."

But he, too, had a hard time.

"You either caught a great big one or you're caught on something."

"Caught on what?" she asked.

"It's hard telling. Maybe a log. Maybe an old tire. Who knows."

He tugged on the line again and again, and then it seemed to give a little. "There we go," he said. He handed the pole back to her. "We'll reel her in together." They reeled the line in and Danny grinned, excited to see what she'd caught. Even if it was an old tire, she'd be ecstatic. It was her first time catching anything.

"There we go," her daddy said. "It's coming now."

"I can't wait to see it," she said, hopping up and down.

"Hold your horses," he said.

The line gave again, this time completely, and Danny would've fallen over had her father not been there. "Whoa," he said.

She squinted out into the murky water as something surfaced.

"What in God's name?" her daddy said. He set down the pole and took a few steps out into the water.

"What is it, Daddy?" And then the smell hit her. She plugged her nose and stared at the pale form in the water. It drifted closer and her daddy suddenly turned and scooped her up.

"Come on," he said.

"Where we going?" She kept looking out into the water.

"To the truck."

"But I wanna see what I caught."

"No, you don't, baby," he said.

"Yes, I do."

That's when the object in the water turned. And she saw the bloated face and dead, pale blue eyes.

She screamed.

Danica's eyes flew open and she sat straight up. It took her a moment to realize she was no longer at the water's edge with her father. She was home, in her bed, with a pounding head.

A knock at the door came and she wondered if that was what had woken her. She'd been in and out of sleep all evening and really needed some rest. The knock came again, and she grabbed her phone off the nightstand and looked at the screen. There were no new texts or missed phone calls. So, who the hell was at her door?

"God damn it, Devereaux. If that's you...." She swung her legs off the bed and slid her arms into her bathrobe. She rubbed her eyes as she headed for the door. "Yeah, I'm coming," she said. She looked out the peephole and saw Lyra standing there. "What in the world?"

She unbolted the door and eased it open.

"Hi," Lyra said. She was wearing a hoodie and a pair of jeans. She appeared to be cold, with one of her hands shoved into her hoodie pocket and the other holding a basket of some sort.

"Hi," Danica said.

"Sorry, did I wake you?"

"No, no of course not," she lied.

"I was sitting at my brother's house, and I thought about you and wondered if you had all you needed. So..."

"You thought about me?"

"Of course. I think about you all the time. Plus, Eleanor said you still haven't been doing well, so I thought I'd drop by and check on you and bring you some things."

"Okay." Danica was pleasantly surprised at her arrival. She wished she'd thought to invite her over herself. She'd just been so busy with the case, that she'd put it, along with everything else in her life, on the back burner as of late.

"I brought you a get-well basket," Lyra said as she held it up for inspection. "It's got a heating pad, an ice pack, some Aleve and some chicken noodle soup. I wasn't sure what you liked as far as candy so I got you an assortment." She seemed nervous. Like maybe she felt like she was intruding.

Danica took the basket. "Thank you," she said. "That was really nice of you."

Lyra shrugged. "It was no big deal."

"Apparently it was," she said, eyeing all the goods. "You really put a lot of effort into this."

"I'm worried about you," she said.

"I'm okay," Danica said, waving her inside. She motioned for her to sit, and she sat alongside her, placing the basket on the coffee table, amongst all the strewn files, photos, and papers from the case.

"You don't look okay," Lyra said. "You look beat. Like you haven't slept in days."

"I sleep," Danica said. "Sometimes."

But Lyra didn't appear as though she believed her. She inched closer and, while holding her gaze, she reached out and lightly brushed her fingers along her cheek.

"You don't look like you sleep at all," she whispered.

Danica trembled beneath her touch. "I—" But words did not come. She was lost in Lyra's eyes, lost in her hypnotizing trance of empathy and understanding.

"It's okay," Lyra said. "You can rest now."

"Rest…" Danica whispered. She closed her eyes, wanting to get lost in the feel of her fingers forever.

"Yes," Lyra said. "You can relax and rest. Right here, right now."

"I'm so tired."

Lyra kept lightly stroking her cheek. "I know."

"Will you…stay?"

A ringing came. As if she were in a dream again. Distant yet close. What was it? Where was it? Did she care?

"Danny?"

She opened her eyes. Lyra had dropped her hand, leaving her skin tingling from her touch.

"I think your phone's ringing."

Danny blinked, still swimming in her languid dream. "Come again?"

"Your phone."

"Oh, shit." She hurried to her bedroom and grabbed her phone, but she wasn't in time to answer the call. She headed back into the living room where she found Lyra standing, looking antsy. "It's okay, I can call her back later," Danny said.

"Eleanor?" Lyra asked as she sank her hands into her hoodie pockets.

"Yes."

She walked toward the door. "I should probably get going."

"Wait."

"I just came by to bring you the basket and to make sure you're alright. Which you are. Sort of." She offered a smile, but it fell flat.

"You don't have to go."

"It's late. You need, more than anything, more than time spent with me, to rest."

"I really wish everyone would stop telling me that. I'm—" She palmed her forehead and sighed. "Fine."

"Maybe you should listen to them," Lyra said, trying again for a smile. "They only mean well. I only mean well."

Danica reached for her hand. She tried to pull her back in, but Lyra resisted.

"Plus, you have a phone call to return."

"It can wait."

But Danica could see that, in Lyra's mind, she was already gone.

"I'll see you later, Danny," she said.

"Promise?"

"I do." She smiled at her and this time, though subtle, it reached her eyes and Danica believed her.

CHAPTER THIRTY-TWO

Eleanor pulled on a pair of gloves and shrugged into her lab coat. She walked to the nearest table and adjusted the arm of the light and then switched on the camera. When she was satisfied with the picture, she looked across the table to Allison and forced a smile.

"Good morning," she said. "What have we got?"

"Morning," Allison said. It took her a moment to focus on the bones laid out before them. She seemed to be sussing Eleanor out. It made Eleanor uncomfortable, so she dove right in, carefully arranging the bones in anatomical position on the table.

"Uh, remains were found along the shoreline of Mullet Lake in Biloxi. Medical examiner couldn't identify it so they sent it to us."

"Hm. Well, it seems we have a male. Probably mid-twenties." She lifted a portion of the skull. "Looks like a bullet wound."

"That's what I thought."

She continued to examine the remains of the skull, looking particularly at the jaw. "Got a chipped tooth here."

"We've got animal disturbance. A lot of teeth marks on the femur and the tibia."

"Mm, some on the ribs as well."

"We'll get everything measured and get Dr. Ray in here for the teeth."

Allison didn't respond.

"Got it?" Eleanor asked. "What is it?"

Allison shrugged a shoulder. "Just wondered why you're not working the Sugar Mill Farm case."

"I am. Just not at the moment. Besides, I'm waiting on Detective Wallace to get back to me on some things."

"And Dr. Aarden?"

Eleanor averted her gaze. That was what she was really asking about. Lyra. Her absence had been noticed by others besides Allison. So, she gave the same answer she'd given everyone.

"She's out at the cane field. She seems to like being on scene." *And probably likes being with Danny. But I can't say I blame her. Or Danny for that matter.*

"Oh."

"So, let's get to work, shall we?"

"Yes, ma'am."

They continued working on the latest case, only speaking about the bones at hand. Soon, it seemed, that Allison had forgotten all about Lyra and her whereabouts. Eleanor wished that she could as well, but Lyra kept returning to her mind. They hadn't spoken much since Friday night, despite leaving things on good terms, with Lyra only calling her to report in from the crime scene at the cane field. She'd sounded like the professional she was, but gone was the friendly chitchat. Now it was as if Lyra was more business. Perhaps that was better.

But what about Danny?

What about her? It's none of my business.

She tried to refocus on the bones. But it was more than difficult. The thought of Lyra and Danny was still a menacing thought.

Eventually, she replaced the bone back on the table and peeled off her gloves. Allison glanced up at her questioningly.

"I'm going to go out to the farm. I need to see how the investigation is wrapping up." She really didn't owe her an explanation, but her guilty conscience saw that she did. Although she was going to go out to Sugar Mill Farm, she wasn't solely going for the investigation. She was going to do a little investigating of her own, even if she did know it was wrong and even futile.

"Okay, boss. I'll hold down the fort here."

Eleanor offered her a smile. "Thanks. Call me if you need anything." She shrugged out of her lab coat and went in her office to retrieve her purse and phone. Then she headed out, leaving the lab and her students behind.

The scene at Sugar Mill Farm wasn't nearly as crowded with personnel as she'd thought it would be. Eleanor slowed her car and parked amongst the others. She saw Lyra's neon green Jeep and she sat and took some deep breaths. She was trying to calm her racing heart. When she felt like she had a hold of herself, she glanced up and allowed herself to stare out at the cane beyond the white tents. There, she saw a bloodhound examining the area, being walked by its handler, a couple of deputies walking behind, and some technicians dressed in their protective gear. She didn't see Lyra right away, but when she did, her heart rate accelerated yet again.

She emerged from a tent, peeling off the white garb and gloves. She had on rugged-looking cargo pants, work boots, and a tight-fitting flannel. She couldn't look any more lesbian if she tried. And she was, Eleanor had to admit, sexy as hell.

Eleanor climbed from her car and walked toward her. She realized as she took several steps in, that she should've gone home to change herself. Her heels just weren't doing the job, but she'd been so focused on getting there that she hadn't even thought of changing clothes.

What's wrong with me? Am I losing my mind?

She tripped a little but steadied herself. *Yes, apparently I am.*

Lyra caught sight of her and excused herself from the fellow technician she was talking to.

"Dr. Stafford," she said, sinking her hands in her cargo pants pockets. "What brings you by?"

"Dr. Stafford? What happened to Eleanor?" She wobbled some but again managed to steady herself. She straightened her spine and smiled, trying to remain somewhat in control and professional.

"I'm just trying to be professional," she said.

Seems I'm not the only one.

"I see."

"So, what's up?"

"Just wanted to see how it was going." She purposely looked beyond her and stared at the hound and the deputies out in the field.

"Well, it's going," Lyra said, turning to follow her line of sight.

"Anything new?"

"Not yet."

"Where's the ground-penetrating radar?"

"Not here yet." Lyra checked her watch. "It's early yet."

"I didn't notice."

They stood in silence for a moment. "We're almost to the edge of the cane," Lyra said. "Almost completed the grid as far as the hound goes."

"And the radar?"

"Still have a bit to go. But the bodies we've found have been relatively shallow, so the hound is doing most of the work. The radar hasn't found much of anything."

"Well, it's best to make sure."

"Of course."

Eleanor fought for another question, for something else to say. "Where's the detective?"

Lyra didn't budge. She just kept squinting out into the cane. "Which detective is that?"

Eleanor laughed. "Come on, Lyra. You know who I'm referring to."

"If you mean Detective Wallace, she's not here." She finally turned to look at her. "Neither is Detective Devereaux in case you're interested."

I'm not, but that's okay.

"Any idea where she—er—they are?"

"No. Should I have?"

"I don't know. I thought maybe Danny—er, Detective Wallace had been in touch."

Lyra crossed her arms over her chest. "Not recently."

"She hasn't been in touch with me either."

"Didn't she talk to you Friday night?"

Eleanor blinked. "Friday night?"

"Yeah, you called her."

"How did you know that?"

Lyra shifted, looking uncomfortable.

Eleanor heated. "Were you—there? At her house?" Her stomach clenched as she waited for the answer. "I'm sorry, I didn't realize. It wasn't my intention to interrupt."

Lyra didn't respond right away. "It doesn't matter."

"Yes, it does," Eleanor let out.

Lyra whipped her head around. "Why?"

"Because. I don't want to hinder your relationship with her in any way."

Lyra chewed her lower lip. "Okay. I appreciate that. I really do."

Eleanor nodded but inside she was on fire. Lyra had been at Danny's. At night. What had they been up to? Oh God. Nothing had ever hurt like this. Not even the breakup between her and Danny. "If you see her, have her call me. I need to speak to her." She turned to leave, needing to escape back to her car.

But Lyra called out to her. "Eleanor."

Eleanor faced her once again.

She appeared to have softened. She lowered her arms and came toward her. "Look, it's obvious that things are complicated here. If you think it's best I leave the case to you and Detective Wallace, I will."

Eleanor was stunned. She never expected her to offer to leave. The woman loved bones and her job too much to just up and leave.

"No," Eleanor said. "We need you."

"Are you sure? What about you and Detective—"

Eleanor held up her hand. "Forget about it. Everything is fine." She chastised herself for acting the way she had. They had a case to focus on. She couldn't allow her emotions to get in the way of that.

And it seemed Lyra and Danny were both doing a better job of it than she was so far.

"Eleanor, everything isn't fine."

"It is. Or it will be from here on out. You have my word."

"Okay."

"I'll see you back at the lab."

"Hey," Lyra said. "How about lunch later?"

Eleanor smiled wistfully. "That would be nice," she said. "But I don't think it's a good idea right now. We still have a lot of work to do." It was a lame excuse but Lyra nodded as if she understood.

"I'll see you later," Eleanor said. She walked quickly back to her car, slipping her heels off to do so. When she got inside, she started the engine and backed out onto the dirt road. Then she tried her very best to not cry on the way back to the lab.

CHAPTER THIRTY-THREE

The trailer was old and worse for wear. Danica stood at the door alongside Devereaux. They were at yet another home of a missing girl, ready to question close relatives. While calling would've been easier, Danica had learned that some things were best done in person.

She and Devereaux both studied the wall next to the trailer door. Missing person flyers for Beatrice Cormier were taped all over it. They, unlike the trailer, appeared new and well kept. Danica wondered how often they changed them out.

Someone pulled open the front door.

"Hello," Danica said, looking down at the little boy who'd answered. "Is your—" She stopped as her heart wrenched. She couldn't ask for his mother. His mother, Beatrice Cormier, was missing. "Is someone else home?"

The door opened farther and an older woman peered out. Danica recognized her as Beatrice's mother, Teri Cormier. "What do you want?" she asked.

"Mrs. Cormier. We're from the state police, remember? Detectives Wallace and Devereaux? We were hoping we could talk to you about Beatrice."

She peered at them through narrow, suspicious eyes. "I remember ya."

"We just have a few questions," Danica added.

She looked down at the little boy. "Talon," she said. "You wanna come outside and play?" He nodded and she ushered him out the door. "Come on, then."

Danica and Devereaux made room for them to step onto the porch. Talon took off down the wooden stairs to play with his battery-operated car on the lawn. It was a little blue Jeep and he immediately crawled inside and pressed on the gas pedal.

"Cute," Danica said.

Mrs. Cormier motioned for them to sit in one of the few folding chairs, while she eased down into a tattered cushioned one herself. "Ya'll wanna talk, go ahead." She reached for her pack of cigarettes and lit up. She inhaled hard, her cheeks caving in, and then exhaled, blowing smoke toward them.

Danica looked to Devereaux and began. "Mrs. Cormier, as you've probably heard, we've found some remains out at Sugar Mill Farm. We're now in the process of identifying those remains."

"You telling me you found her?" She crossed her skinny legs and bobbed her bony foot.

"No, ma'am. Well, we don't know for sure. That's why we're here." A breeze came through and blew some more smoke in Danica's face. She tried not to cough.

"We still put up flyers, ya know." She motioned toward the flyers on the wall. "Put 'em up all over town. Been two years since she disappeared, but we still put 'em up." She pointed her finger at Danica. "I called you people the day the article came out about the bodies ya'll found out at Sugar Mill. No one ever called me back."

Danica heated. She felt awful about not being in better communication, but they'd honestly, at the time, had nothing concrete to report. "I'm sorry about that, ma'am. We've been very busy trying to identify the remains," Danica said. "We didn't want to give you misinformation."

She huffed. "A phone call woulda been nice."

"We'll do better to keep in touch."

She didn't respond.

"We need to ask you some things about Beatrice."

She again narrowed her eyes and sucked on her cigarette. Danica began. "To your knowledge, was there ever a period where Beatrice didn't eat, or would eat very, very little?"

Mrs. Cormier sat quietly. Her foot stopped bobbing. She flicked some ash off of her cigarette into an ashtray next to her. "I took good care of my daughter," she said. "And I take good care of that boy out there, too."

"We're not suggesting otherwise," Devereaux said.

"We just need to know if she was ever malnourished. Like say, from an eating disorder?"

Mrs. Cormier turned her head. Smoke rose from her knobby hand where she held her cigarette.

"What you wanna know about that for?"

Danica leaned forward in her chair. She spoke softly. "Mrs. Cormier, please. It will help us in identification."

"We're not suggesting you did anything wrong," Devereaux said.

Mrs. Cormier shook her head. "It didn't matter what I did. What her daddy did. What we cooked, what we bought for her to eat. She just wouldn't do it."

Danica reached for her small notebook. She began to make notes as Mrs. Cormier continued.

"The girl just wouldn't eat."

"When was this?" Danica asked.

"She was fourteen. Started smoking cigarettes and dabbling in drugs then, too. Sneaking off at night."

"That must've been a very difficult time," Danica said.

"It wasn't any fun, I can tell you that."

"Doesn't sound like it," Devereaux said.

"About how long did her lack of eating last?" Danica asked.

"Two years," Mrs. Cormier said. "She got down to ninety-five pounds. Thought we was gonna have to put her in the hospital."

"What happened to make her change?" Devereaux asked.

"She got a damn boyfriend."

Danica scribbled some more. "Is this the father of her child? Talon's father?"

"Mm-hm."

Danica flipped through her notes. "And his name is…Brian Ball."

"Yes."

Danica quickly read over the notes she'd previously taken on Brian Ball from her initial visit with the Cormiers. They'd questioned him and eventually cleared him as a suspect. But that didn't mean that she liked the guy.

"You'd said previously that Beatrice no longer did drugs, correct?"

"She hasn't gone near the stuff in years. She'd seen her friends get all messed up on them. Said she didn't want anything to do with them anymore."

"And you said previously that Beatrice would never get in a car with someone she didn't know, correct?"

"That's right. She weren't no fool."

Danica checked her notes. This had become the norm in her interviews with the families. She was beginning to think the suspect incapacitated them somehow, like Tina had said had happened to her.

She checked her notes and then pulled out her phone. She showed Mrs. Cormier the photo of the hummingbird necklace.

"Did Beatrice ever own anything like this?"

She shook her head. "Never seen that before."

Danica slid her phone back in its holder.

"Why?"

"We believe it's related to the case," Devereaux said. "But we can't tell you more than that."

She snickered. "Figures."

Danica looked to Devereaux. "I think we've got all we need, Mrs. Cormier," she said. "We appreciate your time."

"You think it's her?" she asked. "You think it's my Bea?"

"We'll let you know as soon as we know something," Devereaux said. They both stood to leave.

Mrs. Cormier, a woman Danica knew to be as tough as nails, wiped her eyes just like she'd done the very first visit. "Make sure you do."

Danica bid her farewell and walked down the steps with Devereaux. Talon drove his car over to them. He squinted up at them.

"Ya'll gonna find my mama?"

Danica's heart sank. She knelt and brushed her hand over his head. "We're sure gonna try."

He gave a nod and then drove off toward his grandmother who'd also stepped down into the yard.

"You thinking those remains are her?" Devereaux asked as they climbed in the car.

Danica sat behind the wheel and looked back at Talon and Mrs. Cormier in the rearview mirror. "Probably."

"But we gotta go pay a visit to the doc?"

Danica started the car. "Yes. Yes, we do."

Danica took Devereaux with her to Eleanor's lab at the university. She was hoping that maybe Eleanor wouldn't get as irritated with her for stopping by if he was with her.

They wove their way between students in the hallway, and then entered the lab with a quick knock. A few of the students looked up as they walked in, but Eleanor, curiously, did not. She kept her eyes on the remains in front her.

"Hey," Danica said as they came to stand across from her.

"Detectives," she said, finally glancing up to examine them over the lenses of her readers. She sounded firm and direct, and the scowl on her face hinted at her cross mood. So much for Devereaux's influence working wonders.

"We've got news about that victim with the eating disorder," Danica said. "Victim number one."

"Oh?" She looked back down at the bones. She continued to measure and enter the numbers into the computer.

"Aren't you curious?" Danica asked.

"I don't have time to be curious. I only have time for facts."

Danica glanced at Devereaux who shrugged.

"Turns out, that one of our missing girls, Beatrice Cormier, was anorexic from age fourteen to sixteen. Her mother said she just wouldn't eat. Got down to ninety-five pounds."

"That seems to fit," Eleanor said. "Thank you for the info."

"That's it?" Danica said.

"What else were you hoping for, Detective? A celebration?"

"Well, something along those lines, yes. I mean, we just pretty much identified a victim."

"And again, a phone call would've sufficed."

Danica almost shivered at the cold in the room. Devereaux shifted and she could sense his discomfort.

"I'm gonna go get a drink from the vending machine. You two want anything?" he said.

"No, thanks," Danica said.

Eleanor smiled at him. "Thank you, Devereaux, but no." Then she looked back to her bones.

Devereaux left and Danica made sure they weren't within earshot of the other students working.

"What is wrong?" she asked. "Are you pissed at me or something?"

"Why would I be pissed at you? Is there a reason I should be?"

"None that I can think of, no."

"Then reason suggests that I'm not pissed at you."

"Come on, Eleanor. What's going on?"

"I told you, I'm just needing the facts. And that being said, you'll be glad to know that we've identified another victim through dental examination."

"You're kidding? Why didn't you call me?"

She looked at her again over her lenses. "Because I literally just found out before you got here."

Danica pulled out her notes. "Who is it?"

"Carroll Reynolds."

Danica sighed. Another one of her girls. "You're sure?"

"Yes."

"Thank you."

"We should have DNA back on victim two relatively soon. I'll keep you posted."

Danica put her notebook away. She was already dreading having to go tell a family about their loved one. And she was seriously troubled knowing that they did, indeed, have a serial killer on their hands. Young women were now in more danger than ever. She had to get the word out.

"You sure nothing else is wrong?" Danica asked.

"I'm sure, Detective."

"You're calling me Detective. I know something is wrong."

"I'm merely being professional. Now if you'll excuse me, I have work to do."

Danica considered pressing her but knew it would do no good. Eleanor had made up her mind and the matter was closed.

"Okay," Danica eventually said. "Thanks." She waited for Eleanor to respond, but when she didn't, Danica turned and walked out the door. She found Devereaux sipping on a Pepsi out in the hallway.

"You good?" he asked, obviously concerned with what had gone on between her and Eleanor.

"No," Danica said. "I'm not. Something's up."

"You aren't sure what?"

They headed for the exit. "I have a pretty good idea."

"Yeah?"

"Yes. And her name is Lyra Aarden."

CHAPTER THIRTY-FOUR

*H*e crept up the front walkway and listened at the screen door. Doris Day was singing on the radio and the birds were chirping just beyond him outside. He carefully opened the door and stuck his head inside. His grandmother stood at the kitchen sink with her back to him. As quietly as he could, he stepped inside and tried to walk through the kitchen without her hearing. But the old wood floor creaked and gave him away. He froze, his heart pounding.

"What in the world?" his grandmother said as she turned to face him. She took one look and marched over to him, wiping her hands on a dishtowel and then discarding it on the floor. She grabbed his chin and pulled him to her.

"What is this?" she said, poking at his sore eye.

He started crying, both from pain and fear.

"Huh? I asked you a question, boy."

He struggled to speak between sobs. "Some boys—"

"Some boys, what?" Her eyes were boring holes into his from behind her thick horn-rimmed frames.

"Some boys on the bus—they—they hit me."

She tugged on his face harder. "They hit you, you say?"

"Yes, ma'am."

"What did they go and do that for? Huh? What did you do?"

He cried some more and she smacked him hard across the cheek. The contact stung and he winced and raised his arms, afraid she'd strike again.

"You stop that crybaby bawling, you hear?"

He fought for breath. "Yes, ma'am."

"*Now tell me what you did to make them boys hit you.*"

"*Nothing.*"

She smacked him again. He stumbled backward, but she was back on him in seconds.

"*Don't lie to me, now.*"

"*I'm—they—*"

"*Well, spit it out. I ain't got all day.*"

"*They were—saying things.*"

"*What sort of things?*"

Terror seized him.

"*Well?*" *She raised her hand in a threat to hit him again.*

He winced and cowered but spoke. "*They were saying things about you—Grandmother.*"

She reared back. "*Me?*"

"*Yes, ma'am.*"

"*Like what?*"

"*Ma'am?*"

"*Go on.*"

He tried his best to garner courage. "*They—said you were a crazy old spinster. That you—killed your husband.*"

She placed her hands on her hips and narrowed her eyes at him. "*And you did what?*"

"*I—told them to stop. And they—hit me.*"

She looked toward the door, as if searching for the culprits.

"*And you just came home crying like a little baby? Did you even hit them back? No, of course you didn't. Because you're a weak little coward, aren't you? A pathetic piece of dog turd. That's what you are. You're lucky I even took you in after your whore of a mother abandoned you.*"

"*Yes, ma'am,*" *he said, praying she wouldn't hit him again.*

"*Well, what do you think your punishment should be for being a little cowardly bastard? Huh?*"

He thought quickly, trying for anything to stop the abuse. "*Cleaning.*"

She seemed to like that suggestion. "*Then that's what you'll do. And you can start in here. On the floors. I want them scrubbed and polished, you hear?*"

"*Yes, ma'am.*"

"*And don't you ever come home with a shiner like that again.*"

"*No, ma'am, I won't.*"

She turned and went back to the sink, leaving him to pick up the dish towel.

He awoke on the couch and sat up. He rubbed his eyes, and looked around, fearfully searching for his grandmother. He sighed when he discovered he was alone.

He rose and walked into the kitchen. Dawn was breaking with the light of day seeping in through the windows. He opened the door and the screen and retrieved the paper. But instead of going back inside to where the memory of his grandmother loomed like an angry giant, he crossed to his car and climbed inside. He drove into town and parked at Miss Honey's Café. He carried his paper inside and sat at a nearby table.

"What can I get for you?" a young woman in a yellow flowered smock asked.

He gave her the once-over, liked what he saw, and smiled. "How about your number?"

Her friendly facade fell and she stopped smacking her gum. "Uh, no. I meant what can I get you from here?"

"I know what you meant," he said. "But I was hoping you'd give me your number so we could have coffee sometime."

"I get plenty of coffee here," she said. "You gonna order, or what?"

He scowled. "You don't have to be a little bitch about it."

A look of alarm overcame her. She hurried to the counter and said something to the man behind it.

He knew what was coming, so he stood and left the café. He headed across the street and found an empty park bench. He sat and unfolded his paper. To his great surprise, the headline was all about him.

MISSING WOMAN IDENTIFIED AT SUGAR MILL FARM

He hurriedly scanned the article, his skin on fire with excitement. It seemed they were beginning to identify some of his lovelies.

He grinned at two people walking by. Here he was reading about himself and they had no idea. No one did.

Ha.

It was his little secret still. His little game.

He felt good about sitting there in front of the whole town reading about his lovelies. These people were so dumb. They'd never figure it out.

He kept reading. They were still claiming they had no suspects. And even one of the detectives had issued a dire warning for young women to walk in pairs and be in by a ten o'clock curfew.

Ha.

As if that would help.

He read the article again and then opened the paper, displaying the headline to all that passed by. Would they notice? Would anyone look at him twice?

He hoped so. He could use some attention. But no one did.

Not one person. They all just kept to themselves.

Idiots. Couldn't they see what was right in front of them?

Jesus, did he have to go and read the paper right in front of the police station? Would that finally garner him some much deserved attention?

It might. But that would be the wrong kind of attention, wouldn't it?

He refolded the paper and walked to the newspaper stand in front of the café. He deposited some money and then opened it up and took the entire stack out. He closed the door and looked into the café. The young woman who'd tried to serve him was staring at him.

He grinned at her and walked away.

CHAPTER THIRTY-FIVE

"Dilophosaurus does too have a frill!" Haley shouted at her sister, Daphne. "And she spits venom, too!"

"Does not!" Daphne said with her hands on her hips.

"Does, too! Auntie Lyra, tell her!" Haley crossed her arms in her green and orange dinosaur costume and puffed out her chest.

"Does not!" Daphne said again, wearing her blue butterfly costume. She held her arms out to flutter her wings. "That was just in the movies, dumb-dumb. It didn't happen for real."

"Auntie Lyra!"

"Of course, they had a frill," Lyra said, taking Haley by the hand to lead her down the sidewalk. It was Halloween and the sun had just set. Around them the street was beginning to bustle with kids in costume carrying candy bags and plastic pumpkins.

"And they could spit venom," Haley continued, refusing to let it go.

"Yes. They could spit venom." She wished the girls would stop arguing. It had taken them nearly an hour to get them dressed and out of the house, due to their unfortunate moodiness.

"Nuh-uh. That was only in the movies. We learned it at school," Daphne said, holding Louie's hand. "Tell her, Daddy."

"For tonight the Dil—whatever-a-saurus has a frill and spits venom. Okay?"

"Fine," said Daphne. "But it's not really like that."

"Sweetie, why don't you come walk with me?" Lyra's mother asked.

"That's a great idea," Louie said. "Why don't you go walk with Grandma?"

Daphne slumped her shoulders. "Fine."

"What's wrong, puddin'? You don't want to walk with me?"

"It's not that," Daphne said. "It's that no one believes me about the Dilophosaurus."

Lyra's mother bent down to her ear. "I do."

Daphne perked up.

Lyra returned her focus to Haley and they all crossed the street. They'd left her father back at the house so he could give out candy. He'd been surprisingly friendly to her and Louie and he'd been more than happy to stay behind to hand out the candy. She wondered if her mother had finally had a talk with him about his behavior.

A car approached from the entrance to the street. Lyra secured Haley on the sidewalk and waved as the familiar unmarked cruiser slowed. The window powered down and she peered inside. Danny sat behind the wheel. Funny, she'd just been thinking about her. She hadn't spoken to her since that night at her house when she'd brought the get-well basket. She'd thought maybe it was for the best, considering the whole fiasco between Eleanor, Danny, and her. But nevertheless, she couldn't seem to get Danny off her mind. Especially the way she'd reacted to her touch.

"Happy Halloween," Danny said.

"Back at ya."

"I can see you're busy with family, so I'll let you go."

"No, no. What's up?" Lyra asked, fearing she would leave.

"Not much. Just wondered what you were up to tonight." She looked sheepish and almost a little embarrassed.

"You wanna come with? We could always use an extra trick-or-treater."

"Yeah!" Haley exclaimed. "Tell your friend to come!"

"You heard her," Lyra said.

"You sure?" Danny asked.

"Absolutely."

"Let me park." She eased off the brake and quickly parked the car. Then she jogged across the street to join them. Lyra introduced her to her nieces, brother, and mother. She shook hands with them all and the girls were thrilled to have one more person on their adventure.

"Do you like dinosaurs?" Haley asked as she took Danny by the hand. They were all three walking together, hand in hand, with Haley in the middle. Louie, Daphne, and Lyra's mother brought up the rear.

"I sure do," Danny said. "I can see that you do, too."

"Yep! I'm a dinosaur expert."

"Are you now?"

"Uh-huh."

"Well, that's impressive."

"I'm gonna grow up and dig up bones like Auntie Lyra. Only my bones are gonna be big, huge, dinosaur bones!"

"Wow! That sounds fantastic."

"What do you do, Miss Danny?" she asked her.

"Well, I'm a detective. I solve crimes."

"You find the bad guys?"

"You got it."

"Do you have handcuffs?"

"Uh-huh."

"Can I see them?"

Danny reached into her blazer and pulled out a pair of cuffs. She handed them to Haley.

"Look Auntie Lyra! Real, live handcuffs!"

"Uh-huh. Pretty neat, huh?"

"The neatest!"

They laughed as Haley dropped behind them to show Daphne.

"You're really good with her," Lyra said.

"She's adorable. They both are."

"You don't have nieces or nephews?"

"'Fraid not. I'm an only child."

"Really?"

"Yes."

Lyra laughed. "That explains why you're so hardheaded."

"Come again? I'm not hardheaded."

"I'm just teasing. Sort of." She smiled at her, feeling serene. "So, what brings you by, Danny? I haven't heard from you in a while."

"Remember when you stopped by my house and said you'd been thinking of me?"

"Yes."

"Well, I've been thinking of you."

"You have."

"Uh-huh. I've been thinking about you a lot."

"Then why the radio silence?"

"I don't know. The case, my physical health, and...Eleanor. All of it has been weighing on my mind."

"Yeah, me too."

"But you...you're always right there, front and center, no matter what seems to be going on."

"I know what you mean."

Danny returned the smile and they strolled quietly to the next house. The girls darted ahead and hurried to the door while a group of older kids exited, fresh load of candy in tow.

"Thanks for letting me come along," Danny said, chuckling at a kid in a zombie costume.

"Don't mention it. I mean, I wouldn't want you to miss all this," she said, extending her arms.

"It would be a shame to miss it, wouldn't it?"

The girls giggled happily as they left the house and sprinted ahead to the next.

"Don't get too far ahead," Lyra called.

"So, how's the case going?" Lyra asked. "You getting anywhere with a suspect?"

"Sadly no. But we've identified two of the bodies now, so that's good."

"Yes, I heard. Carroll Reynolds and Gabby Dietrich. But that didn't help with any leads?"

"Not really." She seemed to think for a moment. "Although it is interesting that each family says the victims would never accept a ride from a stranger."

"Hm. That is interesting. What do you think it means?"

"He took them by force."

"All of them?"

"Seems so."

"And no one saw anything?"

"Sounds impossible, doesn't it?"

"You would think someone would've seen something, somehow." They halted at the next house and watched as the girls rang the doorbell.

"Anything else going on?" Lyra asked.

"Such as?"

"I don't know. I guess I'm just a little surprised to see you."

"It's unusual for me to just show up, is it?" She laughed. "I understand."

"I didn't mean any offense. I mean—I'm glad you're here. Really glad." The sentence trailed off as she realized what she was saying.

Danny smiled. "That's nice to hear."

Lyra's heart fluttered. They were standing close together. So close she could smell her cologne and feel her strong arm graze hers.

"So, you wanted to see me again?"

Danny glanced over at her. "I did, yes. Is that okay?"

Lyra ran her hand nervously through her hair. "Yes, of course."

"Because you left in such a hurry the other night at my place, I wanted to make sure I didn't do anything wrong."

"No. It's—it was me. I'm sorry."

They began walking again. "Anything you want to share?"

Lyra had been upset over the whole Eleanor thing, but she didn't want to take anything from the moment. It was a beautiful evening and she had her family, and now she had Danny to spend it with. She decided to leave well enough alone.

"I just thought you should rest. I was really worried about you, you know?"

"No need to be. But I do appreciate it. It's nice to know someone cares so much."

Again, she thought of Eleanor. Didn't she care? She shook the thought way.

"That basket you made for me was nice. It helped a lot."

"Yeah?"

"I've used everything in it. Even ate the Hot Tamales. They were good."

Lyra laughed. "I can't believe I got you those. I just had no idea what you liked."

"Well, candy in general was a safe assumption."

"I see."

"But I used the other stuff, too. Just so you know."

"Good. I'm glad I could help."

"You did." They stopped once again, and the girls hurried up the front walk to an entryway covered in black tarps. A man dressed in a skeleton body suit greeted them and asked if they dared to enter the haunted house. The girls ran back to Lyra and Danny.

"It's haunted!" Haley said.

"We don't want to go by ourselves," Daphne said, looking back over her shoulder as if to make sure the skeleton man hadn't come after them.

"Will you please come?" Daphne asked, and then ran back to her dad to ask him. She clung to him, obviously frightened.

"Yeah, cuz it's scary," Haley said, following her sister.

"Looks like duty calls," Lyra said.

"Let's do it then," Louie said. He led the girls by the hands followed by Lyra's mother.

Danny extended her arm to Lyra. "Shall we?"

"I don't know," Lyra teased her. "It looks pretty scary."

"I've got you."

"Okay," she said. "As long as you promise not to leave me."

"Wouldn't dream of it."

They followed the others into the house and were immediately met with darkness and another person in costume jumping out at them. The girls screamed and held onto Louie while Lyra grabbed Danny's hand.

Danny tugged her close and wrapped her arm around her. Lyra held her in return, loving the feel of her so close. Danny was taller than she was, and firm with muscle. Though she was currently frightened with all the people and props jumping out at her, she was thoroughly enjoying herself in Danny's protective embrace.

When they neared the exit, Danny stopped and faced her.

"Wait," she whispered.

She touched her cheek, lightly grazing it with her fingertips.

"I—I can't wait any longer." And before Lyra knew what was happening, Danny's warm, soft lips were tasting hers. Tenderly, carefully, just enough to be head spinning and tantalizing. Lyra leaned into her, wanting more. Needing more. But Danny drew away just before a horrifying clown jumped out at them to shoo them back outside.

"Oh, my God," Lyra let out as she followed Danny out, holding tightly to her hand. They all stood in the driveway, trying to recover. Lyra touched her lips, still able to feel Danny's on them, as if she'd been stung by the sweetest, most alluring honeybee. "That was…" she started.

Danny raised an eyebrow at her. "Exciting."

"Yeah, it was great!" Haley said as she came bounding up to them. "But Daphne got afraid."

"Did not," Daphne said, wiping away a tear. She was now clinging to Lyra's mother who was doing her best to soothe her.

"Daphne, I got scared too," Lyra said. "It's okay."

"I wasn't scared. I was—just surprised."

Lyra caressed her head. "Me, too," she said. "All those crazy monsters jumping out at us. Whoo. I'm glad it's over."

"I shoulda cuffed 'em," Haley said, holding up the cuffs. "Huh, Danny? They were bad guys."

"They sure were," Danny said.

"You better keep them in case you need them for real."

"Good idea," Danny said, returning them back inside her blazer.

She and Lyra fell back and allowed the others to walk in front of them.

Danny smiled at her. "I always seem to feel better when I'm with you."

Lyra blinked at her.

"You have no idea, do you?" Danny asked. "The way you make me feel. It's—like I'm alive again." She gently touched her hand. "Please, tell me you feel it, too. I've been going crazy wondering if this is all in my head."

Lyra clutched her warm fingers in hers. "I do."

The breeze kicked up again and blew Danny's dark mane across her face. They were inches apart once again when the girls stopped and called out to them.

"Guess we better go," Danny said. "We're being beckoned."

Lyra laughed. "So, we are."

"Can I get a rain check on that?" Danny asked.

"On what?"

"On whatever that was about to be."

"You mean another mind-blowing kiss?" Lyra said softly.

"Yes."

Lyra smiled. "Oh, definitely."

Danny placed her hand on the small of her back and they headed back toward the rest of the family.

CHAPTER THIRTY-SIX

Eleanor drove home from work in silence, grateful to be alone once again. She just didn't feel like being around people lately, and her students were noticing. Allison had tried wholeheartedly to get her to set up a dating profile online. But Eleanor had refused, telling her she just wasn't interested. Of course, her students weren't the only ones noticing her quiet distance. It seemed Danny and Lyra had noticed, too. Both had tried to call and text, but she'd yet to get back to them.

"Damn." She'd forgotten that her mother had been calling as well. God, where was her mind these days?

She knew.

It was with Lyra and Danny. Danny and Lyra. She tried like hell to tear them from her mind, but short of a frontal lobotomy, she worried it wasn't going to be possible.

When she pulled up to her drive she saw her mother's car, but for the tiniest of seconds, her heart fluttered hoping it was Danny or Lyra.

What the hell is wrong with me?

Here I am avoiding them at all costs, yet I hope it's one of them waiting for me in my driveway?

"Shit." She was losing it. "Shit." She really wanted to spend this weekend alone to wallow in her misery, even if she did adore her mother.

She parked and headed for the door. Several children gleefully shrieked as they ran by her on the street. They were dressed up in costumes.

Holy Fuck. It was Halloween. How could she have forgotten?

Her mother opened the door before she could enter her key.

"I'm sorry I didn't warn you, but I figured you'd tell me no, so I decided to come on my own. Surprise!" She opened her arms for an embrace.

Eleanor fell into her, grateful for the contact. "I forgot it was Halloween."

"No need to fret. I bought some candy."

"Oh, thank God."

She really was exhausted. It took all her strength not to completely collapse into her.

"There, there," her mother said as she drew away. "My little Ellie." She held her face. "I knew something was wrong. I knew it when you didn't return my calls."

Eleanor carried her bag and purse farther inside and set them on the coffee table. "I've just been really busy with work," she said. "So, I'm tired."

"You can't fib to me, Eleanor. I'm your mother."

"Maybe not, but would it help if I said I really didn't want to discuss it right now?"

"I suppose."

"Thank you. I just need some space, I think, to deal with it on my own."

"I'm not going to leave," her mother said as she crossed to the kitchen and stood at the stove. She was cooking something. Eleanor could already smell it.

"I would never want you to leave, Mom." She loved her mother and loved her visits. Even if she was currently feeling cranky and tired.

"You remember when you were a child?" her mother asked as she stirred the food.

"I remember many things," Eleanor said as she dropped down to the couch. She dug the Sugar Mill Farm files out of her bag and began to go through them. She wanted to look over them again to see if she could garner any more clues as to identity or the victims' disappearances. But in a flash, her mother was by her side, offering her a glass of wine.

"Oh. Thank you."

Her mother sat and sipped from her own glass. "You were a tenacious reader." She laughed softly. "Your father always said if we were to slam the book real quick, we'd surely take your nose off."

Eleanor remembered the saying fondly. "I miss him," she said.

"I know, love." She grabbed her hand. "I know." She patted it gently. "You were also a bit of a lone wolf. Remember? Always preferring books to friends? Always wanting to solve your problems on your own?"

"Mm."

"I'm afraid much hasn't changed. But I'm thinking maybe now… it should."

Eleanor tried to stand, but her mother stopped her. "You're too wonderful a person to be alone all the time, Ellie."

"I prefer it. Did you ever consider that?" She was getting tired of everyone trying to set her up, or do something to bring more people into her life. People did things, said things, broke promises, broke hearts. Bottom line, she'd recently decided, life was easier alone.

"I have," her mother surprised her in saying. "Which is why I've given a lot of thought to what I'm about to do next."

Eleanor whipped her head around, terrified at her statement. "What, pray tell, do you mean by that?"

She held up a finger. "I'll be right back."

She hurried into the spare bedroom, quietly opening the door and closing it behind her. Eleanor broke out in a cold sweat, worried she might actually have a human being hidden away in there for her as a companion.

She wouldn't, would she?

Oh, God.

The door opened again and Eleanor steeled herself.

"Close your eyes," her mother called out.

"Oh, Mother, for heaven's sake." But Eleanor closed her eyes. She waited quietly, hands resting on her knees.

She heard her mother enter the room. Felt her presence right next to her.

"Okay. You can open them."

Eleanor opened her eyes and saw her mother standing there with a gray cat in her arms. She blinked at her, unsure the sight was real.

"You—got a cat?"

"For you."

"For me?"

"His name is Huck. Short for Huckleberry. He's nine months old and he's a rescue. Someone found him beneath their vehicle."

"For me?" Eleanor repeated.

"Yes, for you." She held him out. Eleanor had no choice but to take him. She held him at arm's length. The cat looked at her with green eyes and meowed, front paws extended.

"Hold him closer," her mother said, gently pushing the cat into her folded arms. "Yes, like that." She clenched her hands together at her chest and grinned like an excited child. "Isn't he beautiful? I know gray and green are your favorite colors. So, I just knew he'd be perfect."

"You got me a cat," Eleanor said, still reeling. The cat meowed again, and she shifted, unsure what to do.

"You have to relax," her mother said, sitting next to her. "Otherwise he feels the tension."

"Really? Huh. Who would have thought that, oh, I don't know, maybe I'm tense in having a wild animal brought into my home without notice?"

"He's not wild. Not feral. He's sweet. And lovable, and I thought you would love him. Remember when you were little and you brought home all those injured and abandoned animals and nursed them back to health?"

"Mom, I was eight."

"The love was there, Ellie."

Eleanor closed her eyes. *God help me.*

And then she felt it. A soft but firm pressure on her chin. A nudging of sorts. She opened her eyes. The cat was rubbing his face against her and purring.

"He likes you," her mother said.

"I don't know about that."

"He does. Look."

He continued to purr. He was resting in her arms, front paws on her chest, looking at her with those slitted green eyes. "What did you say his name was?" Nothing wrong with knowing his name. Didn't mean anything. Certainly didn't mean she was keeping him.

"Huck. Short for Huckleberry."

"Like Huckleberry Finn."

"That's right. One of your favorite books. I took it as a sign."

Eleanor glanced at her. *Sometimes you are so silly. But you love me. It's more than obvious.*

"I'll let you two get acquainted while I go tend to dinner."

"Wait." She stood with Huck in her arms. "You—don't want to hold him?" She wasn't yet used to holding him. He was warm and soft and... kind of cuddly. Things she was not used to.

"No, he's yours. You need to hold him. Get to know him."

"Mom, you don't honestly expect me to keep him, do you?"

"Of course, I do." She turned to stir the pot. "Why wouldn't you?"

"Because I—" But she couldn't come up with a reason. *Don't want a cat?*

Was that true, though? She did have a profound fondness for animals. And she *was* lonely. Painfully so. Even though she was trying to keep everyone at arm's length, her heart ached.

Maybe her mother was right. Maybe a pet was the perfect solution.

"Hm?" her mother said.

"Nothing."

She looked over her shoulder and smiled. "I knew he'd grow on you."

"Oh, you did not. And I'm not saying he has."

"He has a litter box and litter in the bedroom, along with a carrier and blanket. Though they said at the shelter he'd probably prefer to sleep with you. He's a lover."

Eleanor fought rolling her eyes. *Christ. What have I gotten myself into?*

But she looked into his eyes again and saw him blink slowly, as if he were sleepy, and her entire body softened. Maybe he was rubbing off on her. Maybe he would help with her stress level. Maybe...God willing... this could end up being a good thing.

She returned to the couch and sat. She released Huck and he walked along her lap, back arched and tail in the air. She couldn't help but pet him. Rub him along his back and hips. He seemed to really like that. She even caught herself smiling a little.

"He's an angel," her mother said as she reentered the living room.

"Mom, it's too much," she tried. But she knew she didn't sound convincing. And Huck was purring again and turning back and forth across her lap, wanting more petting.

"Cher, baby. He'll be fine. You'll be fine."

Eleanor scratched his hips and he stuck his rear end in the air. She laughed.

Her mother said nothing, just sat back and smiled, as if she were pleased with herself.

"Don't get used to this," Eleanor said. Though she wondered who she was trying to convince.

"Oh, I won't."

"I mean it. I may take him back."

"Uh-huh."

But she knew that her mother was on to her. There was no way she'd take Huck back. He was hers now. Like it or not. *Damn it.*

She sat him on the couch between them. "I have to get some work done." She sifted through the files.

"That's a lot of work," her mother said.

Eleanor sipped her wine and replaced the glass on the coffee table. "It's the Sugar Mill Farm case."

"Oh." She shifted. Eleanor could sense her unease.

"Danny working that one?"

"Mm-hm."

"You working with her?"

"When the occasion calls."

"Not speaking to her, eh?"

"Mom."

"I know you so well."

Eleanor tossed the files onto the table, barely missing her wine. Huck immediately crawled back onto her lap. She started to push him away but then changed her mind. Instead she began to pet him, completely giving up.

"She just—ah, hell."

"That bad, huh?"

"It's a mess, Mom. The whole thing."

"The case, or something more…personal?"

"All of it. We have no leads, no suspects. Only bones."

"And?"

"And—Danny is—" She fevered at just the thought of Danny and Lyra. "Danny is interested in someone."

"I thought you and Danny were no longer an item?"

"We're not."

"Then, what's the issue?"

"The person she's interested in…it's the woman helping me on the case. She's a bioarchaeologist. From Arizona State."

"And you think that's cutting it too close."

Eleanor just looked at her. How could she confess how ridiculous she was feeling?

"Oh, I see. You like her, too."

Eleanor shooed Huck away and buried her head in her hands. "I'm lost, Mom. I mean, how do I get over this? I've been trying so hard. I've even told them both that I'm letting my feelings go so they can pursue a relationship. But it's still gnawing at me. I feel like I'm going crazy."

"Well, it's simple, really. Do you love Danny?"

"Yes."

"But you didn't want to be with her, correct?"

"No, we just didn't work."

"Do you think you could work now?"

She palmed her forehead. "No. Most likely not. I mean, it might be good for a short while, but then…"

"Then there's only one thing to do."

Eleanor waited.

"If you love Danny, then you have to do what you say. You have to let her go so she can be happy. Same goes for this other woman. If you care for her at all, then let her go where she's happy. Even if that's with Danny."

Eleanor sighed. "God, I hate it when you speak reason."

"I know you do."

"Oh, Mom. Come on. I just wanted to sit here and wallow in my jealousy-filled misery."

Her mother laughed. "Which is why I came. I had a sneaking suspicion something was up."

"You're bloody psychic is what you are."

"No, I'm just really good at my job, sweetheart. I read people for a living. It becomes a habit, I'm afraid."

"Well, stop it. You're forcing me to take the high road here and I don't like it. Not yet."

She patted her leg. "There is something else you can do that will make you feel better."

"Yeah?"

Her mother lifted Huck. She eased Eleanor back against the couch and placed him in her lap. "You're gonna drink your wine, relax, and love on your new cat. That's what you're gonna do. And you're going to forget all about Danny and this other woman."

"Mom, I can't, I—"

"I mean it."

The doorbell rang, interrupting them. Her mother grabbed the bowl of sweet treats she'd bought and headed for the door. She greeted the kids with a light-hearted hello and gave them some candy. Then she closed the door and walked back to Eleanor where she continued their conversation. "It's Halloween and you need a break from all this work and your heartache. A big break."

She handed her the bowl. "Let's go sit on the front drive and eat our soup and hand out the goodies."

"What about Huck? Shouldn't we stay inside with him until he gets settled? I mean, you know, in case I decide to keep him."

Her mother grinned like she knew very well that she'd keep him. "Didn't I tell you? I bought him a leash too."

Eleanor couldn't help but laugh.

CHAPTER THIRTY-SEVEN

Danica held the framed photo of her father in her lap. It was late. Well past midnight. The headaches were still a nuisance, but she had to keep going, keep working. Keep trying to find this fucking killer. The elusive suspect now haunted her dreams, along with the dreams of her father, which she was having more frequently lately, since she'd stopped drinking. She felt like her subconscious was awakening from a long, deep slumber. And she didn't always like what surfaced. But tonight she'd come home and instead of tossing and turning in bed, longing for the peace that only a drink could seem to bring, she'd put on her father's favorite record to sit and ruminate.

He'd passed away when she was thirteen, a pivotal age for any young girl. He'd been shot in the line of duty, trying to chase down a burglary suspect in a grocery store parking lot. His death had been all over the news for weeks, with the small town community of Sugar Mill Farm up in arms over the whole ordeal. The suspect, the young man who'd shot him, was only sixteen. Not too much older than she'd been.

She skimmed her thumb across the glass of the photo, wishing she could touch her father's face for real. She still recalled how he'd held her in his lap when she was little and she'd laughed and giggled at his rough beard as she'd played with his face, curious as to how it was she looked so much like him.

"Why did you have to go? I needed you. Need you now."

Otis Redding kept crooning about the dock of the bay as she recalled the most heart-wrenching memory of all, other than his death. It was the day they'd gone fishing down at the lake. The day she'd caught a body.

She'd been in shock for hours after seeing the dead, bloated young woman bobbing in the surface of the water. Her father had taken her to the police station, and she'd sat staring straight ahead, convinced the killer was going to come after her next. Her father's colleagues would check on her, one after the other, until finally, a female detective, Detective Charlotte Van Ness, approached her and saw what was happening. She'd immediately called Danica's father over and told him to take her to the hospital, that she was in shock. But her father hadn't. He'd taken her home to her mother. And a new nightmare had begun, her mother not exactly being the warm, nurturing type. Instead of tending to Danica, she'd yelled at her father for over an hour, and then sent Danica to bed with a shot of her father's whiskey, to help her relax.

She laughed. And her mother wondered why she drank? She glanced at the whiskey bottle still sitting on her coffee table. She considered putting it away once and for all. But if she did that, she feared she'd be putting her father away once and for all. Could she handle that?

She took a deep breath as she set the photo on the table next to the whiskey. She would know when it was time, and right now, it didn't feel right. Not yet.

She rose and retrieved her beeping phone from the kitchen counter. It was Eleanor, texting her about the remains of Gabby Dietrich. She'd have to pay another visit to Mrs. Broussard. The case was finally coming together with the victim's identities. Unfortunately, it wasn't helping them find the killer. Her sergeant, in response to the community's fear, was threatening to allow the FBI to take over. Something she did not want. Sugar Mill Farm was her town. Her community. She and her task force could solve it. She knew they could. They just needed a clue. Just one clue that would blow the case wide open.

She stared at Eleanor's name. Eleanor had been avoiding her. Was she still that upset?

She made a mental note to reach out to her again. She had to keep trying. Eleanor's friendship meant too much to her.

Another text came in as she was walking to the bedroom. It was from Lyra.

Dinner tomorrow tonight? My place? The girls want to make spaghetti for you.

She smiled. Lyra really did know how to cheer her up.

She stripped and slid into her usual pajamas of soft boxer briefs and a sleeveless tee. She no longer felt the need to sit and think of the past. She eased down onto the bed and relaxed onto her pillow. The record was still playing, but she let it. Only now instead of bringing tears, it brought peace.

❖

The meeting the next morning lasted over an hour. Danica, as lead detective, went over all the evidence in the case, just as she'd done back when the women first started to disappear. Her team seemed eager, though many had dark circles beneath their eyes from the countless long hours. They all quietly took notes and asked questions. She'd excused them with the threat from her sergeant about the FBI wanting to take over. They, like her, did not want that to happen.

"We'll get him, Danny," Rita said as she exited the conference room.

"Yeah, we'll get him. No matter what it takes," fellow detective Lawrence Raabi added. He patted her on the shoulder.

She sighed as Devereaux brought up the rear. "They're still willing and able," she said as they headed for their desks.

"For now. Give them another couple of weeks. With the hours we've all been keeping, we'll be lucky if any of us is able to walk upright by then."

"I hope we won't need another couple of weeks." But that was wishful thinking.

They sat at their desks and Devereaux cracked open his morning jolt of Pepsi. He slurped loudly. "You wanna go see Ms. Broussard?"

Danica moved her mouse and brought her computer screen to life. "It's too early. Right now I want to go over more footage from the businesses on State Street."

He leaned forward, causing his chair to creak, and clicked on his mouse. "You got it."

They both brought up the surveillance footage from the State Street businesses and spent the next few hours combing through it. After numerous yawns, Danica caught sight of something that intrigued her.

"Hey. Which footage are you looking at?"

"The one from the Dollar Store. Again. Why?"

"Pull up the one from Marty's Meats."

She came around his desk to stand behind him. "Fast forward." She touched the screen to signal when to stop. "Here," she said, and Devereaux paused. "Play at normal speed." He did, watching closely. "Here. Stop it." She pointed again. "You see this vehicle?"

"Yeah."

"If you fast forward again, to here. There. Is it me, or is that the same vehicle?"

"Okay. Could be something. Could be nothing. We've done the best we can with identifying the cars we could. Rita and I have gone over and over these—"

Danica chastised herself for not going over the footage herself.

"We have to do better," she said.

He sighed and pinched the bridge of his nose. "You get a plate number?"

She shook her head. "Not clear enough."

"See?"

"But look here. There's lettering on the vehicle."

He moved and clicked the mouse again. "Looks like a smudge to me."

"Zoom in."

He did. He leaned closer to the monitor. "Maybe. But we still can't read it."

"We need to read it, D. We need to absolutely rule out everything we can. I'm hoping some of the other footage will show us a little more."

"I'll get on it."

Danica hurried over to the printer and grabbed the photo of the vehicle, along with the children's book *Flying Home*, and slid them into her satchel. She then slipped into her blazer and grabbed her car keys.

"Hold off. Right now, we need to go see Ms. Broussard."

Ms. Francine Broussard answered the door in silence. She looked Danica and Devereaux up and down before pushing the door open farther to let them in. Then she sat in her old recliner and lifted a fat cat onto her lap.

"You come to tell me you found her," she said. "Well, I don't wanna hear it."

Danica and Devereaux, who was trying his best not to cover his nose from the stench of cat urine, settled down onto the plaid couch.

"Miss Francine," Danica tried. "I'm afraid we have to talk."

"I don't wanna know."

Danica felt for her. The older woman was all alone now, save for her cats. This couldn't be easy, not for anyone, much less a woman living all on her own. "Miss Francine, is there someone we can call for you? Someone who can come be with you?"

She covered her face. "Just say it. Just go on ahead and say it. Then I can get on with it."

Danica glanced at Devereaux. He was feeling the same empathy for Ms. Broussard that she was, she could tell by the sad look in his eyes.

"Miss Francine, we've made a positive identification. We've found Gabby."

Ms. Broussard choked up with her face still covered. Danica knelt beside her. She placed a gentle hand on her arm. "I'm so very sorry."

She continued to cry. "My Gabby. My sweet Gabby."

"Is there someone we can call? Maybe a friend, or a neighbor?"

She wiped her eyes. "I don't want nobody here." She looked at Danica and sniffled. "Nobody but Gabby."

"I know," Danica said, her own heart tearing to bits.

"Can we do anything for you, Miss Francine?" Devereaux asked softly. "Do you need food, a ride to the store, anything? We can get someone to help."

She grabbed Danica's hand. "You can catch this monster. Catch him and string him up."

Danica could see the fierceness in her eyes. "We're doing our best. I can promise you that."

"You ain't got nobody in mind?"

"We can't really discuss it. But what we can do is show you some more things. See if they strike you in any way."

She nodded solemnly, and Danica glanced back at Devereaux. He brought the two items to her. Danica first showed Ms. Broussard the children's book. "Have you ever see this before?"

She shooed the cat from her lap and took the book in her trembling hands. "I haven't seen this in a long, long time."

Danica perked up. "You know it?"

"Why, yes. I used to read this to Gabby when she was little."

Danica fished out her notebook and began making notes.

"She loved it. Loved that the hummingbird finally found his way home."

"But you haven't seen that hummingbird recently? Like on a necklace?"

"No. Done told you that."

Danica pressed her lips together. "Do you still have the book?"

"Lord, I don't think so. It's been years. But you know…" She tapped the book. "Gabby mentioned something about this book just before she disappeared. She said she saw it at the library and a man came up to her asking her if she'd read it. Said they had a whole conversation about it."

Danica couldn't write fast enough. "Did she mention his name or anything else about him?"

"No. She just said he was nice."

Danica couldn't figure out the significance. Devereaux, who looked as dumbfounded as she felt, pointed at the photo of the vehicle she'd printed. It was black-and-white and grainy, but it was all they had.

"What about the car?" he asked. "Does it look familiar?"

She took the photo. "No, I can't say it does."

Danica stopped scribbling. "You never saw this car lurking near your home?"

"No."

"What about with Gabby? You ever see her get out of a car that looked like this?"

She thought for a moment. "Gabby got a ride one time, in the rain, but I didn't see the car."

"Was it a ride share?" Danica asked. "Like Uber or Lyft?"

"She wouldn't pay for those. Couldn't afford to."

"But you said before she would never get into a stranger's vehicle?"

"That's right. She was wise that way."

Danica sat back on her haunches. "Who gave her the ride home, Miss Francine? Do you know?"

"I don't."

"A friend, maybe?" Devereaux asked.

"No. She just said she got a ride home 'cause of the rain. And when I asked her about it she kind of snapped at me. Said, 'It was safe, Nana, I know what I'm doing.' And that was it."

Devereaux scrubbed his face. Ms. Broussard hadn't mentioned this before when asked.

"That was the one and only time she got a ride home," she said, staring off into the distance. She looked to Danica.

"You think that was him? The man that took her?"

"I'm not sure, Miss Francine."

"If it was him, why didn't he just take her that time?"

"I don't know."

"You go," she said, touching Danica on the forearm. "You go and you find him. The both of you."

Danica took the book and photo from her and straightened. "We will," Danica said, meaning it. They left the house and Devereaux kept eyeing her on their way to the car.

"What?" she finally asked.

He shook his head. "You," he said.

"What about me?"

"Making promises again."

She opened the car door and climbed inside alongside him. She buckled her seat belt and looked him dead in the eye.

"This one, I'm gonna make damn sure I keep."

CHAPTER THIRTY-EIGHT

*H*e huddled beneath the covers and switched on the flashlight, illuminating his favorite book. A creaking noise came from the hallway. He stilled, covering the light with his palm. His heart raced as he listened.

Nothing.

He exhaled and uncovered the flashlight. His belly fluttered with excitement as he read. The little hummingbird, lost and alone, after days of searching, finally found its way home. Not the home it had, but a new home. A better home.

He flipped back to the first page to read the book again. He wanted so badly to be that hummingbird. To find his way to a new home. A better home. Where he'd be safe and loved and live happily ever after. That would be his Flying Home.

He gripped the book tighter, sounding the words out softly as he read. First the hummingbird was lost and sad. And then the other birds were mean to him. Then—

He heard it again. A creaking. He covered the flashlight and listened with his heart pounding in his ears.

Silence.

But he didn't dare move. He exhaled, trying to breathe as quietly as he could. Was it just the wind? Or the old house moaning in the middle of the night? That happened sometimes. But no, this sounded like her.

Grandmother.

He closed his eyes, saying a silent prayer.

And just as he opened them to uncover his flashlight, the covers were ripped off of him and strewn aside.

He shrieked as his grandmother flicked on his bedside light and snatched his book from his hands.

"Look at you!" she said. "Sneaking around in the middle of night. To what? To read? To read this little baby book?" She threw the book against the wall, and he jerked at the noise it made. Tears streamed down his face and he hugged his knees up to his chest, terrified.

"Get up," she said, ripping the rest of the bed clothes off of the bed. She grabbed him by the wrist and yanked him off the bed. "You want to read your little baby book? You want to stay up late past your bedtime? Then you can stay up, you little twerp. Come on." She pulled him down the hall into the kitchen. "On your knees, baby," she said.

He fell to his knees and wept. She smacked him upside the head. "Quiet." She left him to open the broom closet where she retrieved the bucket and brushes used to scrub the floor. She tossed them to him, but he wasn't quick enough to catch them. Instead they hit him in the head and chest. He continued to cry.

"Please, Grandmother," he said.

She stood over him with her hands on her hips. "Please, what? Get you some water? I can do that." She snatched the bucket and went to the sink. She filled it with water and brought it back to him steaming. It sloshed as she dropped it to the floor. "There. Get busy."

He trembled as he took a brush in his hand and hesitantly dipped it in the water.

"Get it good and wet," she said.

"But it's hot," he cried.

"It's hot," she said, mimicking him. "Baby."

He dipped the brush in again, but the water was so hot his hand stung and reddened.

She kicked the bucket, startling him. "You going to continue being a baby? Alright. You go ahead." She strode back down the hallway and returned with Flying Home in her hands.

"What—what are you gonna do?" he asked.

She walked to the sink again and grabbed the matchbox over the windowsill.

"No," he said, heart hammering. "No, please, Grandmother."

She struck a match and held the flame up for him to see. A wicked grin crawled across her face. She lifted the book and lit the bottom of the pages.

"No!" He stumbled to his feet and ran to her, crying. "Please, no!"

She laughed as she held the burning book over the sink. "Say good-bye. Good-bye, little baby book. Good-bye, little hummingbird."

He sat straight up on the couch and rubbed his face. Sweat dampened his skin despite the chill in the air. "Grandmother," he whispered as he tried to shake her from his mind.

He glanced at his watch, hoping it was time. He needed something to distract from the nightmare.

He hurried down the hall to the bathroom. There, he turned on the bath facet and switched on the shower. He stripped and stepped inside the tub. He adjusted the water to cold, needing to shock his system in order to better wake. The chill took his breath away, but it felt refreshing and satisfying. Quickly, he scrubbed his skin with Irish Spring and rinsed. Then he washed and rinsed his hair and climbed from the tub. He dried as he walked to the bedroom to put on his clothes. After pulling on his boxers and socks, he opened the closet and retrieved a freshly pressed pair of slacks and a crisp button-down shirt. Then he combed his hair in the mirror and dabbed on his favorite cologne.

He smiled at his reflection. Now he was ready.

"Question is, are you ready for me, Lyra Aarden?"

CHAPTER THIRTY-NINE

Lyra ran down the dirt road that bisected the Sugar Mill Farm cane field. After turning around at the police barrier, she checked her Fitbit, and increased her speed. She needed to push herself more. Her knee was feeling better, so she really needed to build up her endurance.

She pushed harder and concentrated on the sound of her sneakers crunching the dirt. Thunder cracked in the near distance.

That was another reason why she needed to increase her pace. She needed to beat this oncoming storm.

Louie had said she'd never beat the rain, but she'd argued with him, convinced she could get in a good run before the onslaught. She had so much excited energy in knowing that Danny was coming for dinner that she really needed do something to calm it. A good run was the perfect solution.

She looked up at the sky as rain began to fall.

"Shit."

She ran harder. The rain seemed to follow suit and fell harder. She was in for it now.

She was halfway back down the dirt road when thunder cracked again over head. It was so loud it frightened her, and she jerked and nearly fell, hurting her knee.

"Fuck me," she said. "No, no, no." She tried walking but it hurt like hell.

She knelt with her hand on her knee. "Come on, don't do this to me. Not now."

But it was no use. Her knee was toast.

She instinctively searched her arm for her phone where she had it strapped.

She called Louie, knowing he would give her an earful about trying to run. But the phone rang and rang and finally went to voice mail. Quickly, she texted him, asking for him to come pick her up from Sugar Mill Farm. Then she started the trek home again, limping badly.

She was soaked by the time she reached the main road. She wiped the pouring rain from her face and searched for oncoming cars. Hopefully, Louie had read her message and was on his way. But there was only one car on the road, and it wasn't Louie's. She checked her watch again, worried about having enough time to clean up before Danny arrived. The car slowed as it pulled up from behind, causing her to glance up from her watch. The passenger window eased down and a man leaned over.

"Looks like you could use a ride," he said with a smile.

She rested against the door as she trembled from the cold rain.

"Yeah?" she said.

"Of course," he said. "Hop on in."

She glanced back up the road. No sign of Louie. She looked back to the man in the car, considering his offer. But then she shook her head, recalling all the warnings she'd heard from Danny and her brother.

"Thanks, but no. My brother is on his way to get me."

"You sure?" he said as he slowly accelerated alongside her slow and painful stride.

"I'm sure," she said.

He frowned but gave her a wave. Then the vehicle stopped abruptly, turned around, and drove off, leaving her all alone in the rain. She wondered briefly why he'd turned around to go in the opposite direction, but soon refocused on trying to walk with her hurt knee.

She checked her phone and looked for a response from Louie.

Nothing.

She kept walking, the pain growing more intense. She worried she'd really done it this time, possibly reinjuring it completely. She checked her watch again. At this rate she'd never make it home in time to be ready for Danny. She imagined the girls there waiting for her to return so they could start cooking the spaghetti together. Her heart ached, and she hoped Louie would come so the girls wouldn't be let down.

She heard a car coming from behind. She turned and saw the same vehicle coming toward her again. Startled, she picked up her pace, wincing from the pain. The car kept coming, accelerating. Her eyes grew wide as he sped right for her. She screamed as she tried to run. But her knee gave out and she went down. Hard.

Panicked, she scrambled, trying to regain her footing. But it was no use. The man was on her in seconds, wielding a tire iron over his head. She turned to scramble again, clinging at the wet grass on all fours. Then she felt the impact. A sharp, heavy blow to her head.

Everything went black.

When she opened her eyes again, she grabbed the back of her head and felt something warm. She brought her hand to her face and saw that it was blood. Her skull throbbed and she tried to sit up. She realized she was in the back of a car. The man she recognized from the road was driving, staring straight ahead.

The man. The man. *The* man.

Fuck.

He had her. The killer had gotten her.

She forced herself to sit up and reached for the door handle. There wasn't one. She touched the window, looking outside as the cane farm sped past in a near blur. Then, another car drove past them. It was Louie.

"Louie!"

She called his name over and over and pounded on the window. But he couldn't hear her and didn't see her. She stared at his car through the back glass, seeing his form, along with the little heads of the girls in the back.

Tears came.

She turned to face the man.

"Let me go!" she said.

But he didn't respond.

"You hear me? Let me go!"

Again, no response. But this time, he glanced at her in the rearview mirror. The rain had slowed, sprinkling lightly upon the windshield. The seeking sunlight glinted off something hanging from the mirror.

She tried to focus on it, but she had trouble. Her body felt very heavy. Extremely heavy. And she was having trouble keeping her eyes open.

"What…" She couldn't even finish her sentence.

She trained her eyes on the shimmering charm hanging from the mirror as she tried to hold herself up. And as her eyes began to close again, she was able to see what it was.

Fear bloomed throughout her chest.

There, hanging from the mirror, was a necklace, with a tiny silver hummingbird dancing in the sunlight.

Then everything went black once again.

CHAPTER FORTY

The rain had stopped completely by the time Danica pulled her vehicle alongside the Aarden house. She gave herself a once-over in the mirror, silently cursing herself for not leaving the station in enough time to go home and shower and change. But she'd been so engrossed with the security footage from the businesses on State Street that she'd lost track of time. And she hadn't wanted to be late for dinner.

Thankfully, her time studying the footage had possibly paid off. She'd found the suspicious vehicle on two other bits of footage. While she hadn't been able to make out the writing on the side, she'd been able to send the footage of the vehicle to her lab, asking if they could clean the images up.

She hadn't heard back yet, but she was anxious to know what they'd find, if anything.

She flipped up her vanity mirror and exited the car to walk up to the front door. She'd considered bringing wine, but then had thought better of it since they were spending time with Lyra's nieces. And there was also the fact that she was no longer drinking. So instead, she'd brought dessert. A peanut butter pie. She'd remembered how much the girls had liked the peanut butter cups on Halloween. They'd even fought over them.

She smiled as she recalled how much fun she'd had with the Aarden family that evening. She hadn't spoken much with Lyra's father, but her mother had been very kind and friendly. So had her brother. And the girls? Well, they had been the most fun of all.

She rang the bell and waited for an answer. She didn't have to wait long. The door was yanked open almost immediately, tiny little faces coming into view as the girls hopped up and down with excitement.

"Danny!"

"Danny's here!"

Daphne motioned for her to come inside, while Haley yelled again.

"Daddy, Danny's here!"

Danica said hello and laughed as the girls tugged her farther inside the house.

"We don't have dinner ready," Daphne said.

"Yeah," Haley said. "That's cuz we can't find Auntie Lyra."

"What?" Danny said.

She looked over at Louie as he entered the room. The look on his face was one of grave concern and Danny immediately stiffened.

"What's wrong?" she said.

"Lyra went out for a run and then texted that she needed a ride. She'd hurt her knee and it was raining. We went to get her, but we couldn't find her. Not anywhere along her route."

Danny swallowed the rising ball of burning coal in her throat. "You checked the cane farm?"

"Everywhere."

She felt the blood drain from her face.

"I was just getting ready to call you," he said. "We got home just a few minutes ago."

"How long ago did she text?" Danny said, already retrieving her phone.

"Half an hour."

She dialed Devereaux as she headed back toward the front door. When he answered, she relayed the news to him and began to coordinate a search. She hung up, not feeling any better. Her heart was racing so hard she felt sick.

She turned to face Louie. "Stay here in case she shows up. If she calls or texts, call me right away."

"Okay."

"You're leaving?" Haley asked.

Danica knelt and placed her hands on the girls' shoulders, looking them both in eye.

"I'm going to go find your auntie," she said. "Okay?"

"And we'll eat spaghetti when we find her?"

"Sure thing," she said, touching Haley's little cheek. "You two stay here with your daddy and keep an eye out for Auntie Lyra, okay?"

They nodded and Danica gave Louie one last concerned look before she headed out the door.

❖

Danica sped away from the Aarden house and drove back toward the main road that ran alongside Sugar Mill Farm. She slowed when she turned onto it, creeping along, searching for Lyra or clues as to where she may have gone.

Realizing that she couldn't see very well due to the high grass, she pulled off the road and climbed from her car. Carefully, she began walking along the side of the road, where she saw a trail of trampled grass. She walked alongside the trail, not wanting to disturb any evidence.

In the distance, thunder rumbled as if it was exhausted from the storm. One single car drove by as she walked the shoulder, but other than that, it was quiet.

"Come on, Lyra, where are you?"

She paused as her eyes homed in on something. Slowly, she approached. She knelt as she came upon the object.

It was a phone.

She recognized it at once as being Lyra's. She choked up as she realized what this meant. She covered her mouth as she stood.

Someone had taken her.

Just then Devereaux pulled up and parked behind her car. He got out and sauntered up to her. She was doing her very best not to completely lose it.

"What's up?" he said, catching her demeanor.

She pointed back to the phone. He walked up to it and nudged it with a pen.

"It's hers?" he asked.

Danica nodded.

"Fuck," he said, looking up and down the road.

She brought her phone to her ear and made several phone calls, alerting the department to Lyra's disappearance. Then she made one last call, this one to Louie, and made another promise, one she was determined like hell to keep.

CHAPTER FORTY-ONE

Eleanor settled down with her glass of wine and tried to relax. The day had been hectic, with her working numerous new cases as well as the Sugar Mill Farm caseload. Things were moving fast now as the DNA results were beginning to come in. They might know who the remains belonged to, but they still didn't have any good leads on the killer. A realization that had been weighing on her a lot as of late. She wanted to help more with the case, help Danny try to solve it, or at the very least, brainstorm with her. But the case belonged to the police. Her part was now nearly finished.

She sipped her wine as she thought about Danny. She hadn't seen her this week at all. And the last time she had seen her things had been a bit tense. She wanted to help her, but it was still difficult to get past the Lyra problem. Danny had been friendly with her, encouraging her to talk to her, but Eleanor had had trouble. She was still a little jealous. So, she hadn't tried or asked if she could help.

While she wasn't positive they were still seeing each other, she suspected as much. Danny was looking a little better, so she wasn't holed up at home in bed as much, and the way she was trying so hard to get Eleanor to talk to her, made her suspect that she was dating Lyra. Danny always did have a guilty conscience.

She sighed as Huck jumped onto her lap and began his nightly ritual of crossing back and forth on her, wanting to be petted. He raised his rear in the air in appreciation as she scratched along his back.

"At least I have you," she said. "Right, bud?" He rubbed his face against her hand.

She took another sip of her wine and then set it on the coffee table as her phone rang. She answered it with a grimace, not wanting to talk to anyone at the moment.

"Hello," she said, sitting back and crossing her legs. She bobbed her bare foot, glad to be out of her square pumps.

"El," Danny said.

Eleanor could hear other voices in the background, along with vehicles and what sounded like a helicopter. Something was going on. She tensed.

"It's Lyra," Danny said hurriedly. "She's missing."

"Missing?" She touched her throat.

"Gone. Someone has taken her."

Eleanor shooed Huck from her lap and stood. "What do you mean? Are you sure?"

"Almost positive. She went out for a run and vanished. We found her phone on the side of the road. And—shit—hang on."

More voices came and the connection muffled. Then Danny was back on.

"We just found her Fitbit. About thirty yards down from her phone."

"Oh, God."

"He's got her, El. I just know it. And I—" she broke off and Eleanor heard her voice hitch.

"I'm on my way," she said as she hurried into her bedroom to grab her boots and a jacket. "Where are you?"

"Right outside the Sugar Mill Farm cane field. El?"

"Yes?"

"I'm scared. For the first time since I was a kid, I'm really scared."

Eleanor paused and ran her hand through her hair as she stood next to her bed. "I know, Danny. I am too."

All feelings of jealousy and resentment left Eleanor the second she pulled up and got a good look at Danny. Her face was drawn and her eyes large and red rimmed, filled to the brim with deep concern and fear. Eleanor had never seen her look like this.

"Any news?" Eleanor asked as she hurried up to her. Red and blue lights reflected off her face as she stared off into the cane field.

"Nothing yet."

Eleanor touched her arm. "We'll find her, Danny. We will."

She choked up. "I'm so sorry, Eleanor."

"Sorry? For what, sweetie?"

"For Lyra, the whole thing. I'm sorry if I hurt you. I just—I really care about her. And I can't bear to think of anything happening to her."

"You don't owe me an apology. You feel the way you feel. And I'm okay. I'm going to be okay." She squeezed her arm. "Alright?"

Danny exhaled. "Yeah."

"Now, let's find Lyra."

Overhead, a helicopter thudded, searching the area behind the cane field and beyond. Darkness was falling. They had little time before they lost the light.

"She's out there. In the dark. With him," Danny said.

"She's smart," Eleanor said. "She'll be okay. She'll find a way to survive."

Danny nodded. "You're right." She glanced beyond Eleanor and swallowed. "Lyra's folks are here. They're a mess. I told them to go stay with Louie, but they are insisting on helping."

"They probably want to stay busy. Helps with the nerves."

"I should go talk to them, but I feel so god damned responsible."

"You didn't do anything wrong."

"I should've had him by now."

"Danny—"

But Danny's phone rang from her hip. She quickly answered and Eleanor waited.

The conversation was brief. And when Danny hung up, her face was flushed with determination.

"Devereaux!"

Devereaux came quickly. "Yeah, what's up?"

"The lab just called. They were able to digitally enhance the lettering on the side of that suspicious car. It's a god damned cab company. The mother fucker drives a cab."

CHAPTER FORTY-TWO

M usic.
        Strange and slow and far away.
As if she were submerged in water.
Lyra blinked. Her eyes were slow to open. She felt heavy.
Everything felt heavy.
Pale light stung her eyes, but she forced herself to focus.
Window. With curtains.
Wall.
She shifted her gaze.
Dresser. Doorway.
She focused on herself.
She was flat. On a bed.
Couldn't move.
She looked to her left.
Wrist tied with a rope.
Same with the right.
Then she remembered.
He had her.
And her gut burned. Clenched. Churned.
She felt sick.
Bile rose.
"He—" But her voice was weak. Her mouth dry.
She tried again. "Help!" But it wasn't loud enough. She knew it and
tears filled her eyes.
In the near distance, she heard a dog bark. It bayed. Others joined
in.

"Help!"

She yanked on her binds, but all it did was hurt. Her arms and shoulders ached from being stretched for who knew how long. She went limp and waited as movement came from beyond the doorway.

A head peeked into the room.

It was him. And he looked plainer than he did before. Just an average guy, existing amongst the masses. An average guy who was also a cold-blooded killer.

"Well, hello, lovely," he said as he entered the room. He was denim clad with a pressed collared shirt. His hair was neatly combed back, and he smelled like his room. Like cheap cologne. It made her gag.

"Oh, no, are we feeling sick?" He sat on the side of the bed and held up a bin. She turned her head. She wanted nothing from him with the exception of her freedom, which she knew she would never get.

"Okay," he said. "Suit yourself." He removed the quilt that was covering her and folded it neatly to place on the dresser. "Can't have you getting sick on Grandmother's quilt, now can we?"

"Grandmother?" Was there someone else there? A woman? Could she help?

He chuckled and returned to the bed. "She's long gone," he said. "But she's still with me every day." He glanced around. "Can you feel her? She's all around." He touched her nose. "And boy, would she like you. You're just the type she'd want for me. You just don't know it yet."

Lyra swallowed. She didn't like the sound of that. It sounded like he wanted her to stick around. Forever.

"Let me go," she said as calmly as she could. "Please. My family. They're worried, I know they are. Please. I won't tell. Won't tell a soul."

He gently stroked her cheek and she fought pulling away. "Now, now. Just relax. You're going to be here for a long time. You and me together." He smiled. "Just the two of us. You'll like that, won't you? I'll cook for you, clean, dance with you, bring you gifts. Doesn't that sound nice?"

Lyra recalled Danny's words about how the killer lived out a fantasy with his victims. As disgusted as she was with the man, she forced herself to smile in return. "It sounds very nice."

His eyes grew wide. He was obviously surprised with her readily agreeing with him.

"Well, well, well. You're just a ray of sunshine, aren't you? I knew you were the one. I just knew it." He slapped his hands on his thighs and stood. "And to celebrate, I'm going to go make us a breakfast fit for a king." He headed for the door.

"Can you—please—untie me? I want to come with."

He smiled again. "In due time, lovely. In due time."

He left her and Lyra yanked on her binds again. They didn't give an inch.

She stared out at the pale dawn and prayed. Prayed that Danny would find her before she ended up in the sugarcane field at Sugar Mill Farm.

CHAPTER FORTY-THREE

What the hell do you mean no one has any record of this cab company?" Danica motioned like she was going to throw her phone down but then thought better of it.

"There's no record," Dennis Ing said. "It doesn't exist."

"I know it fucking exists, Dennis because I'm looking at it in the photo you sent me. It says right fucking there, Hummingbird Cabs."

"Right. But the name is a front. So is the listed phone number. We think this lettering on the vehicle is really a magnetic sign. You can stick them to your car and remove them whenever you want."

Danica closed her eyes. "So, what you're saying is we got nothing?"

"We're working diligently on trying to get some of the license plate."

"Thanks," she said and ended the call. "Fuck."

She took a few steps near the swamp and then stopped. Around her, divers and cops and volunteers were searching the nearby pond for Lyra. She knew in her gut that she wouldn't be found. Not yet. And not there. But her sergeant was going over her head now. Pulling out all the stops. There was nothing she could do about it.

Or was there?

She dialed some numbers on her phone and put it back to her ear. They needed to ask the community for help. See if anyone recognized the vehicle or Hummingbird Cabs. She about threw her phone again when the deputy told her the request for help from the community would have to go through the sergeant first. She killed the call before he could say more.

"This is bullshit," Devereaux said as he walked up to her. "She ain't here."

"Tell me about it," Danica said. She headed for her vehicle, fed up with the meaningless search. "This SOB has her at a house somewhere. We know that from Tina Givens. Why won't anyone listen to me?"

"They're desperate. The deputy superintendent is pissed at the lack of progress and the community is up in arms about it. So he's saving face. Putting on these big searches. Makes the public feel like we're doing something. Makes them feel safer."

"But they're not safer. He's still out there. And he has Lyra."

"What can we do? Search every shotgun house in the county?"

"It's better than this," she said, looking around.

They climbed in the car and Danica started it up and put it in drive. They sped away from the swamp toward the only hope they had.

CHAPTER FORTY-FOUR

Eleanor hadn't slept. And she was pretty sure Danny hadn't either. Nor had most of the town. Lyra Aarden was missing and presumed kidnapped. Everyone was worried, and the search had been all over the local news.

She climbed in her car, fresh from a shower but hardly fresh in mind, and drove into town. She had no idea where Danny was, she wasn't answering her phone, so she was on her own. The first thing she needed to do was to grab some coffee. And rather than waiting till she got closer to Danny's station, she decided to head to the local café.

The parking lot was full at Miss Honey's Café so she had to park by the hardware store and walk. It was a beautiful Saturday morning, and if someone didn't know any better, they'd say it was an ideal day for early winter. But she knew better, and by the hushed quiet along Main Street, she reckoned everyone else did as well.

The bell on the door clanged as she entered the small café. The two-seated tables, like the parking lot, were full. When she entered, folks stopped their idle chitchat and looked up at her.

"Morning," she said, feeling uncomfortable. She was used to the stares and the silence. Most folks didn't know what to say or how to act around her. She was just the "bone whisperer." And that, for reasons she understood but disagreed with, was just the way things were. People feared what they didn't understand. And she was not understood.

"Any word, Doc?" someone asked from a table near the wall in the back.

"No," she said. "Sorry." The hush remained for a few more minutes and then, when she failed to offer more, they began their chitchat again.

Eleanor wove her way to the front counter where she waited in line. A young college student, one she recognized but whose name she couldn't remember, helped her.

"What can I get for you, Dr. Stafford?"

"I'll have my usual," she said. And then blinked when the young woman looked at her cluelessly.

"Oh, I forgot I'm not at the university café." She laughed at herself and then stopped as she remembered the mood of the room. "I'll have a praline latte, please."

"Sure thing. Coming right up."

She waited patiently for her coffee and tried texting Danny again, asking if she wanted one. But she got no response.

The young woman, whose name tag said Amy, brought her her drink. "Here you go, Doc."

Eleanor handed over her debit card, but the girl waved her off. "It's on the house."

Eleanor hesitated, confused for a moment. But then said, "Okay, thank you."

"No problem," she said. She glanced around like she was about to share a secret. "Actually, can I talk to you for a second? Maybe outside?"

Eleanor grew alarmed. She had no idea what the young woman could possibly want to talk to her about. "Okay, sure."

Amy came out from behind the counter, and they walked outside. They headed around the side of the building where there were no people. When they faced each other, Amy sighed.

"So, you're like really smart, right?"

Eleanor blinked again. "I suppose."

"And you work with, like, the police and stuff?"

"I do."

"Well, I need to tell you something. I've told my boss and some other people, but they keep telling me that my imagination is running wild and that my head is always in the clouds and—"

"What did you have to tell me?"

She cleared her throat. "Right. So, about a week ago this guy comes into the café. No one special, just some guy. I didn't know him, and he didn't know me. But he starts acting really flirty, you know? Asks me for my number. Anyway, I tell him no and he gets pissed. Says I don't have to be a bitch about it. Really caught me off guard."

She took a deep breath and placed her hands on her hips. "He leaves, right? So, I shake it off and figure he's just an asshole. But then later on, I see him again. He's outside the café at the newspaper stand. And get this. He opens it up and takes out the whole stack of papers."

Eleanor waited.

"And guess what the headline was that day?"

"I don't know."

"It was about the women being identified out at Sugar Mill Farm. I know because I saw the paper that day. The customers always leave them at the tables."

Eleanor studied her, considering what she'd just said.

"It's weird, right? I mean, the guy really creeped me out and overreacts, and then he goes and takes all the papers? Why? I think it's because he wanted them. Like as a keepsake. Because of the headline. Because he's the, you know, guy."

Eleanor held up her palm. "Okay, slow down."

"You believe me, don't you?"

"Yes. I believe you, Amy."

"And you think it's weird, right?"

"It is weird. But let's not get ahead of ourselves."

She sighed again. And Eleanor tried to calm her nerves.

"You said you didn't recognize him?"

"No. I'd never seen him before."

"Did you get anything else? Maybe a credit card receipt from his order? Did you get his name?"

"No. But I got this." She reached in her back pocket and pulled out a paper napkin.

"What is it?"

"His license plate number."

Eleanor took it and smiled. She had another phone call to make. This time, she really needed Danny to answer.

CHAPTER FORTY-FIVE

I don't want you to bother her. She's been through enough," Oliver Givens said, as he stood guard at his front door.

"Please, Mr. Givens. It's vital we talk to her. Another woman is missing and time is running out."

He pushed out a breath. "Fine." He moved aside and Danica and Devereaux entered the small home. Oliver brought up the rear. "Have a seat. I'll go get her."

Danica and Devereaux sat on the couch and waited. Mrs. Givens was nowhere to be seen. Oliver returned with a very weak looking Tina wearing a pink terrycloth bathrobe and worn slippers. She eased down into the wingback chair that her mother usually favored.

"Ms. Givens, good morning," Danica started. "We really appreciate you seeing us."

She got herself settled and stared straight at them but said nothing. Her eyes were glossy but clear, but there were significant dark circles beneath them. She hugged herself as if she were cold.

"How are you feeling?" Devereaux asked.

Her gaze shifted to the window. "I've been better," she said.

"It's going to take some time," Danica said. "To heal."

Tina pressed her lips together. "Yeah."

"Ms. Givens, we're here because we need your help," Danica said.

There was silence before the young woman spoke again. "He's got another one," she said. "I knew he would."

Danica glanced at Devereaux. "What do you mean by that?" Danica asked.

She kept looking out the window. "He…he's looking for the perfect woman. The perfect woman for him."

"You mean as a partner?" Devereaux asked.

She looked at him. "As a wife."

Danica felt queasy, thinking of what the man might be doing to Lyra. Tina continued.

"I wasn't the one. I think because I fought him too much. Didn't do what he wanted."

"What did he want?" She was almost afraid to ask.

"He wanted me to eat, to bathe, to dance with him. Tell him I loved him and would never leave him." She swallowed and studied her hands. "But I couldn't bring myself to do it. So he would get angry."

Danica's heart skipped a beat as it accelerated. *Please let Lyra be okay.*

"Ms. Givens," Danica said. "Is there anything else you can tell us? Anything at all that might help us catch him?"

She seemed to think for a moment. "I don't know."

"Would it help to know that he drove a cab? Is that how he tried to pick you up?"

She looked up at Danica. "Hummingbird," she said as if she'd just remembered. "Yes. It said that on the side of his car." She shook her head. "But I told him no. I didn't trust him. He was too eager to get me to accept the ride. He kept bothering me so I—" She swallowed again. "I walked away. And the next thing I knew, he had hit me on the head, and everything went dark."

She touched the back of her head. "I can still feel the lump."

"Did you see his name? Did he have it displayed in his car somewhere? Or maybe on some mail, in his house?"

"I'm sorry, I didn't. He must've kept stuff like that put away."

"Do you think you're well enough now to meet with the department sketch artist?" Devereaux asked. "So we can get a sketch of the suspect?"

She nodded. "I can try."

"Thank you," Danica said. She and Devereaux stood. "You don't by chance remember the neighborhood you were in, do you?"

She shook her head. "No. When we left that last night, it was dark and I was drugged. Not much made sense."

Danica slipped her notebook back in her pocket. "Okay, then. Thank you again." She crossed to her. "If you can think of anything, please call." She handed her her card and she and Devereaux exited the house.

"We got zilch," he said.

Danica was about to agree with him when her phone rang.

She saw that it was Eleanor and answered.

"Danny, thank God," she breathed. "I've been trying to reach you."

"What's going on?"

"I think I have something for you. A lead."

"Okay. Shoot."

She and Devereaux slid into the car.

"I was at Miss Honey's Café this morning and the young woman who works there told me about a strange encounter she had with a man a few days ago. The man hit on her and when she declined, he got upset. Called her a bitch. Then, sometime later she saw him take all the newspapers out of the newspaper stand."

"Yes, and?"

"The headline that day was about the bodies being identified at Sugar Mill Farm. And he took all of them. Even gave her a creepy grin when he saw her watching him."

Danica rubbed her brow. "Is that it?"

"Yes, that's it. Oh. Wait. She got his license plate number, too."'

Danica fought sighing. It wasn't much of a lead. A man is a jerk and steals newspapers. Hardly something to get excited about.

"Did she say what kind of car he drives?"

"No. And I didn't think to ask. Look, Danny this could be something. I think you should at least check it out."

Danica retrieved her notebook and pen. She wrote down the license number.

"Got it," she said.

"Are you going to check it out?"

"Eventually."

"Lyra doesn't have much time. And the department's wasting that time by searching all the rural areas."

"I'm well aware."

"Is your sergeant not listening to you?"

"Not at the moment, no."

"Well, what can I do? I feel so helpless."

"You're doing more than enough," Danica said. "I'll call you back about the license plate, okay?"

"Okay. Good luck, Danny."

"Thanks. We're gonna need it."

She ended the call and looked over at Devereaux. It was obvious he'd heard at least some of the conversation.

"You gonna run it?" he asked.

She tore the paper out of the notebook and handed it to him. "You do it. I'll be right back."

She walked back up to Tina's front door and knocked. This time Tina answered. "Yes?"

"Do you know if this man got the newspaper delivered to his house or not?"

"Oh, yes. He did. He used to wait anxiously for it sometimes."

"So, he wouldn't have a need to steal papers from a stand?"

She cocked her head. "He might. He would cut out all articles about the crime and put them on his refrigerator."

Danica heated as excitement began to bloom within. Devereaux called out to her from the car. She turned to look at him.

"We got something," he said.

Danica looked back to Tina. "Just a moment." She crossed the lawn to the car. "What is it?" she asked as she knelt to look into the vehicle.

"Son of bitch drives a yellow Chevy Caprice. His name is Donald Allen Greer." He turned the monitor toward her so she could see his photo.

Danica looked back at Tina. "Can you come over here for a second? We've got something we need you to look at."

Slowly, Tina walked down the porch steps and crossed the lawn. Danica moved aside so she could peer into the car.

"Do you recognize this man?"

Tina knelt and peered in at the photo. She sucked in a quick breath and backed away from the car. She tripped over herself and fell onto the grass, crawling backward to get away.

"No," she let out, her face contorting in fear. "No, no, no."

Danica hurried after her. "It's okay," she said, trying to help her up. "He's not here. You're safe now."

Tina stopped crawling. She allowed Danica to help her up. She buried her face in Danica's shoulder. Danica looked to Devereaux who was standing outside the vehicle, looking on with great concern.

They had him. They finally had their man.

CHAPTER FORTY-SIX

I'm sorry, I can't eat anymore," Lyra said as she forced down some of the bacon, lettuce, and tomato sandwich.

The man stopped chewing his own bite and swallowed. "You need to eat, my lovely," he said. "Try another bite."

She lifted the sandwich with a shaky hand. It was nearing midday, and she was still feeling the effects of whatever he'd drugged her with. Her entire body felt heavy, as if she were draped in a lead blanket.

She took another bite and forced herself to chew. She'd already had a big breakfast, the one that he'd promised. And now they were eating again. The man enjoyed cooking for her, that was more than obvious.

She wondered how he stayed so slim.

She chewed her food and studied him cautiously, careful not to seem too obvious. He had a slim to athletic build, dirty brown hair, light blue eyes, and he dressed impeccably, with finely pressed clothes. Even his jeans had a crease down the legs. His home was equally as immaculate. The wood floors shone as if they'd been recently polished, along with the furniture. The rugs were old but clean, the kitchen sparkling. He cleaned up after himself as soon as they were finished eating.

He was a very tidy individual. She wondered what he would do if something were out of place. She didn't want to find out.

So, she was compliant. She bathed as he requested. Though, that had been the toughest thing of all. He'd insisted on sitting on the commode and watching, even insisting on washing her hair for her. The whole thing gave her the serious creeps, but she knew in her mind that's what she had to do to survive.

She had to do what he wanted.

He caught her looking and he smiled at her, sandwich in hand.

"Do you like it?" he asked, referring to the food.

"Mm-hm." She was still pretending to chew. Her stomach just couldn't take much more. The drugs had left her nauseous and so had the man and his requests. She didn't know how much more she could take without the risk of throwing up. Then what would he do when she'd messed up his shiny floor?

She sipped the glass of milk he'd provided.

Ugh.

It didn't help.

He took another bite and happily chewed. "After lunch, I thought we'd read some."

"Read?"

"My favorite book. It's called *Flying Home*."

She felt herself pale. He still read a children's book? And *that* particular book? Things were beginning to make sense.

"My grandmother wouldn't ever let me read it. But it's a great book. About a little bird who finds his way to a new home."

"Is that what you wanted? To find a new home?"

He blinked at her and set down his sandwich.

"I have a home," he said. "Can't you see it?" He motioned to the house.

"But is it the home you wanted?"

"It is now. With you." He smiled again.

"And without your grandmother?"

He frowned. She'd hit a nerve.

"You don't get to ask me questions," he said sternly. "Not yet."

She looked back down at her food. He was getting upset. But she just couldn't eat anymore.

She glanced around the room. Her gaze fell upon the fridge. She'd noticed it before. It was covered with newspaper clippings about the murders at Sugar Mill Farm. He had more covering the walls in the living room, behind the sofa and covering the window. He had them all over it seemed.

The neighbor's dogs began to bay. He straightened, ball of food still in his cheek. He turned to try to see out the kitchen window. The dogs grew louder. He stood and looked out the window. He returned to his seat at the table.

"Dumb dogs," he said. "Barking at nothing."

But they didn't stop. They only grew more excited.

He swallowed his food and stood. The hair on the back of her neck stood up as she saw the angry look come across his face.

"Something's up," he said.

"It's probably nothing." But she hoped, in her heart, that it was Danny. That she'd found her and was coming to save her. It was wishful thinking, but she should still try to distract him. He returned from down the hallway with a rifle.

"You stay back," he said, heading for the kitchen door.

"It's probably nothing," she tried again. "Just crazy dogs. I have one and he barks and barks at nothing."

He turned from glancing out the window on the door. His back was flat against the wall. "You don't have a dog," he said.

She shook, but not from the cold. How long had he been watching her? She looked at the picture of her on the fridge. How long indeed.

"So, stop your lying," he said. He snuck another look out the window.

"No one is there," she said.

But he snapped at her. "Shut up! Just shut up, you!"

She clamped her mouth shut but eased backward down the hallway. It was difficult to stand, her body felt heavy, her head woozy. But she continued on, one small step at a time.

She closed her eyes as the dogs continued to bay.

Please, let it be Danny.

CHAPTER FORTY-SEVEN

Is there any way to shut those damn dogs up?" Danica asked into her mic from her position against the house. She held her gun down in front of her, waiting for the right time for her team to make their move. Her bulletproof vest was strapped on tight, and she winced as one of her guys answered her in her ear.

"Negative. Too late now. Suspect is at the kitchen door, peeking out the window."

"Do you have a clear shot?"

"Negative."

"Do you see the victim?"

"Negative."

"Shit." She pressed herself tighter against the house.

Lawrence was beside her with his gun clasped tightly in his hands. Despite the cool weather, sweat beaded his brow.

"What's our next move?" he asked.

"We need to get a visual on Lyra. I'm going around the back."

She edged sideways along the side of the house until she reached Rita.

"See anything?" Danica asked.

"I haven't snuck a glance yet." She was referring to the back window, directly next to them.

Danica carefully moved around her, closer to the back window. She spoke into her mic.

"Is he still at the kitchen door?"

"Affirmative."

Danica looked to Rita. "I'm going to take a look."

"Be careful."

"Roger that." She bent her knees and walked under the window. Then, as slowly as she could, she rose up on her toes and looked inside. At first, she saw an empty bedroom. There were binds of rope on the bed frame. A dresser nestled against the wall. But then she saw movement from the entrance. She quickly ducked, her mind not yet registering who it was. As soon as she was safe, she realized it was Lyra.

She reported to the team. "Victim is in the back bedroom. I repeat. Victim is in the back bedroom."

"Suspect still at the door," came the reply.

"Think we can get her out through the window?" Rita asked.

Danica considered it. "It will be risky. But I don't think we have much choice." She spoke to her team once again.

"We're going to try to extract the victim from the back window. Distract the suspect up front."

"Copy that."

She and Rita waited for the word to make their move. It came a few minutes later.

"Sending someone to knock on the door. Get ready for the green light."

They heard a knocking sound in the distance. Danica's heart raced and her mind swam with possibilities. They wouldn't have much time to get Lyra to safety. They would have to move fast.

She closed her eyes and said a silent prayer, briefly thinking of Father O'Toole and how he often told her to pray. She hoped with all her might that the praying would work, because she couldn't bear the thought of losing Lyra.

"You okay?" Rita asked, causing her to open her eyes.

"Fine," she clipped.

Just then a voice came through her earpiece. "Go, go, go."

She and Rita scrambled to the window and peered inside. Lyra was still in the entryway, so Danica tapped lightly on the glass. Lyra turned and walked very slowly to the window. She looked clumsy, almost drunk, and Danica realized she was drugged.

She mouthed for her to open the window.

Lyra fumbled for the latch and then struggled to push upward. Danica and Rita helped her until it was up high enough for her to climb through.

"Come on," Danica whispered as she looked into her glazed eyes. "We'll help you out."

"I don't think I can," she slurred.

"Try."

She shook her head, her solemn eyes filled with terror. "He's coming. And he has a gun."

Danica gripped her arm and tried to coax her out.

But before Lyra could even try, a voice came from behind her.

CHAPTER FORTY-EIGHT

"What are you doing?" he asked.

Lyra faced him. "Nothing," she said.

He marched over to her with his rifle in hand and pressed himself against the wall. After a few seconds, he took a brief look out the window. Seemingly satisfied, he took her by the arm and tried to lead her away.

She refused, trying to stand her ground. "I feel sick," she said, doubling over as if she needed to vomit. "I need some fresh air."

He studied her long and hard. She swayed a little for added effect, though it wasn't too far of a stretch, considering her current condition.

"Fine," he finally said. "But sit on the bed. I don't want you falling."

He set his rifle against the dresser and ran a hand over his gelled hair. "Damn salesman, going door to door. He about got shot is what he did."

"I told you it was nothing."

"It wasn't nothing. It was a man. The dogs definitely alerted to him. But it was nothing to us," he said.

The curtains billowed in the breeze and Lyra longed to escape. But her body felt like lead. She knew it would be virtually impossible to escape quickly through the window on her own.

A long sigh came from the man. "I gotta take a piss." But instead of leaving the room for the bathroom, he tied her hands together, and then bound her feet. "I'll leave you in here with the window open, but only if you're tied." He cinched the binds tight and straightened. "You gonna behave?" He stroked her face and she clenched her jaw, trying her best not to pull away.

"Mm-hm."

He dropped his hand. "Okay, then."

He moved toward the doorway, gave her one last guarded look, and then disappeared.

She waited a moment for the sound of his stream to start. When it did, she stood and hopped carefully over to the window. She stilled again, and waited for her head to stop swimming so she could focus. Then, with all the strength she could muster, she leaned out the window, with her hands hanging down.

Danny was at her in an instant, grabbing her arms and pulling. Rita stood cover, her gun aimed at the window.

"Hurry," Lyra whispered. She heard footsteps. "He's coming."

"No!" he cried as he rushed to her. She felt him grab her feet and pull in the opposite direction. "You don't get to leave, you don't get to leave!"

Lyra shrieked in pain and fear as Danny pulled on her and the man wrenched her legs. The splintered ledge of the windowsill was scraping her abdomen and she felt like she was being torn in two.

"Harder," she said to Danny. "Hurry."

Danny grunted and yanked her harder, digging her heels into the ground. And then, the man let go and she was freed.

CHAPTER FORTY-NINE

Danica fell backward onto her rear while Lyra landed with a sickening thump. Danica scrambled to her feet and tried to grab Lyra and drag her away, but Donald Allen Greer was at the window in seconds. With a rifle pointed straight at her.

"Drop your weapon!" Rita shouted, then fired a shot, obviously unwilling to take any chances. Greer stumbled. But he was still able to fire a round, hitting Rita in the shoulder. She careened back, fell to the ground, and dropped her weapon. Danica fumbled to get hers, but not before another shot rang out. She was thrown backward as the bullet slammed into her chest.

"Danny!" Lyra let out.

Danica looked up and saw Greer lowering the gun toward her once again. She lifted her Glock and squeezed the trigger. Another shot followed coming from somewhere behind her. Greer blew backward but remained on his feet. She kept firing, unloading her weapon, until she saw him go down completely. Shots continued to fly from behind until she called a cease fire. Bullet holes peppered the house, black holes in the faded white clapboards. She sat up slowly, hand to her chest, empty gun still aimed at the open window.

Lyra was trying desperately to get to her, still bound by the ropes. Inside the house, Danica heard the team entering through the front. They called out as they cleared each room before finally reaching the bedroom.

"In here!" someone shouted. Her team huddled around what she presumed to be Greer. Then Lawrence leaned out the window.

"He's down," he said.

Danica nodded. She crawled to her knees and went to Lyra. "It's okay now. We've got him."

Lyra looked at her with heavy lidded eyes. Her mouth was slack, as well as her limbs. "You…okay?"

"I'm fine. The bullet hit the vest."

Lyra closed her eyes and began to cry. Danny pulled her close and held her while the soft sobs racked her body.

CHAPTER FIFTY

Donald Allen Greer was dead. Danny and her colleagues had killed him, and frankly, Eleanor was glad. She didn't want Lyra and Tina Givens to have to suffer through a trial. From what she'd heard, both women had suffered enough.

She slowed her car and pulled alongside Lyra's house. She sat for a moment before going in. She checked her hair and makeup in the vanity mirror, making sure she didn't look like she was trying too hard. After all, Lyra was absolutely taken now, and she was in the process of moving on. She was even considering dating again. At some point. Maybe. Yes, maybe.

She laughed at herself and climbed from her car. She walked up to the front door carrying a good bottle of merlot and some snickerdoodle treats for Lyra's nieces. She'd heard all about them from Danny and she couldn't wait to meet them.

She knocked softly on the door and then chuckled as she heard excited giggles.

The door opened and two little girls beamed up at her.

"Hello," the taller one said.

"Hello," Eleanor answered. "I'm Eleanor. What's your name?"

"I'm Daphne and this is—"

"Haley! I'm Haley." She stuck out her hand.

Eleanor took it and then shook Daphne's hand as well. "Very nice to meet you."

"Nice to meet you, too!" Haley said.

Eleanor stepped into the house. She could already smell dinner cooking.

"You're the lady in the paper," Daphne said as she led her into the kitchen. "In the picture next to Auntie Lyra."

"That's right," Eleanor said. "Very observant."

"Are you the bone lady?" asked Haley. "Like my auntie?"

"I sure am."

"Cool! I'm gonna dig up dinosaurs when I grow up."

"That sounds fantastic."

Haley hopped away and Daphne carefully took the wine and cookies. She placed them on the counter and Eleanor swallowed the lump in her throat as she watched Danny and Lyra at the stove, working together to make dinner. A small radio was playing pop music in the corner, so she wondered if they'd even heard her arrive.

She cleared her throat and Lyra turned. Her smile was wide and genuine and she nudged Danny who turned with a dish towel draped over her shoulder.

"El," she said, with a smile of her own.

Lyra walked to her and enveloped her in a big hug. "It's so good to see you," she said.

Eleanor hugged her back, giving her one tight squeeze. "It's doubly good to see you. All safe and sound."

They drew apart and Lyra wiped tears. She laughed. "It is, isn't it?"

Eleanor held her shoulders. "It is."

"I know I've said it before, over the phone, but thank you, Eleanor. Thank you so much. Your tip saved my life."

"You don't have to say it again."

"I want to."

They looked at one another for a long moment before Danny came for her hug. "How about one for me?"

They embraced and Eleanor inhaled her woodsy scent. She closed her eyes, silently wishing her former lover all the happiness in the world. Even if it did still feel bittersweet.

"And you did save the day," Danny said. "Somehow you always do."

Eleanor blushed and changed the subject. "Who wants wine?"

"I do," a man said as he entered the room from the hallway. He was handsome and striking, and resembled Lyra with his blond hair and high cheek bones. "I'm Louie," he said as he shook her hand. "Lyra's brother."

"Right. I'm Eleanor."

"Ah, the infamous Dr. Stafford. We finally meet at last."

Haley and Daphne entered the room and Haley bounded up to her. "He's our daddy," she said.

Daphne elbowed her. "She knows that already."

"Does not."

"Does so."

"Hey, girls? Who wants to help me put the bread in the oven and add the spaghetti noodles to the pot?" Lyra asked.

The girls hurried over to her with Haley looking back. "We're the cooks tonight!" she said with a big grin.

"Yeah, we make good spaghetti," Daphne said.

"I bet you do," Eleanor said. "I can't wait to eat."

The girls helped Lyra finish dinner while Eleanor talked with Louie and Danny. Danny reported that the Sugar Mill Farm case was now officially closed. They had positively identified the remaining victims and Donald Allen Greer was dead. Louie thanked them both profusely for all their work in solving the case and finding Lyra before it was too late.

Eleanor opened the wine in celebration as the doorbell rang and the front door opened.

"Knock, knock," said an older woman as she crept inside, followed by an older man. With their familiar looks Eleanor pegged them to be Lyra's parents. The girls took off from the kitchen to jump in their arms.

"Grandma! Grandpa!"

They loved on the girls and then made their way into the kitchen. Lyra hugged and kissed her mother and then paused at her father.

"Dad," she said.

"Lyra," he said. "How are you?" He reached out tentatively and rested his hand on her shoulder.

She teared up. "I'm okay, Dad. I'm okay."

He brought her in for a hug and Eleanor got the sense that it was a long time coming.

Then Lyra introduced her. "This, Mom and Dad, is Dr. Eleanor Stafford. The woman who saved my life."

Eleanor flushed again as she shook hands with the older couple. They, like Louie, thanked her, and then Haley stood in the middle of the kitchen and announced dinner like she was king of the court. It was undeniably adorable.

Eleanor joined Danny and the Aarden family at the table in the dining room and they all dug in and ate the spaghetti with plenty of wine and garlic bread. Eleanor felt right at home, and she realized as she watched Danny and Lyra playfully interact, that she was no longer jealous. She was just happy that they were happy, and that everyone was safe, and that Donald Allen Greer could no longer hurt anyone else.

She thought perhaps it could've been the wine affecting her mood, but she didn't really think so. She was genuinely happy. For everyone. Even herself. She had her job, which she loved, good friends, her mother, and now Huck. She was pretty well off by most standards.

And maybe, just maybe, she'd call up Allison after dinner and ask her to help set up a dating profile on one of those sites. It could be an adventure. The start of something new.

And maybe, she'd meet that someone special.

Maybe.

EPILOGUE

Danica stood at her kitchen sink holding her father's favorite bottle of whiskey. She'd been thinking about doing it for days, and after the wonderful dinner that night with Eleanor and the Aarden family, she knew it was time. It was time to let go.

She opened the bottle and held it out. "Good-bye, Dad," she said. "Good-bye whiskey." She turned the bottle over and poured out the contents, watching the amber colored liquid disappear down the drain, along with it all the nightmares and all the pain and regret. She would, of course, still miss her father, but now it would be just that. Nothing more. And no more drinking to numb the pain.

She tossed the bottle in the garbage and wiped away a tear. To her great relief, no more tears came. She headed back into the living room, ready to wind down for the night and maybe watch a movie. She was just getting ready to sit down when the doorbell rang. Perplexed, she rose to answer it. A quick peek outside showed her who it was.

She opened the door. "Mom," she breathed. "What a surprise."

"Is it really?"

"Well, yes."

"It shouldn't be. I've been trying to call you."

"Sorry. I've been busy."

"Too busy to call your mother?"

Danica didn't want to argue. It was getting late and all she wanted to do was relax and have a peaceful night for a change. No more thinking about the case or trying to find the missing women. Just peace.

But, at the moment, it didn't seem like that was going to happen anytime soon.

"So, what's up?" she asked.

Her mother walked in and tossed her purse on the chair next to the couch.

"I came to see how you were? Is that so bad?"

"It's not bad, Mom." Was it?

"You've disappeared since you solved that case. I don't see you, don't hear from you."

"I've been trying to come down. With the accident and everything, I really needed some good rest."

"Well, it wouldn't have hurt you to tell me."

Danica rubbed her brow. "I'm sorry. I should've returned your calls."

"That's better," she said.

The doorbell rang again and Danica furrowed her brow, confused. What was going on tonight?

She answered the door. "Lyra." She was truly dumbfounded. They'd just said good-bye a short while ago. "I—"

"Who is it, Danny?"

Danica motioned for Lyra to come inside. "It's Lyra. My—"

"It's late," her mother said. "What kind of friend shows up this late?"

Lyra stepped inside and twisted her hands as if unsure of herself. "Am I interrupting?"

"No," Danica said quickly. She was actually more than relieved to see her. "Lyra, this is my mother, Linda. Mom, this is Lyra. My girlfriend."

"Girlfriend?" Her mother looked as though she'd been struck.

"Hi," Lyra said, extending her hand. "Lyra Aarden. It's very nice to meet you."

Her mother limply shook her hand. Then she looked at Danica. "Well, that explains it. Rest my left foot. You've been with her. That's why you haven't called."

Lyra appeared dismayed. Danica fought to explain, but then she saw the look on her mother's face. It was one of strong disapproval. There was not going to be any explaining where her mother was concerned. And suddenly, she didn't feel the need to.

"I'm not going to argue with you, Mom."

Her mother guffawed.

"Lyra is my girlfriend and she's come to see me. So, if you'll excuse us…"

"I see." She quickly gathered her purse. "I will assume however, that you're going to pick me up for mass tomorrow morning?"

Danica glanced at Lyra. She looked so beautiful standing there in the warm light, all nervous and earnest. She had good reason to believe that Lyra had come for more than just a quick visit.

"No," she said and straightened her shoulders. "I won't be able to make it tomorrow."

Her mother glared at her and then at Lyra. "Don't you do this, Danny. Don't you do it."

She'd never stood up to her mother before and her nerves were on edge. But the pounding in her heart didn't frighten her. It moved her. And she couldn't take her eyes off Lyra. As if she were giving her strength with just her gaze.

"Maybe some other time, Mom," she said. She walked back to the door and opened it. Her mother stood still for moment, glaring at her. Then, with a huff, she hurried across the room to the door. She gave Danica one last look.

"I won't forget this," she said. "I will not forget it."

"Good night, Mom," Danica said, giving her a smile. "Drive carefully."

She walked out into the night without another word.

Danica closed the door, bolted it, and then turned her attention back to Lyra.

"Hello," she said. "And what brings you by?" She took her hands in hers and kissed them.

"I—I'm so sorry. I didn't even pay attention to the car parked on the street. Is she upset?"

"Shh." Danica put a finger to her lips. "She'll be fine. Or she won't. It doesn't matter. All that matters is that you're here. Right here. Right now."

"I just couldn't stop thinking about you," Lyra said.

"The feeling is mutual." Danica said. "You sure you're okay though? I thought you needed to rest?" Lyra was still recovering from her ordeal with Donald Allen Greer, and it had taken a few days to get the drugs from her system. Danica had been insisting that she rest and take all the time she need.

"I can't possibly rest any more. If it's one thing I've learned, it's that I don't want to waste any more time. I want—you. And I don't want to wait any longer."

Danica brushed her fingers along her jawline. "God, it's good to hear you say that."

"Then I'll say it again. Danny, I want you."

Danica slid her hands along her hips and drew her closer. Then she closed her eyes and leaned into her. "And I want you, Lyra Aarden." Gently, she pressed her lips to hers and kissed her. The world seemed to spin, and Lyra moaned and kissed her back, wrapping her arms around her neck. Danica had the urge to kiss her harder, deeper, to explore her every corner, but she refrained, choosing instead to take her time. She played with her lips, taking them between her own, truly and fully tasting her. There were no distractions now, nobody dressed in Halloween costumes ready to jump out and scare them. No bones to be examined, no killer to find. There was just the two of them. Finally.

She lifted her and Lyra wrapped her legs around her, and they headed for the bedroom. Danica eased her down on the bed and then crawled atop her. But to her surprise, Lyra rolled onto her and held her arms above her head. She breathed down upon her, a sly grin on her face.

"Mm, I think I like this position," she said.

"I think I do, too."

Lyra released her and pushed herself up so that she was straddling her. Quickly, Lyra pulled her hoodie off over her head and did the same with the shirt beneath. Then she unhooked her bra and freed her breasts. Danica reached up to touch her, but Lyra pinned her back down. "Not yet," she said, and she climbed off the bed and removed her shoes and socks. Then she undid her jeans and pulled those off, along with her panties. She climbed back onto Danica and took hold of her hands.

"Now," she said as she brought them up to her breasts. "Touch me."

Danica's breath caught as she felt the warm fullness of her beneath her fingers. Lyra moaned softly and tilted her head back to expose her delicate throat.

"Feels so good," she said as Danica gently caressed her, bringing her nipples to rapt attention. "Oh, Danny, yes. Touch me, baby."

"Look at you," Danica whispered. "So beautiful. So beautiful moving atop me."

"Mm. I want more," she said, looking down at her. "Can't wait for more."

"We have all night," Danica said.

"I know, but I can't wait. I want to *feel* you, Danica Wallace. Inside me."

She took Danica's hand and slid two fingers into her hot mouth where she lightly sucked them, making Danica's toes curl. Then she traced Danica's hand down her abdomen to her center and shifted so that Danica had access to her most sensitive place.

"Go inside me," she said. "Hurry."

As carefully as she could, Danica slid her fingers up inside her and they both groaned in sheer pleasure. Lyra was hot, wet, and tight down around her, and she began to move, to gyrate, and to grind, riding Danica's fingers.

"Yes," she said, eyes closed. "Oh, God yes. Like that. Just like that." Her eyes opened as Danica curled her fingers and she gripped Danica's shoulders and then thrust backward, arching her back. "Baby!" She cried. "Oh, Danny, baby. Yes."

Danica pushed up into her, matching her rhythm. "I love you," she said, truly amazed at the sight and feel of her.

"Oh, Danny. I love you, too." She knelt and kissed her, thrusting her tongue into her. Danica met it with her own and they danced together there as Lyra danced atop her fingers.

"Mm. I want to feel more of you," Lyra said as they drew apart, breathless. "This way," she said, stopping her movement to open Danica's robe. "Right here," she said as she shifted back and traced her hand down to her center. She slipped her fingers inside her folds and Danica sighed and arched, the feel of her talented fingers causing her eyes to roll back in her head.

"Yes, baby," Lyra said. "Can you feel me?"

"Yes," Danica hissed.

"Good. Now come with me."

Danica pressed her lips together, trying to hold on as Lyra expertly played her like she'd been playing her all her life.

"You're so slick," Lyra said. "Feel so good."

Danica opened her legs, allowing her better access.

"I'm close," she said, lost in the view of Lyra grinding down on her fingers. "I'm so close."

"I am, too," Lyra said, panting.

"Now?" Danica said, gripping her hip.

Lyra nodded. "Mm-hm. Yeah. Now. Ah! Oh, God! Oh, God, I'm coming! I'm coming, Danny!"

"Lyra!" Danica called. "Lyra, yes. Yes, come! I'm coming!"

"Danny!" Lyra threw her head back and convulsed in climax. She rode Danica out, jerking her hips, with her free hand entwined in Danica's. When she eventually stilled, and Danica's hips had stopped bucking, she collapsed on her, breathing heavily into her neck. Her skin was warm and moist with sweat and the scent of her made Danica's body heat all over again.

"God, I love you," Danica said.

Lyra laughed. "I love you." She eased her fingers inside Danica, causing her to buck once again.

"Oh, yes, you're ready for more."

"Mm, in a minute. I want to enjoy this for a moment."

"This?"

"You, resting on me like this. All sweaty and spent, like you just had the best sex of your life."

"It was pretty darn good," she said.

"I agree."

She pushed herself up. "But it could be so much better." She kissed her, warm and soft and careful, as if she were just tasting her for the very first time.

"You've convinced me," Danica said.

"Yeah? You're ready for more?"

"I'm ready for forever. Forever with you."

Lyra touched her face. "Danny," she said. "Don't make me cry."

"Don't cry, Lyra. Just say yes. Say yes to us. To forever making love."

She kissed her lips and then drew away with a soft smile. "Yes," she said.

"Really?"

She nodded. "Yes."

"Come here." Danica brought her back down for another kiss. Then, with her heart pounding, she rolled Lyra over onto her back and got busy giving her forever.

THE END

About the Author

Ronica Black lives in the desert Southwest with her menagerie of animals and her menagerie of art. When she's not writing, she's still creating, whether drawing, painting, or woodworking. She loves long walks into the sunset, rescuing animals, anything pertaining to art, and spending time with those she loves. When she can, she enjoys returning to her roots in North Carolina where she can sit back on the porch with family and friends, catch up on all the gossip, and relish an ice cold Cheerwine.

Ronica is a two-time Golden Crown Literary Society Goldie Award winner and a three-time finalist for the Lambda Literary Awards.

Books Available from Bold Strokes Books

Coasting and Crashing by Ana Hartnett. Life comes easy to Emma Wilson until Lake Palmer shows up at Alder University and derails her every plan. (978-1-63679-511-9)

Every Beat of Her Heart by KC Richardson. Piper and Gillian have their own fears about falling in love, but will they be able to overcome those feelings once they learn each other's secrets? (978-1-63679-515-7)

Grave Consequences by Sandra Barret. A decade after necromancy became licensed and legalized, can Tamar and Maddy overcome the lingering prejudice against their kind and their growing attraction to each other to uncover a plot that threatens both their lives? (978-1-63679-467-9)

Haunted by Myth by Barbara Ann Wright. When ghost-hunter Chloe seeks an answer to the current spectral epidemic, all clues point to one very famous face: Helen of Troy, whose motives are more complicated than history suggests and whose charms few can resist. (978-1-63679-461-7)

Invisible by Anna Larner. When medical school dropout Phoebe Frink falls for the shy costume shop assistant Violet Unwin, everything about their love feels certain, but can the same be said about their future? (978-1-63679-469-3)

Like They Do in the Movies by Nan Campbell. Celebrity gossip writer Fran Underhill becomes Chelsea Cartwright's personal assistant with the aim of taking the popular actress down, but neither of them anticipates the clash of their attraction. (978-1-63679-525-6)

Limelight by Gun Brooke. Liberty Bell and Palmer Elliston loathe each other. They clash every week on the hottest new TV show, until Liberty starts to sing and the impossible happens. (978-1-63679-192-0)

Playing with Matches by Georgia Beers. To help save Cori's store and help Liz survive her ex's wedding they strike a deal: a fake relationship, but just for one week. There's no way this will turn into the real deal. (978-1-63679-507-2)

The Memories of Marlie Rose by Morgan Lee Miller. Broadway legend Marlie Rose undergoes a procedure to erase all of her unwanted memories, but as she starts regretting her decision, she discovers that the only person who could help is the love she's trying to forget. (978-1-63679-347-4)

The Murders at Sugar Mill Farm by Ronica Black. A serial killer is on the loose in southern Louisiana, and it's up to three women to solve the case while carefully dancing around feelings for each other. (978-1-63679-455-6)

Fire in the Sky by Radclyffe and Julie Cannon. Two women from different worlds have nothing in common and every reason to wish they'd never met—except for the attraction neither can deny. (978-1-63679-573-7)

A Talent Ignited by Suzanne Lenoir. When Evelyne is abducted and Annika believes she has been abandoned, they must risk everything to find each other again. (978-1-63679-483-9)

All Things Beautiful by Alaina Erdell. Casey Norford only planned to learn to paint like her mentor, Leighton Vaughn, not sleep with her. (978-1-63679-479-2)

An Atlas to Forever by Krystina Rivers. Can Atlas, a difficult dog Ellie inherits after the death of her best friend, help the busy hopeless romantic find forever love with commitment-phobic animal behaviorist Hayden Brandt? (978-1-63679-451-8)

Bait and Witch by Clifford Mae Henderson. When Zeddi gets an unexpected inheritance from her client Mags, she discovers that Mags served as high priestess to a dwindling coven of old witches—who are positive that Mags was murdered. Zeddi owes it to her to uncover the truth. (978-1-63679-535-5)

Buried Secrets by Sheri Lewis Wohl. Tuesday and Addie, along with Tuesday's dog, Tripper, struggle to solve a twenty-five-year-old mystery while searching for love and redemption along the way. (978-1-63679-396-2)

Come Find Me in the Midnight Sun by Bailey Bridgewater. In Alaska, disappearing is the easy part. When two men go missing, state trooper Louisa Linebach must solve the case, and when she thinks she's coming close, she's wrong. (978-1-63679-566-9)

Death on the Water by CJ Birch. The Ocean Summit's authorities have ruled a death on board its inaugural cruise as a suicide, but Claire suspects murder and with the help of Assistant Cruise Director Moira, Claire conducts her own investigation. (978-1-63679-497-6)

Living For You by Jenny Frame. Can Sera Debrek face real and personal demons to help save the world from darkness and open her heart to love? (978-1-63679-491-4)

Mississippi River Mischief by Greg Herren. When a politician turns up dead and Scotty's client is the most obvious suspect, Scotty and his friends set out to prove his client's innocence. (978-1-63679-353-5)

Ride with Me by Jenna Jarvis. When Lucy's vacation to find herself becomes Emma's chance to remember herself, they realize that everything they're looking for might already be sitting right next to them—if they're willing to reach for it. (978-1-63679-499-0)

Whiskey and Wine by Kelly and Tana Fireside. Winemaker Tessa Williams and sex toy shop owner Lace Reynolds are both used to taking risks, but will they be willing to put their friendship on the line if it gives them a shot at finding forever love? (978-1-63679-531-7)

Hands of the Morri by Heather K O'Malley. Discovering she is a Lost Sister and growing acquainted with her new body, Asche learns how to be a warrior and commune with the Goddess the Hands serve, the Morri. (978-1-63679-465-5)

I Know About You by Erin Kaste. With her stalker inching closer to the truth, Cary Smith is forced to face the past she's tried desperately to forget. (978-1-63679-513-3)

Mate of Her Own by Elena Abbott. When Heather McKenna finally confronts the family who cursed her, her werewolf is shocked to discover her one true mate, and that's only the beginning. (978-1-63679-481-5)

Pumpkin Spice by Tagan Shepard. For Nicki, new love is making this pumpkin spice season sweeter than expected. (978-1-63679-388-7)

Rivals for Love by Ali Vali. Brooks Boseman's brother Curtis is getting married, and Brooks needs to be at the engagement party. Only she can't possibly go, not with Curtis set to marry the secret love of her youth, Fallon Goodwin. (978-1-63679-384-9)

Sweat Equity by Aurora Rey. When cheesemaker Sy Travino takes a job in rural Vermont and hires contractor Maddie Barrow to rehab a house she buys sight unseen, they both wind up with a lot more than they bargained for. (978-1-63679-487-7)

Taking the Plunge by Amanda Radley. When Regina Avery meets model Grace Holland—the most beautiful woman she's ever seen—she doesn't have a clue how to flirt, date, or hold on to a relationship. But Regina must take the plunge with Grace and hope she manages to swim. (978-1-63679-400-6)

We Met in a Bar by Claire Forsythe. Wealthy nightclub owner Erica turns undercover bartender on a mission to catch a thief where she meets no-strings, no-commitments Charlie, who couldn't be further from Erica's type. Right? (978-1-63679-521-8)

Western Blue by Suzie Clarke. Step back in time to this historic western filled with heroism, loyalty, friendship, and love. The odds are against this unlikely group—but never underestimate women who have nothing to lose. (978-1-63679-095-4)

Windswept by Patricia Evans. The windswept shores of the Scottish Highlands weave magic for two people convinced they'd never fall in love again. (978-1-63679-382-5)

An Independent Woman by Kit Meredith. Alex and Rebecca's attraction won't stop smoldering, despite their reluctance to act on it and incompatible poly relationship styles. (978-1-63679-553-9)

Cherish by Kris Bryant. Josie and Olivia cherish the time spent together, but when the summer ends and their temporary romance melts into the real deal, reality gets complicated. (978-1-63679-567-6)

Cold Case Heat by Mary P. Burns. Sydney Hansen receives a threat in a very cold murder case that sends her to the police for help where she finds more than justice with Detective Gale Sterling. (978-1-63679-374-0)

Proximity by Jordan Meadows. Joan really likes Ellie, but being alone with her could turn deadly unless she can keep her dangerous powers under control. (978-1-63679-476-1)

Sweet Spot by Kimberly Cooper Griffin. Pro surfer Shia Turning will have to take a chance if she wants to find the sweet spot. (978-1-63679-418-1)

The Haunting of Oak Springs by Crin Claxton. Ghosts and the past haunt the supernatural detective in a race to save the lesbians of Oak Springs farm. (978-1-63679-432-7)

Transitory by J.M. Redmann. The cops blow it off as a customer surprised by what was under the dress, but PI Micky Knight knows they're wrong—she either makes it her case or lets a murderer go free to kill again. (978-1-63679-251-4)

Unexpectedly Yours by Toni Logan. A private resort on a tropical island, a feisty old chief, and a kleptomaniac pet pig bring Suzanne and Allie together for unexpected love. (978-1-63679-160-9)